CRUSH

THE CRESCENT LAKE WINERY SERIES

LUCINDA RACE

MC TWO PRESS

BOOK 2

Crush
The Crescent Lake Winery Series
Book 2
By
Lucinda Race

Editing by Susan Helene Gottfried at West of Mars
Proofreader Kimberly Dawn

Cover design by Jade Webb www.meetcutecreative.com

Manufactured in the United States of America
First Edition May 2021

Print Edition ISBN978-1-954520-02-8
E-book Edition ISBN 978-1-954520-01-1

INSPIRATION

Wine is not just an object of pleasure, but an object of knowledge;
and the pleasure depends on the knowledge.
– Roger Scruton

1

Anna followed her sister Liza's minivan to their parents' house for the traditional Price family post-wedding brunch hosted by Mom and Dad. The April weather was perfect, warm enough to be outside and enjoy the day, but not too hot so people wanted to be in air conditioning. Today they were celebrating Anna's younger sister Tessa and her new husband Max. Tomorrow they'd be off on their honeymoon.

This turtle pace caused her fingers to tap on the steering wheel. Her car was meant for hugging curves in the road like yoga pants to her backside. The candy-apple red Benz had been an impulse buy to ignite her fun side again and alleviate the humdrum of her life and career. How had she turned into some old lady by her late thirties?

The minivan slowed even further and turned up the long gravel driveway to their parents' home. Daffodils and tulips lined the way, with deep purple pansies adding a splash of contrasting color peeking from under the evergreen and large maple trees.

Ahead of her, the circular driveway was filled with cars: her siblings and extended family, with a few others she didn't recognize. More than likely rental cars from Tessa and Max's out-of-town wedding guests. She parked so she could make a quick getaway, leaving the keys in the ignition before running up the front steps after Liza. Her nephews, Johnny and George, came flying through the door and into Liza's open arms. Despite being six and seven and tall for their ages, she was still able to scoop them up and cover their faces with kisses. The boys looked like their uncles, but the freckles were from their dad. There was a time when Anna thought she'd have a couple of kids wanting to leap into her arms and the familiar pain of regret that she didn't stung.

"Hey, Mom, you'll never guess what." Johnny was first to wriggle from her arms. "Uncle Leo said we can spend the night at his house whenever we want."

George interjected, "But we have to ask you first."

"So, were you good for Mimi and Poppy?" She looked from one sweet face to the other.

They both nodded. "Yup."

She ruffled their hair. "Good."

In unison, they asked, "So when can we have another sleepover?"

"Tonight?" George asked.

Johnny looked up. "Please, Mom? We'll be good."

"It's a school night and you know the rule. No sleepovers during the week, but I'll talk to your uncle and we'll plan something."

Anna was silent while she watched the boys try and change Liza's mind, to no avail. "Hey, boys, I'll bet Mimi is waiting for us to get inside."

"Come on, Johnny. Mimi will set up the sprinkler out back."

As the boys raced away, Liza called after them, "No sprinklers. It's too cold."

Anna looked at Liza. "Really? You sound just like Mom."

Liza placed a hand over her heart and chuckled. "Are you forgetting I am their mother?"

Anna opened the door and they stepped into the whirlwind of brunch where, as happy as she was for Tessa, she longed for someone special in her life.

The afternoon was the usual fun-filled chaos. Laughter filled the rooms, plates overflowed, and glasses were never empty for long. A party at the Price family home was not to be missed.

Anna noticed her dad sitting quietly, watching the kids play outside sans the sprinkler. She wandered over.

"Hey, Dad, whatcha doing out here?" She dropped next to him on the glider.

He looked up. "Just a little tired. I didn't sleep well last night—a touch of heartburn."

"Can I get you something? Antacid or glass of milk?"

He patted her hand. "I just needed some air. Nothing to worry about at all."

"I don't mind. How about I get a glass of water?"

"Stop fussing over me, Anna. I'm okay."

His voice wavered, which did nothing to quiet her growing concern. Sam Price was a tower of strength. He rarely took a day off, let alone got sick—with the exception of a mild heart attack a few years ago.

They watched the grandkids playing.

"Ben isn't one to be left behind by the bigger boys."

Kate and Don's three-year-old son was the spitting image of his mother, with striking green eyes and dark hair. He was tall, but his dimples were all Price.

"They look out for him though." Anna pointed to George, who was racing with Johnny across the backyard. He turned back and saw Ben, who had stopped to try to tie his shoe.

Instead of continuing to chase his brother, George turned to his cousin. He knelt down and tied Ben's sneaker, then checked the other one. Then they both raced to join Johnny.

"He's a good big brother. Do you ever wish you had a couple?"

"Maybe someday I will, but not yet." The last thing she wanted her dad to know was that she wished she was in Tessa's shoes, planning for a real future instead of being stuck —work, home, repeat.

He shifted in the seat and tapped the middle of his chest.

"Maybe I should have some milk. Would you mind getting me a glass?" He grasped her hand. "But don't make this a big deal. I don't want Tessa and Max to miss their flight out tonight."

Leave it to Dad to downplay that he didn't feel good. "I'll be right back," she said, jumping up and hurrying into the house. She went straight to the kitchen, smiling at Max's sister Stella and trying to play it cool. She didn't want to create a situation as she went to the refrigerator and got the carton of milk. Thankfully, most of the guests had gone and only family remained.

Her youngest brother Leo strolled over. "What's going on?"

He knew of her aversion to milk.

Softly she said, "Dad's not feeling well. Complaining of indigestion and asked for a glass."

His brow shot up. "Is that all it is?"

"I'm not sure." She put the carton away and picked up the glass. "Come with me and see for yourself."

He took a cursory look around the room. "Let me get my cell."

Mom had a thing when you came into a party at her house. All cell phones were put in a basket on the breakfast bar. Her theory was you came to socialize and you couldn't if you were always looking at your phone.

"Meet you out back."

"Try not to worry, sis; it's probably nothing. Too much food, wine, and dancing yesterday."

She tried to relax, but she wasn't so sure. "I'm sure you're right."

Making a smooth exit without Mom asking questions, Anna stepped onto the back deck. Her eyes went directly to her father. He was still massaging his chest and shrugging his shoulder. His face was pale.

"Dad." She dropped next to him. "Does your chest hurt?"

He ignored the question and held out his hand to take the glass of milk. He took a small sip and grimaced.

"I feel like I'm going to throw up."

Leo overheard the statement and pulled out his phone. "I'm calling EMS."

"Don't overreact. It's just a little stomach upset. Nothing more." His usual commanding voice was replaced by one laced with apprehension. "Tell your mom before the sirens scare the heck out of her."

She turned and waved a hand at George. "Can you come here a minute?"

He dashed over.

"Run inside and ask Mimi to come out here."

"Sure thing."

He zipped around the outdoor dining chairs and through the open door.

In less than a minute, Mom came rushing out. "Sam," she cried and grabbed his hands, rubbing them as if to warm them. "What's wrong?"

"Maybe I ate something that didn't agree with me." Beads of sweat appeared on his upper lip. "I'm sure I'll be fine."

Leo said, "Mom, an ambulance is on the way. Should I call Dad's cardiologist?"

"Um, yeah. His number is on the fridge." She continued to rub his hands between hers.

Anna looked up. "Go. Tell the others."

Leo went inside. The time dragged and when she checked her watch, it had been only a minute which seemed like a lifetime.

Dad had his eyes closed and Mom held his hand, fighting back tears. Anna took the glass of milk and set it aside. She looked around, anxious to hear sirens. But nothing yet. Don rushed to her side.

"What's wrong with Dad?"

She kept her eyes glued on Dad's face. "I'm guessing a heart attack."

"Should we help him inside?"

"Will you stop hovering." Dad gave him a stern look but his voice wavered. They sat in silence, straining to hear the sounds of an ambulance. He rubbed the center of his chest and then massaged his left shoulder and down his arm, and his face grew pinched.

Time dragged. Finally, a faint wail of sirens could be heard in the distance. They grew closer.

Jack, her other brother, burst through the door. Two men in dark-blue jackets, white shirts, and matching pants were right behind him. Each one carried two cases and strode across the deck.

One dropped to kneel beside Sam. He took his wrist in his hand and studied his watch.

"Mr. Price, can you tell me how you're feeling?"

Anna said, "He was complaining his chest ached and he was nauseous. He said it started last night."

"Do you have a history of heart problems?" He handed Dad a small tablet of nitroglycerin and directed him to put it under his tongue.

"Yes."

"How long have you been having symptoms?"

Dad looked at Mom. "I'm not sure. Since yesterday maybe."

The EMS man strapped a blood pressure cuff to Dad's arm and pumped it up. During this time, his partner wheeled out a chair.

"Mr. Price, we're going to take you to the hospital. I'll help you up and you're going to sit on that chair. Once we get outside, we'll get you into the ambulance and your family can follow us."

Leo piped up. "I've called his cardiologist at Crescent Lake Memorial and he'll meet us at the ER."

Dad didn't argue and allowed himself to be helped into the transport chair. He gave a weak smile to Mom. "I'm sorry, sweetheart. I'm breaking up the party."

She smoothed a hand over his cheek and kissed his forehead. "Nothing to be sorry about, and we'll be right behind you."

She looked at Liza and Anna. "I have to put the food away before I go."

Anna knew this was her mom's way to regain her equilibrium. "Mom, I'll clean up here and follow you in a few minutes. Don and Kate will drive you."

Liza stepped forward. "I'll keep the boys at my house."

Mom looked around, dazed. "I need my purse and keys."

Don took her elbow. "Come on, Mom."

While this was going on, Dad was secured to the chair, which was wheeled into the house. They followed the EMS and Dad out the front door.

Stuffing the worry down, Anna rushed down the front steps to drop a kiss on Dad's cheek.

"I'll see you in a bit. I love you, Daddy." She blinked back the tears that threatened to spill down her cheeks.

"Love you." He was eased into the waiting ambulance. One man climbed in back with him and the other closed the doors, immediately striding toward the driver's door.

Don pulled the car up and Anna rushed over to open the passenger door for Mom. Kate was sitting in the back.

"I'll see you at the hospital." She leaned down. "Call if anything happens."

Don said, "Will do."

Anna slammed the door. She watched, feeling helpless as both the ambulance with lights flashing and Don's car raced down the driveway. Jack, Liza, and Leo were watching the ambulance, their faces blank.

She looked around the group. "Where's Tessa and Max?"

Tessa ran down the steps. "Here. We're headed to the hospital."

Anna threw a frantic look at the kitchen.

Stella ushered the three young boys into the family room. She tilted her head to the door and said, "Go. I'll watch the kids, clean up the kitchen, and take care of the house. We're family now."

"Thanks, Stella." Anna looked at her siblings. "Let's go."

2

Anna paced the long, overly bright hallway; the polished linoleum floor and dull-colored walls were so sterile, along with the antiseptic smell that filled her sensitive nose. It was like this the last time he was in the hospital; that smell made her pulse race, and not in a good way. Her sneakers squeaked as she turned to pace the length again. She couldn't spend another minute sitting and waiting for news about Dad.

Just yesterday, he had been smiling and dancing at Tessa's wedding. Now he was in the cardiac unit, lying in a bed, hooked up to machines monitoring his every vital function. Mom was by his side, waiting for the doctor to tell them the results. The rest of the family was sitting in the waiting room just outside the ICU. How they could just sit there and wait was beyond her. Instead, she walked the halls.

A handsome man who looked very familiar approached her. He had been Dad's nurse after his heart attack a few years ago. He was dressed in green scrubs, was tall, and walked with quiet confidence. She couldn't help but notice his sculpted biceps under his shirtsleeves. A stethoscope was around his neck and a pen and pad poked from the pocket of his shirt.

"Anna?"

"Yes." His voice put her at ease instantly. It was like a good pinot noir, smooth.

"I'm Colin Grant, your father's nurse practitioner."

She stuck out her hand. "I remember you were his nurse when Dad was in the hospital a few years ago." As they connected, a spark gave her heart a jolt.

A smile of recognition flashed over his face. "I remember you too."

She could feel her face flush, as she had definitely remembered how he had made her feel the first time they met. "How's my dad?"

"He's a lucky guy. But he will need a coronary bypass and vein graft. Which means we'll take a healthy vein and bypass the blocked artery."

"Do my parents know?" She glanced down the hall toward the elevator.

"Yes. Dr. Thomas is with them now, and the rest of the family has been updated too. One of your brothers said you were walking the halls and they'd fill you in when you returned but I'm glad I bumped into you." He gave her an understanding smile.

Her eyes slipped to the floor as she exhaled. "I'm not good at just hanging around." She met his kind eyes. "NP? I thought it was RN?"

"Good memory. The first time we met, I was a registered nurse, in school to become a nurse practitioner. My specialty is still cardiac patients. I work with Dr. Thomas and people like your dad. I'll be a part of his care team as he prepares for surgery, and afterward, he'll need to make a few lifestyle changes."

She listened intently. "I'll do whatever is needed to help him recover." Her throat constricted. "Is he going to be okay?

I mean, is the surgery risky?" She didn't want to put into words and ask if her father could die. It was as if that would tempt fate.

"All surgery has risks, but it is absolutely necessary for your father to live a long and healthy life."

"Is he comfortable now?" Absentmindedly, she toyed with the end of her ponytail.

"He's resting, and the surgery will be scheduled for tomorrow morning."

"Why not now? If he needs it, shouldn't it be done right away?" The sense of panic was rising again in her stomach.

"We'll monitor him overnight, but it's important to get his blood pressure stable, and he's a bit dehydrated. Waiting won't pose any additional risk for him and in the cardiac unit, he'll be closely monitored."

He touched her shoulder. It was a comforting gesture that quieted the fear clutching her heart.

"Can I see him now or should I wait with the family?"

"Come on. I'll take you to him and if you have any more questions, I'll be around."

"Thanks for talking with me." She gave him a strained smile. "You're very kind. I'm sure it's just part of the job, but I appreciate it. Well, maybe it's just who you are. Not all medical professionals are as nice." She clamped her mouth closed and glanced at him. "I have a bad habit of rambling when I'm worried or nervous."

He gave her a reassuring smile, and his hazel eyes were kind. "My sister Marie is a lot like that, so I'm used to it."

She could feel her cheeks grow warm and was at a loss for words.

A set of heavy glass doors whooshed open as they walked into the cardiac unit. Her father was in a bed at the end by the window. A few other beds were occupied by people of various ages. Anna was surprised; she thought only older people had heart attacks. But this wasn't the heart attack wing. It was for all types of heart issues.

Walking softly to not disturb anyone, she approached Dad. Mom was by his side. Colin fell behind as she walked the rest of the way alone.

Mom was holding Dad's hand. He was resting with his eyes closed.

She whispered, "Hi, Mom."

"Anna. I wondered where you had gone off to." Her brow was furrowed with worry lines. "Your dad was concerned."

"I didn't mean to upset anyone. I went for a walk, as the sitting around was driving me nuts." She looked over her shoulder. Her eyes sought his. "Colin found me and gave me the update on Dad's condition and told me that he has to have surgery tomorrow." She eased her mom into a chair. "How are you doing?"

"I'll be fine. It's just—" Tears welled up in her mom's eyes and trailed down her cheeks. "I never dreamed we'd be back in the hospital, waiting for surgery. I really did think that we had his heart condition under control. He's been exercising and watching what he eats. Mostly."

"I'm sure there are cases when things like this happen. But he's in good hands with Dr. Thomas and Colin. We'll be bringing him home very soon."

Dad's eyes fluttered and he gave her a tiny smile. "Love your optimism, Anna. You've always been *my glass is three-quarters full* kind of girl."

She placed a hand on the blankets. "Hey, Dad. How are you feeling?"

His voice was weak. "Guess it wasn't indigestion."

"You were lucky. You ignored the symptoms you were having for too long."

Mom looked between Anna and Dad. "What are you talking about?"

"Do you want to tell her or should I?"

He gave a half shrug and looked out the window. "You can."

She turned her gaze to Mom. "Apparently, he was having symptoms yesterday during the wedding."

"Sam."

Anna could hear the anguish in Mom's voice.

"Why didn't you say anything?"

"I couldn't ruin Tessa's wedding. And saying I wasn't feeling well would have put the kibosh on the happy day."

"How do you think Tessa would have felt if you had dropped dead on the dance floor?" Mom's tone ratcheted up with each word.

"Sherry, shush. There are people trying to rest, and your tone can be grating."

Mom pushed the metal chair back. The legs screeched against the linoleum floor. Through clenched teeth, she said, "I can't believe you would risk your health. Yes, it was our daughter's wedding day but really, Sam…" Tears coursed down her cheeks. With a hitch in her voice, she continued. "You could have said something when we got home last night."

"You were exhausted and we had brunch today. I figured I'd wait until tomorrow and call the doctor."

Anna could see why her dad had waited, but his logic was messed up. Mom was right. Things could have turned out very differently.

"Guys, let's just take a deep breath. Dad's in the hospital and on the mend."

Mom moved to stand next to the window. She dried her eyes and Dad snorted. "Easy for you to say. I'm the one who goes under the knife tomorrow, and it sounds like they're going to crack open my chest. That's a long recovery."

Anna moved closer to the edge of the bed. "You're going to do everything the doctor says."

He grumbled, "At least I can count on you and your

brothers to keep the winery buzzing. Spring is not the best time to be sick."

"Don't give CLW another thought." Her heart flipped. So much for making changes to her life or career. She could never leave the winery if something happened to her dad. "Does this mean you're going to move into full retirement mode and stop going into the office five days a week?"

"For the time being, it seems I won't have a choice."

"Good." Anna stood up. "I'm going to find the family and then, Mom, do you want me to drive you home?"

"No, I'll stay here tonight." Sam held out his hand to her. Mom moved to the bed and took it. She visibly softened as she smiled. "I know what you're going to say."

"You do, do you?" Dad squeezed her hand and winked at Anna.

"You're sending me home to get a good night's sleep."

With a soft chuckle, he said, "See, Anna, what forty years of marriage does to a person? We can read the other's mind." His eyes softened. "Drive Mom home, okay?'

"I'll wait outside. Take your time." She leaned over Dad and kissed his cheek. Somehow, he seemed more fragile than he had sitting on the back deck just a few hours ago. She guessed it was the machinery beeping and the IV attached to his arm. "I'll check in later."

She turned to give them some privacy.

He called to her, "Love you, kid."

She turned and looked over her shoulder. "I love you too, Dad." She blinked away the tears. He was the strong and silent type when it came to expressing his feelings. Tears blurred her vision and she walked into Colin.

He reached out and grasped her arms. "Hey, are you okay?"

She nodded and wiped the dampness from her cheeks with the palms of her hands.

"Your father is in good hands so there is no need to worry,

and you can call anytime, twenty-four seven, and check on him." He reached into his chest pocket and pulled out a slip of paper. "Here's the number for the unit."

Without looking at it, she tucked it into the pocket of her capris. "Thanks." She nodded toward the door. "I need to find my family."

"I saw them in the cafeteria a few minutes ago." He pointed to the elevator. "Go to the first floor and turn right. Walk to the end of the hall."

"Colin?"

"Yes, Anna?"

The way he said her name made her believe he cared about her dad and her. "My father's going to be okay, right?"

"We'll do our very best, but in my experience, he's an excellent candidate to make a full recovery."

She dropped her head, hoping he was right and they wouldn't lose Dad. "I'm scared."

"That is completely understandable." He reached in his pocket and withdrew another slip of paper. "This is a bit unorthodox, but here's my number. If you need to talk, give me a call. Anytime."

She extended her hand. He clasped it. The warmth went up her arm and wrapped around her. Surprised, she gasped and stared into his eyes. Time seemed to stand still.

"Anna." The sound of Mom's voice broke the trance Colin's eyes seemed to have trapped her in.

"Um, Mom, are you ready to leave?"

Distracted, she fumbled with her handbag. "No, but Dad wants me to go home so I'm going to let him rest."

"You can come back anytime you'd like, Mrs. Price."

"You'll call if anything changes, won't you?"

Colin's attention was focused on Mom. "Of course." He then looked at Anna as he spoke to her mom. "If you need to come back later, the front door will be locked. Use the ER entrance and tell them your husband is in ICU."

"We will." Anna slipped her arm through the crook of Mom's. "Let's go round up the troops and head home. I'm sure the little guys are anxious to see you." She gave Colin a smile of thanks and steered Mom in the direction of the elevator.

Colin watched Anna and her mother get on the elevator. He remembered her vividly. She had been sitting at the foot of her father's bed, surrounded by her entire family. He had wanted to ask her out on the spot, but that would have been totally unprofessional. After all, her father had had a heart attack and his nurse was going to hit on her? But time hadn't dimmed his attraction to her. How could he have held the torch for her this entire time? It wasn't like he had seen her around the area. He had been immersed in school and work, and Anna, well, she lived the glamorous life on a winery.

The elevator doors slid open and a nurse pushed an occupied bed into the hall. He stepped out of the way to let them pass. Time to get back to work. He walked through the unit doors and followed the nurse pushing the bed. A new patient would hopefully keep him distracted from the tall, beautiful brunette with the soft, chocolate-brown eyes.

3

The sun was just painting the sky from dark grayish purple to magenta, and clouds of peach drifted across the brightening blue sky. The hues of early morning gave Anna hope for the day ahead. She was behind the wheel with Mom in the passenger seat, her head turned to the horizon. Nothing bad could happen after such a glorious start. Could it?

"How did you sleep last night?"

Mom didn't look at her. "I didn't."

Anna's hands tightened on the steering wheel. "You should have called. I would have come over."

"You needed to rest. It's going to be a long day for all of us."

"Did you check on Dad during the night?"

"I called every hour."

The first night had to be the hardest on the spouse. Anna was worried that Mom was holding all her emotions in check.

"He was resting comfortably, so that's all that mattered." For the first time, Mom's voice cracked. She patted the bag in her lap. "I brought his reading glasses and that mystery book he started."

Anna wasn't about to tell Mom he probably wouldn't be up to reading anytime soon. If it made her feel better, it was worth bringing it to the hospital. "Did you bring a sweater and something for you to read to keep your mind occupied while Dad's in surgery?"

"I can read his book but I don't expect I'll be able to concentrate on anything until it's over and I know he's okay." Her hands tightened on the bag's strap. "I'm scared."

Anna slowed the car and pulled over. She put the car in park and faced her mom. "We're all frightened, but we have each other to lean on, and Dad has all of us. Together, we can get through anything." She pulled her mom's cold, clammy hand away from the strap she was clutching. "Mom, you can count on me."

"I know." Her eyes were bright but she didn't shed a tear. "We should get to the hospital. I need to see your father before they take him down at seven."

She gave Mom's hand one final squeeze and turned her attention back to the road. They drove the remainder of the trip in silence, mother and daughter each lost in their own thoughts and fears.

Don, Tessa, and Jack's cars were already in the visitor lot when Anna parked. Liza had to get the boys off to school, and Leo had volunteered to stop over and help. The boys had been off the wall last night once they learned their grandfather had to stay in the hospital and have surgery. Liza was sure it had a lot to do with losing their dad, and Leo was ready to lend a guiding hand. Once the boys were on the bus, they'd join the family.

Mom sat still as a statue after the car was turned off. "I don't want to go inside."

"Why not?" Just minutes ago, Mom had wanted to get to the hospital and now she didn't want to get out of the car.

"If we don't, the clock won't start ticking down to when he goes into surgery."

"You need to look at it another way. Once Dad's out of surgery, he'll be on the road to a full recovery. Surgery is the first step."

A sob escaped her. "I couldn't bear it if anything happened to him."

"He has good doctors and Dad is too stubborn to give up." Anna's heart broke a little. She knew her parents loved each other, but this was the first time she had seen her mother so vulnerable.

Mom tapped her temple. "I know that here but"—she tapped the middle of her chest—"in here, I'm terrified."

Anna placed her hand over Mom's. "You're not alone. You have all of your children to lean on today—and for all the days ahead."

"I'm ready." Her voice was shaky but Mom got out of the car, still clutching her bag as if it were her lifeline.

Anna hit the lock button on her car and walked with her mom, arm in arm, across the lot and through the main doors. She gave Mom's arm a squeeze. "He's going to be just fine."

Mom gave Anna a tentative smile as they waited for the elevator. They rode to the fourth floor in silence. Once they stepped off, they discovered the waiting area directly across the hall. Just as Anna suspected, Don, Kate, and Jack were waiting inside. Tessa and Max came from the opposite direction, juggling cardboard trays of what Anna hoped was strong coffee. Other than wine, her family had coffee flowing through their veins.

"Has anyone been in to see your father yet?" Mom asked.

"We were waiting for you." Don leaned in and brushed his lips against her cheek. "How are you doing?"

"I'm okay." She hesitated and then walked into the critical care unit and paused at the desk while she spoke with a nurse before making her way to Dad's bedside.

Anna could see through the glass walls that there was a different nurse standing next to Dad's hospital bed. She seemed to be taking his vital signs. The family went into the waiting room and sat down.

Tessa leaned forward and massaged her temples. Max slid his arm around her shoulders. Not speaking to anyone, she said, "I feel awful. If it hadn't been for the wedding, Dad would have gotten to the doctor sooner."

Anna's head swiveled in her direction. "I think it's just the opposite. Dad was having symptoms and he was ignoring them. If we hadn't had brunch, more than likely he would have just kept ignoring them, had a heart attack, and who knows if he would have been driving his car, wandering in the vineyard, or what. He might have collapsed without anyone around."

Jack added, "Anna's right. Dad's a stubborn guy. We have no idea how long he was having issues before the wedding."

Tessa shook her head. "No. But."

"No buts." Mom strode into the room. "Each of you need to go spend a minute or two with Dad before they take him to surgery." She pointed to Don and Kate. "We'll go in order of age."

Anna couldn't help but chuckle a little. "You're always going to organize us by birth order, aren't you, Mom?"

She gave Anna the first real smile of the day. "Mothers have been using that particular method for generations. It works, so why change?"

Don and Kate left the waiting area, hand in hand. Anna could only guess what they were thinking. She felt the weight of the world on her shoulders.

"Will Liza and Leo arrive in time to see Dad?"

Max held up his phone. "I got a text from my sister. She's going over to Liza's to get the boys on the bus, so Leo and Liza should be here shortly."

Tessa clasped his hand. "That's really nice of her."

He kissed the back of her hand. "We're family, remember?"

Tessa rested her head on his shoulder. Anna felt the old familiar longing of wanting that too. Someone to lean on in the tough days and have fun with on the good ones.

Colin poked his head around the corner. "Good morning."

Anna stood up and crossed the small space to him.

"Hi. Have you seen my dad yet?"

"No. I was walking in and saw you sitting here, so I wanted to check in. Make sure you're holding up okay." His gaze swept the room. "All of you." But his eyes came back to rest on her.

Mom looked from Colin to Anna and then back to Colin. "That is very kind of you."

Anna stuck her hands in the pockets of her lightweight sweatshirt. "Will you be in surgery with Dad?"

With a shake of his head, he said, "No. I'm not a part of the surgery team, but I'll check on him before he goes down and I'll be here when he comes up from recovery."

"I see." She looked at the floor, disappointed, and realized she'd feel better if Colin was with him.

"I can check in with the operating room if you'd like while he's down there."

She brightened. "You can do that?"

"You can relax. I'll be here all day and you still have my number, right?"

Anna nodded, oblivious that her family was listening intently to this conversation. "I do."

"If you can't find me, just call. If I don't answer, leave a message and I'll find you. I'm assuming you're going to be here for the day?"

"Until Dad is back and resting comfortably, you won't be able to pry me out of here." She gave a half smile.

"You're welcome to stay. The surgery will last around five hours, and then he'll be in recovery while he comes out of anesthesia. Then he'll be in ICU for a least twenty-four hours so we can monitor him. After that, he should be able to be moved to a regular room for another five to six days before discharge."

"Will you be handling his case even after he's moved to a regular room?" She chewed the corner of her lip and glanced in Dad's direction. She only wanted the best for him, and having Colin around bolstered her confidence that Dad was getting the best care possible.

He gave her a reassuring smile. "Yes. I'm not restricted to the ICU, so I'm part of his care team while he's in the hospital, which means you can't get rid of me that easily."

"Anna, it's your turn to see Dad."

"Oh." She tossed a look to Tessa as she rushed from the room. Over her shoulder, she said, "I'll be right out."

Liza and Leo stepped from the elevator as she hurried by.

"Hey, Anna, where's Mom?"

She jerked a thumb at the waiting room. "In there."

Colin walked next to her as she made her way to her dad. Her heart was heavy in her chest and her footsteps became lead weights as she approached him. Despite what was ahead of him, Dad greeted her with a tired smile.

"Anna."

"Hey, Dad."

He gave Colin a quizzical look. "Do I have to go down already?"

"No, Sam. I just came in with your daughter."

She gave him a quick kiss on the cheek. "I love you, Dad, and I'll see you in a little while." She blinked away the tears that formed before she walked out of the unit. She was overwhelmed. Despite what she had said to her mom earlier, this was very serious.

4

The digital numbers on Anna's watch clicked in triple slow motion. Dad had been taken into surgery six hours ago. Colin walked into the waiting room and Anna got to her feet so quickly, the chair crashed against the wall.

"What's going on? It's been hours since you've given us an update." She could hear the accusatory tone in her voice. Like Colin was the reason things had taken so long.

"I'm sorry. I got called away for an emergency." Colin sat next to Mom. "Mrs. Price, I've just come up from the recovery room, where your husband is resting comfortably. Dr. Thomas was called into an emergency and asked for me to let you know the surgery was more complicated than he had anticipated but feels confident your husband will have a complete recovery. He'll be up to see you as soon as he can, but he didn't want you to have to wait unnecessarily for an update."

Mom clutched the front of her sweater. "When can I see him?"

"He'll be brought up in about an hour. Once his nurses get him settled, you can see him for a few minutes."

Anna watched as he looked around at the rest of the family, who were uncharacteristically silent.

"Does anyone have any specific questions?"

She asked, "Can we see him tonight or would it be better to wait until tomorrow?"

"I'll defer to your mother. He will be sleeping, so if you want to see him, you can, but he more than likely won't know you're there."

Anna knelt next to Mom. "I'll wait to take you home."

She shook her head. "I'm not leaving. You can all go home and I'll call if there are any changes."

Anna swiveled toward Colin. "Do you think we should stay?"

"Honestly, there won't be much you can do tonight, so getting a good night's rest is the best thing you can do for your parents."

"What about Mom?"

"I'll find a sleep chair to put next to your dad's bed." Colin looked at Mom. "You'd rest better in your own bed. ICU is pretty noisy."

She shook her head and rose to her feet, her lips in a thin, determined line. "I'm not going anywhere until I know Sam is out of danger."

Anna gave Colin an apologetic smile. "She's hardheaded."

He seemed to have to tear his eyes away from Anna—or was that her wishful thinking?—and said, "I understand. Mrs. Price, let me check with the recovery room and see if they're still on schedule."

Anna slipped her arm around Mom's shoulders and got a smile of thanks in return. Relief washed over Anna. Watching Colin walk toward the desk, her heartbeat quickened. He wore scrubs well.

"Mom, you haven't had much to eat today. Let's go to the cafeteria and we'll grab a bite while we wait for news."

Mom allowed herself to be steered toward the elevator

with the family around her until she saw Colin. "I want to hear the update first."

"Sherry, it looks like you were on your way out. But everything went well and Sam will be brought up in just under an hour."

"We were going to get something to eat."

"You have plenty of time." He gestured to the elevator.

"Thank you. I just need a break." Mom looked at Anna and said, "Are you coming with us?"

"You all go ahead and I'll join you in a bit."

Colin watched as the Price family got on the elevator, except for Anna. She slowly turned and walked toward him. The smile slipped from her lips to her eyes. Damn, she was beautiful. He had to remind himself her father was his patient. That had to be his main focus. Maybe after Sam was discharged, he'd find a way to run into her and ask her out, or maybe he could ask her if he could call.

"What did you find out?"

"Find out?" He was confused, and then the fog cleared. "Sorry, my mind was elsewhere." There was no way he was going to ask for her number right now, no matter how hard his heart was hammering in his chest.

"It's okay."

"I expect your father back in about forty-five minutes, and he's doing well."

She nodded. "That's good." She pointed to the elevator but seemed to be reluctant to follow her family. "I'll be in the cafeteria. So if anything should change, you know where to find me," she stammered. "Us."

"Right." He picked up a chart. "I have rounds to make. Patients to see."

"I'll see you later then?"

Did he detect a note of hopefulness in her voice? "I will definitely be around."

"See you later." She made her way down the hall to the elevator and pressed the button. He stood there, unwilling to move. Just in case she had another question. Or at least that was what he told himself.

She glanced over her shoulder, her face flushed the prettiest shade of pink. He moved quickly down the hall in the opposite direction. Nothing like getting caught staring. Well, maybe she'd give him a second thought. Then he groaned. He wanted her to not only give him a second thought but take a good long look and then agree to go on a date.

For the next hour, he focused on his patients, checking on a woman who was scheduled to be discharged the next day, and following up in the cardiac rehab center on several others. One of the many things he loved about working in the hospital was his hands-on contact with patients. It wasn't like an office, where people drifted in and out every fifteen minutes. This setting was more conducive to his way of being a staff healthcare provider.

He glanced at his watch as he finished up the chart note on his last rehab patient. It was time to get back to the unit and check to see if Sam Price was up from recovery yet, and thinking of Sam led his thoughts to Anna.

What did she like to do to have fun? How could he find out? He pushed through the door and sauntered into the cardiac unit. Several nurses were surrounding Sam's bed. They had just finished adjusting the monitors when he approached.

Sam was alert and looking around for, Colin assumed, Sherry.

He picked up the chart and glanced at the recorded vital signs. Everything looked good, especially for someone just fresh from open heart surgery.

"Sam, how are you feeling?"

He croaked, "Not bad." He smacked his lips. "Dry."

"I see you had some nausea in recovery. How about you have some ice chips to start with?"

Sam gave a slight nod.

"Are you ready for Sherry to come in?"

Again, he gave a single nod. His eyes were heavy.

"Your family is waiting and if you're up to it, they can check on you very briefly. But if you're not, they'll certainly understand."

His eyes fluttered as he struggled to stay awake.

"Sam, you rest and I'll get your wife."

He didn't answer, which was completely normal, given the circumstances. One of the nurses came back with a cup of ice chips and a spoon. She placed it on the tray next to Sam's bed.

Colin thanked her.

As soon as he walked into the waiting room, everyone stood up. Anna held on to her mother's arm. Sherry looked worn out from worry.

"I have good news. Sam's vitals look good and he's resting comfortably. He suffered from nausea and a bit of vomiting in recovery, but that is pretty normal. Mrs. Price, he's asking for you."

She brightened and took a step forward. "Can I see him now?"

Anna said, "What about the rest of us?"

"I'd like Sam to rest and you could see him tomorrow. But I'm sure you'll all sleep better if you see him for a moment or two for each of you to say good night." Why did he phrase it that way? There were rules for patients after surgery in the cardiac unit. Here he was trying to be some kind of softie.

Don said, "We'll wait until tomorrow. He knows we're here and that if he needs something, all Mom has to do is ask." Everyone was slow to agree but after a sharp look from Anna, they nodded in agreement.

Relieved, Colin said, "Mrs. Price, are you ready?"

She slung her handbag across her shoulder and, without a backward glance, followed Colin down the short hallway. Her sure and steady steps propelled her through the busy unit, where machines were beeping and nurses were checking on other patients. She stopped next to the open curtain, where her husband lay with his eyes closed.

"Are you sure he's okay? He looks so pale and frail."

Colin could hear the tremor in her voice. "He's sleeping off the anesthesia and once that gets out of his system, he'll do much better." He guided her to the chair and said, "When he wakes up, you can give him some ice chips. Go slowly, as we don't want him to become nauseous again."

She nodded. "Will you tell everyone to go home and let them know I'll call later. I don't want them to see their dad like this. They'll worry too much."

He had to wonder how they would take that directive from him. But he had faced tougher moments in his career. Sadly, when they left, that meant Anna would leave too.

He left Sherry sitting by the bed, holding Sam's hand. She wasn't talking but waiting for him to open his eyes. Colin gave her an encouraging smile. "Be patient. He'll wake up again soon."

Thank you, she mouthed.

Colin went directly to the waiting room. Members of the Price family were milling about the room. Anna's head was in her hands. "Hey, are you okay?" He knelt down next to her.

"Just a little overwhelmed."

Kate rubbed her shoulders. "I don't think she had enough water to drink today."

"I'll be right back." He hurried from the waiting room and went to the efficiency kitchen in the unit and grabbed a bottle of water.

When he got back, Colin handed her the water. She gave him a grateful smile. "I guess in all the hustle of the day, I may have neglected a few things—like good hydration." She drank about half the bottle.

"Are you feeling better?" he asked.

"Yes, thank you."

Well, at least this incident would support Sherry's request.

He clasped his hands together. "Your mother asked me to tell you to go home. If she needs something, she'll call."

Anna shook her head. "I'm staying. The rest of you go home." She looked at one of her brothers. "Don take Kate home and have dinner with Ben." She then pointed at her other brothers and the sister who had kids. "Jack and Leo, you guys can help Liza with the boys, as I'm sure they'll be more than a handful."

Tessa stepped forward. "Max and I will stay with you."

Anna shook her head. "You're supposed to be on your honeymoon, so the least you can do is get out of here and have a romantic dinner." She grinned at the couple. "You're welcome."

Colin marveled at the way she dispatched every member of her family with expediency. There was a quiet strength emerging, and she was quite the enforcer of Sherry's wishes. With promises to call if there were any issues or concerns, Anna and Colin waited until the elevator doors closed on the family.

She then turned to him. "Now. Was there something you didn't want to say in front of my family?"

5

Anna's heart pounded in her chest. She steeled herself for bad news. Why had Colin encouraged everyone to leave? Surely if Dad were in bad shape, he would never have done that, right?

"It's nothing, really. Your mother wanted to be alone with your dad and she was concerned that the rest of the family wouldn't leave if I didn't suggest it."

"You're being straight with me? There's nothing wrong with Dad?"

He looked her in the eye, his voice steady, and she could hear the sincerity in his words. "He's resting comfortably."

She sucked in a deep, ragged breath and her hand rested at the base of her throat. She turned away. All she wanted to do was sink into a chair and cry. Her emotions had been on a roller coaster since yesterday when Dad left the house in an ambulance.

Colin steered her to a chair by the window. It was then the tears began to flow unchecked. He put his arm around her and comforted her until she had no more tears left to shed.

She wiped her cheeks with the back of her hand. Embarrassed, she kept her eyes on the floor. "I'm sorry. I don't know what set me off." He withdrew his arm. Suddenly, she felt chilled to the bone, as if he were a cozy blanket.

"You've been under a lot of stress and needed to release it."

He was handsome with hazel eyes that were flecked with gold; high, chiseled cheekbones; and a small scar just above his right eyebrow. She couldn't help but notice his scruff of a beard; it suited him and she liked it. The red in his closely cropped strawberry-blond hair was echoed in his beard. "You're a nice man." She clasped her hands in her lap. "Do you think I could peek in on my parents and just double-check to make sure Mom really wants to stay here for the night?"

"Come on. I'll walk you down." He seemed to hesitate before asking, "I was wondering if you'd like to have a cup of coffee sometime?"

She stopped midstep. She wasn't sure if he was asking because he felt bad for her after watching her sob her brains out. She stammered, "Sure. Anytime."

He grinned. "You have my number, so let me know when you're free."

Her heart skipped and she fumbled with her bag. He wanted to have coffee. She withdrew her cell and looked at him from the corner of her eye.

His cell pinged and he withdrew it to glance at the screen. His smile grew.

She placed a hand on his arm; her fingertips tingled at the connection. "Your schedule is much busier than mine, being in the medical field, so now you can give me a call when you're free."

"I will. You can count on it." He opened the door to the ICU and they walked in the direction of Dad's bed. All the while, thoughts raced in her head. She couldn't even turn to look at Colin since it was uncharacteristic for her to be so forward, especially since she really liked him and the first time they had met, she had been tongue-tied. She inwardly groaned and reminded herself it was just coffee. Not a big deal.

Her footsteps slowed as she grew closer to her father's bed. Her mom's eyes were closed. It was then her heart melted—Mom's arm rested on the bed and her fingers were entwined with Dad's. She could feel Colin watching her. Anna stepped away and pointed toward the door, and he followed her again.

"Since they're both asleep, I'll go home and come back later. I can pick up some food for her."

"That sounds like a good idea." He pushed the automatic door button.

Unsure what to do, she said, "I'll see you tomorrow, I guess."

"I'll be here."

"Are you here all the time?"

"It seems like it, but my shifts can be from eight to twelve hours depending on staffing, and I work one weekend a month."

"That's a busy schedule. I thought the wine business was demanding. I work a lot of hours too, but mine are more seasonal. Not that I'm comparing what you do. Caring for people and me blending wines isn't the same category at all."

"Some people would say what you do is more important than my job. Red wine keeps the heart doctor away and all."

Anna stepped in front of him and lightly touched his arm. The warmth of his body flowed into the tips of her fingers. "Thanks for everything. It was comforting to know we could turn to you for answers."

"It was my pleasure." He gave her a gentle smile.

"I know it was your job and all, but you went above and beyond."

"Anna. I wanted to help you. This is tough stuff and I'm glad to be a part of your father's recovery."

He seemed to add emphasis to the *you*. "Alright then." She took a halting step toward the elevator. "See you later."

"Bye." He continued to stand there as she took a few steps away from him.

Feeling self-conscious, she jabbed the elevator call button and stared at the metal doors until they slid open. Once inside, she turned and Colin gave her a wave.

She put a hand out to support her knocking knees. He was so good-looking and kind, and he had asked her for coffee. She was definitely going to answer that call.

She crossed the lobby and as she got close to the exit door, her cell phone rang. She grinned when she saw the caller ID. "Hello, Colin." She could feel the smile spread across her lips.

"Hi, Anna. I was wondering if you'd like to have coffee with me on Saturday."

"I would love to."

"If for any reason we can't do it Saturday, would you give me a rain check?"

"Absolutely." She grinned. He really did want to go out with her. Sweet! She did a two-step jig as she walked into the last gleam of sunlight.

"Great. I'll look forward to seeing you here tomorrow."

"Me too. Goodbye, Colin."

"Good night, Anna."

There was a soft click and the line went silent.

She grinned as she stopped and drank in the sweet, earthy smell of spring. Her mom always had said that out of something bad comes good. Boy, was she right.

Anna woke with a start the next morning. The sun was poking through the slats of the wooden blinds on her living room window. She stretched to work out the kink in her neck. So much for sitting down for a few minutes. She grabbed her phone from the floor and checked for messages. Nothing.

She punched in the direct line to the cardiac unit and waited. A woman answered on the second ring.

"Cardiac. This is Sonia."

"Good morning, Sonia. This is Anna Price. I wanted to check on my father, Sam Price."

"Hold a moment, please? I just came on duty so I need to check the chart."

Anna got up and crossed the room, pulling up the blinds to let the sun stream in. It was a glorious morning, full of possibilities.

"Anna, it was an uneventful night. Would you like me to ask your mother to give you a call?"

"Not needed. I'll bring her some breakfast soon. Can Dad have something to eat from the bakery?"

"Unfortunately, no. He has to start with liquids. We'll introduce something more solid tomorrow."

Anna could almost see the nurse on the other end of the phone—crisp, efficient, and all business. "Thank you for the update and I'll see you later."

She tossed the phone in her vacated chair and took the stairs two at a time. A shower, coffee, and then the bakery for breakfast sandwiches and more steaming hot coffee.

She carefully applied makeup after blow-drying her hair and securing it in a barrette. She checked her outfit in the mirror. Typically, she didn't fuss over clothes and makeup unless she was going out on a date, but she wanted to look nice when she saw Colin.

She frowned at her reflection. "What am I thinking? My father is lying in a hospital bed and I'm looking to impress his NP." Gathering up her cell phone, laptop bag, and her denim jacket, she dashed through the door and ran lightly down the front steps. The April morning was crisp and cool with the sun rising in the crystal-blue sky. It was a good growing day for the vines.

Once she pushed the ignition button in the car, the engine purred to life. Since there were no voicemails or text messages, she needed to get the family phone tree going on the way to the bakery to give the update.

Using hands free, she called Don. He could pass along what she knew. Kate answered on the first ring.

"Morning, Anna. Have you heard from the hospital?"

"I called when I got up and Dad had a good night."

"Good. Don called around midnight and he was keeping water down but dealing with some discomfort, so they changed his pain medication."

"Oh. I didn't know that." Anna wished Don had sent her a message to fill her in. "Is my brother around?"

"He just got Ben up. Hold on a minute and I'll get him."

Anna could hear Ben's sweet little voice in the background talking about his fruit choice for his oatmeal.

Don said, "Hi, Anna-banana."

She smiled at the nickname. "Hi, Don. Kate said you checked in on Dad last night."

"It was right before we went to bed. I couldn't stop worrying. Kate suggested I call."

"I wish you had sent me a text or better yet, a group text. I'm sure it would have eased everyone's minds." She wasn't successful in keeping her tone neutral and annoyance bled through.

"I'm sorry. I didn't think about it."

He did sound genuinely sorry and she regretted her snarky comment. "I'm sorry, Don. I should haven't been short with you. We should agree from this point forward to keep the family all in the same loop."

"Sounds good. Did you talk to Mom this morning?"

"No. I called the hospital and talked with a nurse. He's

doing well and should be on a liquid diet today, easing into something more solid by tomorrow."

"That's good news."

She could hear the genuine relief in his voice. "Can you either call or group text that I'm headed there now and when I go into the office, maybe someone else wants to stop over. I think if we keep it to one kid at a time, we can make sure Mom's getting something to eat and maybe even some rest."

"I like that idea. And I'll send the text with both the update from last night and this morning."

She turned into the parking lot of the bakery. "I gotta let you go. I'm picking up breakfast for me and Mom. But I'll be sure to send you a text once I see Dad with my own eyes." And maybe she'd grab a coffee for Colin too.

"You know the old man is tough and he'll get through this. It's just..."

"Hard." She finished for him. "I'll check in later."

She turned the engine off and sat with her hands gripping the steering wheel. What would the family do without Dad? He was demanding and at times unyielding, but he was their dad.

Her phone pinged with a text from Mom.

Any chance you can bring me a decent cup of coffee?

With a chuckle, she texted her back. *Once step ahead of you. Bringing coffee and breakfast. See you shortly.*

A return thumbs-up emoji was her reply. Anna smiled. Her mom had really embraced the whole texting thing. Whereas Dad never answered a text; he called. He was an original.

Her phone pinged again.

Can you bring something sweet and savory?

Anna laughed out loud. *Got ya covered.*

6

When Anna walked into the cardiac unit, she quickly surveyed the area, hoping to catch a glimpse of Colin. It seemed quieter today, with fewer patients. Hopefully that was good news and not the unthinkable.

She made a beeline for Dad's bed. He was propped up and smiling as she approached.

"Hello there. You certainly do look better today than the last time I saw you." She handed Mom an insulated cup and the bag with breakfast sandwiches and muffins. "Dig in."

Dad's bushy gray-blond eyebrows wiggled. "Got anything in there for your dear old pop?"

With a snort, she said, "Per doctor orders, you're on liquids for a bit longer. Then I'm sure we can find you something to eat that will taste mighty good." She perched on the corner of the bed and turned to her mother. "Did you get any sleep last night?"

"I did and actually, this chair is pretty comfortable."

Dad gave them both a stern look. "You should have taken your mother home last night."

"Now, Sam," Mom admonished, "you would have done

exactly the same thing if the roles had been reversed."

"Don't be so sure of yourself. If I had to choose between our nice comfy bed or a vinyl chair, I don't think it would have been a difficult choice."

Anna playfully tapped the bedcovers. "Dad, this would have been your choice and you know it."

Dad looked around Anna and gave a welcoming smile. "Good morning, Colin. I was just trying to convince my daughter to give me something out of that bakery bag."

"Hello, Sam." He was talking to Dad but his eyes met Anna's before focusing on Sam. "How are you feeling today?"

"Not bad considering you guys cracked open my chest and did a graft." He tried to shift on the bed and grimaced. "I know it can be dicey; we do something similar with grape vines." His eyes got a mischievous look. "You should swing by our winery and Anna can show you what I'm talking about."

Colin's eyes once again met Anna's and he smiled. The gold flecks were more pronounced today. "I'd like that."

She didn't need her father playing matchmaker from his hospital bed. She held out a to-go cup to Colin. "I wasn't sure how you took your coffee, so there's cream and sugar in the bag."

"Thank you." His smile caused her heart to skitter in her chest.

He flipped open the laptop in his hands. "Sam, let's talk about you, though, before we make other plans." He scrolled down. "I see your vitals are strong. Pain meds are controlling your discomfort." He nodded. "All good signs."

"When can I get up and walk around?"

"Did they get you up last night?"

"I stood by the bed but I didn't walk."

Colin held Dad's wrist with his fingers. "How did it feel? Okay?"

"Yeah, I used that heart pillow over my chest and they had me move very slowly. But I'd really like to get moving. I know the sooner I do, the sooner I can go home."

He released Dad's hand. "Your pulse is good. I'm going to listen to your heart and then answer all your questions." Colin stepped closer to the bed. "Can you lean forward for me?"

Dad sat up. A flash of pain crossed his face. Anna was ready to assist with supporting him but the look on his face told her that was the last thing he wanted. It would make him appear weak.

Colin draped the stethoscope around his neck. "Here's our plan. Today, you'll sit in the chair for your meals and walk up and down the hall a few times, with help from a couple of nurses. Please do not try to get out of bed without help. At least not yet. Tomorrow, you'll spend more time out of bed and do a few more walks than today. Each day, you'll get stronger and in a few days, we'll talk about your discharge plan."

"That quick? Good." Sam tried to scooch forward to the edge of the bed. "Guess it's time to get up."

"Dad, Colin just said you need help getting out of bed."

He cocked his head to one side. "You're both here. So, you can help me."

Colin gave a short laugh. "I wish all my patients had your grit."

He gave a quick wave to the desk nurse and then adjusted a recliner chair close to the bed. "We're going to slide Sam from the bed to the chair, and try not to worry." His eyes locked on Anna's. "We've done this a few times before today."

Anna's insides clenched. She appreciated his attempt to lighten the mood but was Dad ready to make the move? Standing was one thing. Getting up and taking a few steps was another. But she had to trust that Colin knew best.

He gave her an encouraging smile as if reading her thoughts and said, "Trust me."

With those two simple words, her worry fell away. In the very short time she had spent with him, she knew without a doubt that she could trust him with her father's safety. She wondered if she could trust him with more than just medical issues. Could she trust him completely?

"Sam, we're going to wait for one of the other nurses. She can show Anna and Sherry the correct way to move you, but I strongly caution you; do not attempt this without one of the nurses here. At least until you're stronger."

Dad grumbled. He never liked being told anything.

Mom pushed back from the bed and her eyes darted between Anna and Dad. "Are you sure he's ready?"

"Mom, it's okay. They wouldn't be getting Dad up if it wasn't safe." She glanced at Colin and continued to speak to her mother. "Let's get out of their hair for the moment and then if it goes well, Colin can show us as soon as we're back." She eased Mom away from the bed. "We should go have our breakfast in the waiting room. We won't be gone long."

Dad gave an impatient wave with his hand. "Good idea, Anna. Your mother could use a change of scenery."

"Sam." She gave him a steady gaze. "I want to be here with you."

"I've just had surgery and in case I fall flat on my face, I'd rather you didn't witness that."

A woman in blue scrubs approached them. With a cheery smile on her face, she focused her attention on Sam. "Hello, I'm Sonia. I'm going to be one of your nurses today, Sam."

Anna flashed her a smile. "Hi. We spoke on the phone this morning. I'm Anna."

She took the bakery bag from Mom, who had been clutching it so tight, it ripped a little as Anna withdrew it from her hands. "Break time."

Mom reluctantly walked down the hall with Anna.

Looking back over her shoulder, she said, "Are you sure he's going to be alright?"

"Yes, I'm sure." Anna ushered Mom into the bright and sunny waiting room. She set the bag on a small table. "Let's eat here."

Mom sat down, seemingly unaware of her surroundings. As if in a daze, she fiddled with her coffee cup. "Can I tell you something?"

Anna waited patiently. "You can talk to me about anything."

"This time, Dad being in the hospital was a kick in the pants. For the first time, I thought this could be history repeating itself, like with Grandpa Donald. He died young and so could your dad."

"He's going to be fine. You have to believe that."

"I know the surgery was a success. But I've had time to think about our family, you and Leo in particular."

"Why the two of us?" *Now, this should be interesting.*

"You and your brother are the only two who don't have someone special by your side. I don't want you to miss out on the most important adventure in life."

"What about Jack?"

"Everyone knows he's still in love with Peyton. There's still time for those two."

That made some kind of sense. "When the time is right, Mom, we will. It's not something you should be worrying about now." The last thing Anna wanted to do was feed into what was apparently her mom's worst fear—that she would live her life alone.

But wait a minute. That was her choice. She wasn't going to settle for just any guy. He had to be the right guy for her. So far, her dating experience had left her wanting more from the men she had met.

"Mom, I'm sure Leo would say the same thing." She took the top off her coffee cup and set it aside. "What about Liza?"

"She was lucky to have been married and has two wonderful sons. And since Liza found it once, I know she'll find it again."

"Thanks for your vote of confidence." Anna hung her head. Wasn't it nice that her mother thought she was inept at finding love?

"I didn't mean that how it sounded. What I'm trying to say is when the time comes, she'll recognize it. At times like this, one tends to look at life a little differently. Dad and I have been so blessed. We have each other and six wonderful children, and now grandchildren. My life is rich beyond measure. Is it so wrong to want all my children to find happiness?"

"No, it's not. But don't you think I would like to have someone special in my life?" She sipped the lukewarm coffee.

"Are you happy, Anna?"

Her head snapped up. "What makes you ask?"

"I have eyes." Mom dug into the bakery bag and set a paper-wrapped sandwich on the table. "You haven't been yourself in quite some time, and I haven't known how to help."

"Don't worry about me, Mom. I've been a little off-kilter but I'm working my way back."

"Buying a red-hot sports car won't bring you happiness. It's just an object, a substitute, if you will."

"I'm not having a midlife crisis, if that's what you're inferring." Anna could hear the defensiveness in her voice.

Mom laughed. "You're not old enough to have a midlife crisis." She patted Anna's hand.

She debated if she should tell Mom about her coffee date. Maybe it would help her relax and stop worrying. "Now, I don't want you to make more of this than what it is, but I do happen to have a coffee date for Saturday, depending on what you and Dad might need from me."

"Indulge your mother. I could use the distraction." Mom's

smile warmed her eyes. "Someone we know?"

"I'm not going to tell you any more other than he's a very nice man and I'm looking forward to it."

"I can't wait to hear to all the details, and you have all the time in the world on Saturday to enjoy your date. You have five brothers and sisters who can help us if we need something."

Sam sat on the edge of the bed, the heart-shaped therapy pillow clutched against his chest. He gave Colin a searching look.

"Are you married? Or in a relationship?"

Colin wondered where this was coming from. "No. Why?"

Sonia gave him a rare smile as she tucked her hand under Sam's elbow. Colin did the same.

He said, "Let me know when you're ready, Sam."

"Anna's not dating anyone." He gritted his teeth as if preparing for pain. "You should ask her out for a drink."

"I'll give it some thought." He gave Sonia a slight nod. "On three, Sam, I want you to keep the pillow tight and push off with your legs."

He gave a slight nod. "Ready."

"Sam, focus. Now. One. Two. Three." Colin held tight, and he knew from years of working with Sonia that she did the same. Sam grunted. As he rose to his feet, beads of sweat appeared above his lip.

Sam gave him a half smile. "Look at me on my feet." With a sidelong look, he grinned. "Now, about Anna."

Colin shook his head in disbelief; Sam Price was not a man easily dissuaded. He pretended not to have heard the comment as he eased him to the chair. *Sam trying to meddle won't stop me from dating Anna, and Saturday can't come fast enough.*

7

Saturday morning arrived, warm and sunny, as Anna pulled up to the front entrance of the hospital in Dad's oversized SUV. Her sports car was not going to cut it for bringing him home. Besides, he wanted to have some bulk around him. Since the surgery, he felt vulnerable to so many things: falling, keeping pain in check, getting a cold. The list seemed so endless Anna had lost track of everything. When she asked Colin if this was normal, he said every person dealt with open heart surgery in their own way and to have an extra dose of patience with him.

She peered through the windshield. The glass doors slid open and a nurse pushed her father in a wheelchair. He held the heart-shaped pillow to his chest. She hopped out and went around to the passenger side. She glanced behind Dad, hoping to see Colin, and was disappointed when she didn't.

"I'll bet you're ready to go home." She noted his face had a healthy glow instead of that gray undertone he'd had last Sunday at brunch.

She tossed her shoulder bag into the back seat and left both the front and rear passenger doors open.

The nurse locked the wheels on the chair and flipped up the footrests. "Are you ready, Sam?"

He looked at Anna, Mom, and then the nurse.

He cleared his throat and rubbed the palms of his hands on his jeans. "As ready as I'm gonna be." He hunched his shoulders down and over his chest. "I'm going to go slow."

The nurse was ready to assist him. Anna stood in front of him just in case he fell forward, and Mom was on the other side.

"Don't worry, Dad. We've got you covered."

He leaned forward and eased to his feet. He paused and pulled himself upright. "So far, so good."

The nurse pulled the wheelchair back so that Dad could step forward and Anna took over, holding on to his arm as she mirrored his halting steps.

"Kind of a big step up." Dad gave her a sideways glance. "Maybe you should have brought Mom's car."

"You wanted me to bring the SUV. Remember?"

His brow furrowed. "Do you always have to listen to me?"

She couldn't help it and let out a half snort, half laugh. "Will you always micromanage what I do?"

He clutched her hand tighter. "As long as I'm breathing, I will."

Taking his time, he climbed into the passenger seat. Anna secured his seat belt and waited for Mom to get into the back. She took the vases of flowers and balloons from the nurse and a tote bag with cards and pictures from the boys, along with the hospital gear he'd need at home, and thanked her again for her help.

Before getting in, Anna sent a quick text to the family asking for some help when they got home. It would be better if her brothers helped Dad out of the SUV. He was a big guy and if he stumbled for any reason, Anna wouldn't be able to hold him up. She didn't bother to wait for an answer but checked the time before she stowed her phone in her jacket pocket. She was still planning on meeting Colin at two and things were going much slower than she had thought. Maybe she should cancel.

"Anna-banana, are we going to stay here all day?"

Even though he used her nickname, she could catch the impatience in his voice. Dad was more than ready to go home. During the drive to her parents' house, he remained silent.

"Are you in pain?" She glanced at her dad and then Mom in the rearview mirror.

He shook his head and continued to stare at the passing scenery. At this point, they were driving past acres of vines. Crescent Lake vines.

She kept one eye on Dad and watched a lone tear trickle down his cheek. This wasn't like him. Something had to be terribly wrong.

"Daddy." She touched his arm. "What's wrong?"

In a gruff voice, he said, "I'm happy to be going home."

"I'm glad they didn't have to keep you any longer too."

Dad remained silent. Mom reached over the back of the seat and put her hand on his shoulder.

A simple touch. Anna marveled at how Dad relaxed with the small gesture.

"I wasn't sure I'd have the opportunity to see my land again."

"Dad," she gasped. "What are you talking about?"

He reached up and patted Mom's hand. "This heart attack put my life in perspective and I've come to some decisions."

"Which are?"

"I'll tell everyone together, but suffice it to say there will be changes."

Anna gripped the steering wheel. Just as she suspected, more work and less freedom at the winery was about to be unleashed on them all. Any hope of making a change in her career had evaporated. She was the enologist of CLW. Suddenly, it didn't sound exciting. She'd be working with Jack, growing the grapes and then blending the different varieties for the rest of her career, something she could do in her sleep.

The driveway to the house came into view, pushing all other thoughts aside. There would be time enough to dwell on her dull future later.

Cars ringed the circle drive but had left a large space open at the base of the stairs. She gave the horn a quick toot. The front door opened and the family spilled out onto the large wraparound porch.

Dad turned in his seat. "Why is everyone here?"

Anna knew her voice held a gentle warning tone. "Everyone is happy to see you come home." She parked the SUV and turned it off.

Mom unbuckled her seat belt and pushed open her door. "Sam, everyone has been very worried and I'm sure they won't be staying long, so be nice." She got out and closed the door.

"Wait until I get around to the other side before you go hopping out," Anna said.

"No hopping for your old man." He gave her a tired smile. "And as soon as I'm inside, go home and get ready for your date."

Her mouth went slack. "Huh?"

Dad gave her a wink. "I happen to know you have a date with my NP. Not that it matters, but I approve."

She was at a loss for words until she muttered, "Is there anything you don't find out about?"

His expression was innocent and his brown eyes shone with happiness. "Enjoy your date. He really is a stand-up kind of man."

"You all need to stay out of my personal life."

Before Dad could respond, Jack opened the passenger

door and joked, "What's taking you guys so long? Waiting for us to roll out the red carpet or something?"

Dad winked at her and Anna knew her date would be kept just between them, at least for now.

"I thought you'd never get over here. Your sister was kind enough to pick me up and now she's turning me over to you." Dad carefully unbuckled his seat belt. "I gotta keep this pillow close to my chest as I move. It protects the incision." He held up the heart-shaped pillow. "Cute, huh. It's a heart to protect my heart." He gave a soft chuckle and turned so he could slide off the seat.

Anna watched as Jack took Dad's forearm and held it firmly. After a couple of deep, calming breaths, Dad leaned forward and his feet slid to the ground.

"Huh. That wasn't so bad."

As Dad started up the walkway, Mom was next to him. "Coming, Anna?"

"Yes, ma'am."

Dad made her head spin. He seemed to like that she was the steady, single daughter, able to work all kinds of hours that were needed and didn't have outside interests that would interfere with her job. Now he was actually encouraging her to date Colin. Did he feel sorry for her or, worse, think that Colin was her only option? He was a good-looking guy and nice, but maybe the attraction had been amplified from her concern over her father.

She was the last one in the house and walked to the back of the home, where everyone always seemed to gather. Something baking made her mouth water and if she were to guess, Kate, the chef in the family, had been cooking. The smell of coffee teased her senses. She headed to the pot to pour herself a mug. Her nephews were crowded around Dad's chair, asking a ton of questions, but the most important one to them was about his scar.

Johnny was standing to one side when he said, "Poppy.

It's okay that you got a big scar." His face was solemn. "Mommy says scars are the road map of our life and when you get a cut or sumthin, it just shows that you did stuff." He glanced at Liza. "Right, Mommy?"

Dad pulled him into a very careful hug. "Johnny, you're right. This scar shows that I want to keep on going for years to come."

He beamed. "See, Mom? Poppy gets it."

Everyone seemed to think the analogy about scars was cute and Dad looked content but tired. He was starting to droop.

Liza said, "Hey, everyone, we should go and let Dad get some rest. I'm sure he didn't get as much sleep as he could have in the hospital."

Dad slowly scanned the room, almost as if he were really seeing his family for the first time in a very long time. His face grew flushed and he dropped his gaze.

Anna rushed to his side and dropped down on one knee.

"Dad, what's wrong?"

"It's nothing." He patted her hand.

"I strongly disagree. Talk to us."

He lifted his head. "I'm a lucky man. A wonderful family that supports each other and an amazing woman who has shared my life for forty years. I'm going to do a better job of taking care of my health so I can be here for a long time."

Relief coursed through her. She was worried that he was having pain, or worse. "You scared me." She placed a kiss on his cheek.

He said, "I am tired. Do you think one of the guys can help me down the hall? I'd like to lie down for a while."

"I'll walk with you."

He shook his head and dropped his voice for her ears alone. "No. You've done enough. Go home and get ready to meet Colin." He squeezed her hand. "Don't forget what I told you."

"I won't, but I'll come back later and we can have dinner and watch a movie together."

"You're banned for the next twenty-four hours. It's time for you." He gave her a warm smile. "Have fun and don't worry about me. Promise?"

So much for keeping her date off the radar with the rest of the family. She waited while Don and Jack stepped forward, waiting for Dad to be ready to stand.

Anna pulled Mom to one side. "Call me if you need anything and I'll come right over. We're meeting at Sawyers so I can be here in ten minutes. Fifteen, tops."

"I agree with Dad. Have fun and don't worry about us. Your brothers and sisters are backing you up."

Mom trailed behind her sons and husband.

Liza and Kate steered her to a chair and Liza's smile warmed her eyes. "So, what was Dad talking about? Do you have a date?"

There was no getting out of this conversation without giving them a few details. "I'm meeting someone for coffee in a little while." She crossed her fingers behind her back when she said, "It's no big deal. Just trying to shake up my dull life."

"At Sawyers? Kind of upscale for coffee." Liza's eyebrow quirked up.

"I chose it so it was close to home, just in case." Anna felt the need to defend herself.

Kate said, "It doesn't matter where you go. I agree with what Sam and Sherry said. Have fun. You deserve it."

Liza looked at Kate. "Anna hasn't had a decent date in a long time. I hope she and Colin have a nice time."

"Why does everyone keep saying that? And I never said the date was with Colin."

"Call it a lucky guess. I like him; he's different in a good way." Liza continued. "To be honest, sis, I saw how he was looking at you a couple of times at the hospital when he thought no one was watching, and that's how a guy should look at you."

Anna could feel her cheeks grow hot. "I'm going to leave now, and no one had better drop by Sawyers to check up on me."

Liza flashed her a broad grin. "The thought hadn't crossed our minds until now."

Anna muttered as she left the room, "Yeah, right. And for the record, you guys need to find something else to do other than keep track of my dating life."

8

Butterflies raced in her stomach as Anna made her way up the walk. She paused before pulling open the door. What if this wasn't such a good idea? Maybe it was better to leave their flirtation as just that.

The first time she had met Colin, she was too shy to even think about asking him out. She had just broken up with Vic, and that relationship had sucked all the joy from her life. He had been borderline verbally abusive, and Anna knew the only reason he had dated her to begin with was because of the door her father could open for him. She hated the idea she might find Colin not who she thought he was and then she'd have to break it to him that she didn't want to see him again. Or worse, what if he rejected her? There was so much pressure for a first date. Did she look okay or was she too casual? *Here goes nothing.* Her forward motion caused her to almost walk into the door as it opened and a couple came out. She stepped to one side and waited for them to pass.

At least they look happy. She needed to snap out of this lack of confidence. Where was the woman who used to look at her from the bathroom mirror? She was a smart and funny woman and Colin was lucky they were having coffee together.

She straightened her shoulders and pressed a hand to her stomach in hopes of quieting the flutter, then stepped into the foyer. The heels of her sandals were muted on the deep carpet runner. Alan Waters, the owner of Sawyers, came over and welcomed her with a warm smile. He clasped her hand. "Anna, great to see you today. What brings you in?"

She took his hand and searched what she could see of the dining room. "I'm supposed to be meeting someone for coffee." She tried to hide her disappointment when she didn't see Colin.

"A tall guy with short blond hair and a beard?"

Typical guy description. "Yes, that sounds like him."

"He's in the bar."

"Thanks, Alan." She never thought to check the bar.

He released her hand with a squeeze. "Tell the family I said hello."

"Will do."

Colin saw Anna the moment she entered the bar. She was beautiful. The way she carried herself was confident but totally oblivious to how pretty she was. He liked that she was dressed in a simple white t-shirt, jeans, and a pale-green cardigan sweater. She had clipped her hair off her face. Those eyes were pools of melted chocolate he wanted to dive into and savor. As she approached, he stood up.

"Hi, Anna. You look very pretty." He gave her a friendly hug and noticed her perfume was soft and floral. It suited her.

"Thank you."

He held out her chair at the table. "I hope you don't mind we're in the bar. I thought it would be more relaxing and if you wanted something stronger than coffee, it would be readily available."

She flashed a smile. "Coffee's good." She placed her bag on the floor next to her feet. "Unless you'd like something else?"

He didn't want anything to dull his senses for their first date. He wanted to remember each moment. Damn, he sounded like a sap. Who had he become since meeting this woman? It was like he had a crush on a girl in middle school, the way he was reacting.

Before Anna had arrived, Alan had already brought the carafe of coffee to the table. Colin picked it up to pour. She gave him a warm but shy smile.

"Is there any cream?"

He passed her the small pitcher that was close to him and then poured his coffee. He watched as she added a packet of sugar, making a note of how she liked it.

"I'm so glad we're doing this."

"Me too." Her spoon clinked against the coffee mug.

There was an awkward silence.

Anna sipped her coffee and scanned the room. "Have you eaten dinner here?"

"I don't go out much because of my work schedule but I've heard it's good."

"My brother Don and Alan were in school together. He's been a friend of our family forever."

"He seemed like a nice guy when I came in."

She nodded and took another sip. Setting her cup down, it clattered against the spoon. "I'm just going to say this. I suck at first dates."

Colin couldn't help but laugh. Not the soft, polite kind either, but a deep belly laugh that filled the room and began to crack the tension between them. He didn't care who was watching; Anna's honesty was refreshing.

"Now that's good news. I was feeling like that pimple-faced kid—you know, when his parents drive him to the diner to meet a special girl for ice cream."

She flashed him a wide grin. "Where you feel all nerdy and stuff? I was that girl." With another laugh, she leaned back into the chair.

He sat forward. "You? I don't believe it. I would think you had lots of guys interested in you."

"For helping them with their math or chemistry homework, sure. But as dating material, definitely not."

"What are you talking about? You're beautiful."

"I had a bit of an acne problem and being at the top of the class, teachers liked me and would say things like, *Well, Anna, that is an excellent answer or hypothesis* or whatever. So I was not popular."

"Then I'm going to say that is a good thing for me."

She wrinkled her nose. "How so?"

He lightly touched the back of her hand, and a definite zing flowed into him. "If one of those guys from school discovered how awesome you are, we might not be sitting here now, having our first date."

"I guess that's true. So, tell me more about yourself. I know you have a sister and you're all about the heart. What do you like to do outside of work?"

He tapped the rim of his cup with his finger. "I'm kind of dull." He groaned. "I shouldn't have said that either."

Her fingertips grazed his arm. "I like your openness. Tell me more."

He decided if this was going to turn into date two, he might as well confess a few of his more geekier habits. "I'm a Trekkie, the original *Star Trek* series and *The Next Generation*, not so much *DS9*."

Her eyes grew wide and he was ready to explain.

"What about *Voyager*, and what is your favorite movie?"

He leaned in. "Are you a Trekkie?"

She held up her right hand and created a V, the pointer

and middle fingers and the fourth and pinkie together. With a coy look, she said, "Live long and prosper."

"Ah, Spock."

They launched into the merits of the different Star Trek series and which was their favorite movie. Totally absorbed in conversation, the coffee had long since run out and what remained in their cups was cold. The superhero movies and Star Wars franchise were also thoroughly dissected too.

Alan approached the table. "Excuse me, but would you like a bar menu or to move into the dining room?"

"What?" Anna glanced out the window. "I'm sorry, Alan. We were so caught up in conversation, I had no idea it had gotten so late."

Colin watched her cheeks grow a shade pinker. "Would you like to have dinner with me, or do you have other plans?"

She twisted her napkin in her hands. "I'm not trying to wrangle a dinner…"

Alan moved away, giving them privacy.

"That's not what I meant, Anna. I'm having such a good time, and I would love to move this right into dinner, but if you have something else you need to do, can I have a rain check?"

Her smile warmed and her eyes grew wider. "That does sound nice." She turned and fluttered her fingers at Alan. "Can we have a table in the dining room?"

Colin was quick to follow her until she made a detour toward the ladies' room.

Over her shoulder, she flashed him another megawatt smile. "Grab a table and I'll be right back."

Alan was holding two menus and a wine list near the dining room entrance. He walked Colin to a corner booth. He slid in, facing the direction so he could see Anna.

Handing the menus to Colin, Alan said, "She's a really nice lady."

"I knew that the first time I saw her."

"What, like a week ago?"

Colin wasn't sure where Alan was headed, but then he remembered he was a friend of the family. "No, the first time I met her was a couple of years ago, when Sam had his first heart attack."

"Hmm," Alan said. "Do you have a specific variety in white or red you'd like me to bring out? We have an extensive wine cellar."

"Either. I'm not a big connoisseur."

Alan gave a chuckle. "Oh, my friend. You have a lot to learn. I'll bring out a bottle of Sand Creek, on the house, and I'll walk you through the tasting." He was still chuckling as he moved in the direction of the kitchen. Anna came around the corner and Colin stood up.

"Is the booth okay?"

With a slight nod, she asked, "Did Alan seat you here?"

"Yes. Would you rather sit somewhere else?"

"This is fine. It's one of the more secluded tables."

"Ah, so it's more romantic." He tapped his temple. "I see what he was up to."

"Buckle up. I hope there won't be any more *treats* in store for us tonight." She eased into the booth.

"Would you rather go to another restaurant?"

"Not at all; the food is really good."

Alan came back with two glasses and a bottle of wine. He held it out for Colin to see. He had no idea what he was supposed to do.

"Thank you."

Alan set down the glasses and uncorked the bottle. He poured a little in Colin's glass and waited. Anna was watching him. Alan gave him a half nod and his eyes dipped to the glass and back to his face. Was he supposed to taste it? Guessing that was the right move, he did.

His eyes widened. "Wow. This is good."

Alan poured some for Anna and then refilled Colin's glass with a smile of approval. He mentioned that the waiter would be over to take their order when they were ready.

Anna sipped the wine. "Fuse. This is a special blend Tessa and Max produce at their winery, Sand Creek. It happens to be one of my favorites."

It all clicked into place. Alan was doing his best to give him some credibility when it came to wine. There was no way he was going to take the credit for this. "Anna, there is something you should know about me."

She took another tiny sip and smiled at him over the rim of the clear glass. "What's that?"

He swallowed hard. "I know absolutely nothing about wine. Beer, I can hold my own, but the wine selection was all Alan."

She gave him an encouraging smile. "Take a sip. Close your eyes but don't swallow."

He sat at the table, eyes closed and with a mouth full of wine.

"Now let it slip down your throat."

He did as she asked.

"Now open your eyes and tell me, did you like it?"

When he opened them, he saw her warm brown eyes, soft and sensual. A small smile played over her lips.

"I did." Oh wow. He was in trouble, as his heart did a double flip in his chest. If she could make sipping a glass of wine such an intimate moment, what else was there in store for him?

With a tinkling laugh, she said softly, "Then you've passed your first test."

9

Dinner was amazing. Anna closed her journal after writing those three words. She didn't want to break down her first date with Colin into a bunch of phrases recounting the afternoon that rolled into a long dinner, capped with dessert. It had to have been the single most romantic day of her life. Unexpected but exceptional. She liked how he was upfront about the wine. But how could someone live in this area and have zero idea about it?

She tossed the book onto her nightstand and wandered downstairs through the comforting darkness. The wood floors were icy, but it felt good to be grounded after floating on air all the way home. She knew Colin had enjoyed their date too. He had asked if she'd like to go out again, and without hesitation, she said yes.

Despite the late hour, she shot a text to Liza. *Coffee?*

Her phone pinged. She read Liza's response. *YES, tomorrow?*

She replied with a thumbs-up emoji and then got a glass of water before going back to bed. Sleep might be fleeting, but at least she'd be horizontal. She checked her phone one last time, wondering if Colin would send her a text. But there was nothing new. Just as well. She didn't want to rush anything, preferring to let things evolve slowly.

Anna waited for Liza while relaxing on her front porch swing. Still nothing from Colin, but she never thought to ask if he had to work today. The life of a nurse practitioner in a hospital must mean there were times when he was on call.

The toot of a horn caused her to look up as Liza's minivan came around the last bend in her driveway. She crossed the wide front steps and opened the passenger door.

"Hi." Anna secured her seat belt. "Thanks for driving."

"I need to pick up a few things at the Gear Up Sporting Goods store before coffee. The boys are going fishing with Jack." Liza let her gaze roam up and down her sister. "You don't look different."

Anna scrunched up her face. "What are you talking about?"

"You went out with the perfect guy. I thought you'd look, you know, different."

"Ha. He's not perfect."

"He might be for you." Liza navigated the circle drive and down the long gravel road. "Why do you have to live so far back from the main road?"

"Simple. I like the quiet."

"How could you ever get used to it? Growing up, there was always a lot of noise and people in and out of the house even though we were in the middle of a vineyard. Out here, you don't have any close neighbors, no road noise at all, and —worse—no streetlights."

Dryly, Anna said, "You're such a big city girl."

Liza laughed. "I know. We live in an area with less than

fifteen thousand people but there are amenities that I like. Ten minutes from everything. You're at least what, thirty?"

"It's not Siberia, and different strokes."

Liza waited less than ten seconds and demanded, "Are you going to spill your guts about the date or do I need to call Alan and get the lowdown?"

Anna looked out the window so her sister wouldn't see the grin on her face. "It was okay."

Liza banged the steering wheel with the palm of her hand. "You're a pain in the arse."

Now Anna couldn't hold back the laughter. "Is that a word you use around the boys?"

"Well, of course. I certainly couldn't say ass; then they'd think it's alright to use. You'll find out when you have kids of your own."

Anna didn't give her usual response that she probably wouldn't have any. For a long time, she had liked to pretend she didn't want them, but Liza knew her heart. It was something she longed for. And maybe if she had a family of her own, she might not feel like the odd one out in hers.

She half turned in her seat. "I was kind of surprised no one showed up last night."

"Everyone was under strict instructions to stay away. But we all wanted to be flies on the wall."

"Mom running interference for me?"

"Actually, no. It was Dad. Right after you left the house yesterday, he called everyone together and said, *Sawyers is off-limits for the day and night*. And that was verbatim." She cleared her throat and dropped her voice for effect. "And then he said, *If I find out that anyone took it upon themselves to go to Sawyers to spy on Anna, they'll have to answer to me*. Needless to say, we left you alone to enjoy your date."

Anna grew thoughtful. "Really? Dad said that?"

Liza's head bobbed. "Yeah, and he was serious."

"That's weird."

"I get the feeling Dad really likes Colin and wanted the date to go well."

"I'll bet he thinks I'm incapable of finding a nice guy." She felt her cheeks grow warm. "After all, I haven't brought home one guy that he liked since college."

She didn't continue that train of thought to the Vic disaster. All he had been interested in was working for CLW after graduation, and he thought dating the owner's daughter was the way to secure a high-profile job. The sad thing was that Dad hadn't seen right through him as usual. He bought his line of bull hook, line, and sinker for quite a while—until he heard Vic trying to leverage his experience at a bigger winery in Napa Valley.

"Are you mad about Vic?"

"I don't want to be used again." She gave a curt nod. "Dad liked him."

"Until he figured out the truth."

"Dad fired him for lying. That had nothing to do with me."

"Anna, that's not true. I heard Mom and Dad talking the day Dad escorted him off our property and told him not to come back. You didn't know, but Dad called his friend in Napa and gave him the scoop about Vic. He was finished before he even got off the plane in California."

"What are you talking about? Vic told me Dad gave him a glowing recommendation. That he had called and smoothed the way." It suddenly dawned on Anna what had really happened. She had been in such a hurry to get rid of him, she hadn't questioned why her dad had arranged a job for him on the West Coast. But now Liza was saying that Dad had only pretended to do so and had sent Vic out to the Coast, only to arrive and learn there was no job there for him. "Huh. Dad had my back the whole time."

"Of course he did." Liza shot her an incredulous look. "Did you think he wouldn't?"

"He liked Vic. He was a good worker, excellent at creating blends and—" Her voice died off. "Oh, Liza, how could I have thought Dad would have ever helped Vic?"

"Dad was upset, but not because Vic left. He hurt you and obviously left some pretty deep scars. You haven't dated anyone seriously since then." Her voice softened. "Dad told Mom that he blames himself for that. He should have seen through Vic sooner. Before you had gotten so involved with that loser."

Anna remained quiet the rest of the drive. She had a lot to process. All this time, she had thought Dad had chosen to help Vic obtain a new position, all the while keeping her tied to beakers and grapes. She had that all wrong.

The van slowed and Liza pulled into a partially full parking lot. The store looked pretty busy for a Sunday.

"Did you bring your list with all the stuff the boys need for fishing?"

Liza nodded. "Sunscreen, new poles, tackle boxes, nets. Yeah, Jack gave me a long list, including bait."

The sisters crossed the parking lot and entered the huge store. In front of them was an enormous indoor trout pond. At least that was what the sign said was swimming around. Anna wasn't big on fishing. To the left were realistic-looking trees with metal platforms hanging off the branches. Beyond that were rows and rows of fishing gear as far as the eye could see. Being in the midst of the lake region, that was to be expected.

"Where do you suppose we can find kid-size gear?" Anna looked around the area.

"I have no idea. Do you think someone can point us in the right direction?"

Another fake tree was placed along a walkway. It had arrows and departments listed. Anna scanned and found the information they needed.

"Come on; we need to go to the right."

The girls took their time picking out everything the boys needed, right down to new life vests, as they had grown a lot since last year.

"When are you giving the boys their new gear?"

"After dinner tonight. Jack wants to take them out for a little while after school tomorrow, just to whet their appetite for the season. You know Jack loves to fish with them and it gives me a break, which I'm going to spend in my flower beds."

Anna steered them in the direction of the pond. One of the store clerks mentioned they could feed the fish and she wanted to give it a whirl and Liza was amenable.

After a few minutes, Liza's cell phone pinged. She pulled it from her back pocket and read the text. "I hate to cut this short, but that was Mom. She asked if we can pick up a few things for them at the store. We can have coffee at Mom's."

"Then let's go." Anna dusted the fish food off her hands and picked up her bag. Her heart stilled as she stared down an aisle. Colin was there with a tall, slender blond girl.

Liza finished her text and put her phone back into her pocket. "Ready?"

Anna slowly nodded as she continued to watch Colin and the blonde out of the corner of her eye.

Liza's eyes drifted in that direction. She grabbed Anna's arm and muttered, "Come on. Let's get out of here."

Her feet were rooted to the floor. They'd had such a nice time yesterday; was he on a date with another girl? They certainly looked like they knew each other well, laughing and having fun while they looked at golf clubs. She wanted to walk over and say hello, but on the other hand, she didn't want to embarrass herself. It would just be too much.

"Anna," Liza urged, "come on."

She followed her sister through the checkout line and then out of the store. The other girl was very pretty and they looked like they were having a great time.

"I'm such an idiot," she huffed and tossed the bags into the back of the van and got into the passenger seat. "Will you drop me at home before picking up the boys?"

"Nope. You're not going home to stew. You have no idea who that girl was and until you do, you're not going to worry about it. She could be a co-worker who needed advice on buying her husband a gift."

Anna stared out the window. "Or he could be dating more than one person. It's not like we're in a relationship and have stated we're exclusive."

"True."

But despite Liza's attempt at distracting her with logic, Anna still wondered. Was this why she hadn't heard from Colin today? Because he had other plans with another woman?

"Liza, it's official. I'm one of the insane crazy women who meets a guy and imagines after the first date it went great and he'll call." She smacked her forehead with the palm of her hand. "Please don't tell anyone that I'm neurotic."

"Your secret is safe with me, but you know the man is going to call. Are you going to tell him that you saw him?"

"I'll make that decision when and if he calls me."

Liza said, "Better make up your mind ahead of time. I've seen how he looked at you, and the man is going to call."

10

Anna got home after an early dinner of pizza with Liza, the boys, and her parents. She stood on the porch and watched as the taillights disappeared from view. Ninety-nine percent of the time, she loved the solitude, but tonight she kept seeing Colin with the woman at the store and she was annoyed with herself for feeling jealous. Maybe a quick run on the treadmill and then a hot shower would help. If that didn't do the trick, there was always yoga and meditation. Or she could forget about all of that and watch an old Star Trek movie.

Before she could make a decision, her cell phone rang.

When she answered, she heard Colin's smooth voice as he said, "Hi, Anna."

"Hello, Colin." She pushed the green-eyed monster away and played it cool.

"I'm sorry I didn't call you earlier, but today was pretty hectic."

"It's okay. I spent the day with my family." Why she felt the need to give him an explanation was beyond her.

"Sundays are good to spend with the family."

"Did you have to work today?" She twirled a lock of hair around her finger, a habit she had from when she was a kid.

"No. Actually, I went shopping for some new golf gear."

She tried to sound nonchalant. "That sounds like fun. Do you play?"

"My parents gave both my sister and me lessons. They said no matter how old you get, you can always enjoy playing a round of golf on a beautiful course."

"I never learned." She could hear the clipped tone in her voice.

"I could teach you. We could go to the driving range and hit a bucket of balls."

She was dying to ask him who the woman was but choked back the question. "I don't own clubs."

"That's an easy fix. You're about the same height as my sister. I'm sure she'd lend you a set."

"Does she have more than one?" This really was an odd conversation.

"As of today, she does. I helped her pick out a new set this afternoon. So, what do you say?"

Anna sat on a wicker chair. She was his sister. Her shoulders slumped as she shook her head. "Sure, I'll give it a try." Should she tell Colin she was a bit of a klutz or let it be a surprise?

"I look at golf as more about being outside, away from phones." He gave a low chuckle. "And you haven't seen me play yet. There's a reason why I'm not on the PGA tour."

"What about shoes? I don't want to embarrass you by showing up in the wrong gear." To say nothing of the fact that wearing the wrong clothes and shoes would put a spotlight on her.

He laughed softly, which caused her heart to soften. "We'll start with the driving range at Crescent Lake Golf Club, and your sneakers will be just fine. If you like it, then you could buy a pair of spikeless golf shoes. But before you invest too much, we should play nine holes."

That was two different dates. She perked up in her chair. "Sounds like a plan."

"Let's agree to say it's a date." Again, his chuckle was low and very masculine. "So are you in for the night?"

Her heart skipped in her chest. Was he going to suggest they meet up? She'd love to see him but made a snap decision to slow things down. "Yeah. I've got a busy day tomorrow and since I spent more time at the hospital last week than in my lab, I have some catching up to do."

"Completely understand. Any chance you'd want to meet for a drink after work one night this week?"

"That would be great." Should she ask when he wanted to hit the driving range? No. She would wait for him to broach the subject again.

"What are you doing this weekend?"

"Liza and I are going for a bike ride on Saturday. We're on this whole get-out-and-do-things kick. I'm not sure if you remember she's the sister with two boys?"

"I do. She's very nice."

Anna laughed. "With her kids, heck, she's a saint. I love my nephews dearly but they can try anyone's patience and as a single mother, she never gets a break. Mom said she'll keep the boys and we can disappear for a while." Once again, she babbled on.

"Would you like company?"

Shoot. She hadn't been extending an invitation, and alone time with her sister was important to both of them.

"I hope you understand, but it's a sister kind of thing."

"Of course I do. But if your plans change, let me know. We could try out the range, hit a bucket of balls, and maybe have lunch too."

"I'll keep that in mind." She smiled and hugged herself.

He definitely wanted to see her again. "Maybe you're available on Sunday for the driving range?"

"I'm free and can pen you in."

"Huh?" What did he just say?

"You know. Pen's permanent."

She could hear the smile in his voice. "Ah-ha. You're cute, Mr. Grant, and yes, pen me in. I'm going to warn you though. If it's raining, I'm not going to stand around and hit a bunch of balls."

"There is an indoor range near Rochester. So," he said casually, "we could go there."

"Sounds like fun. Rain or shine, we'll do something golf-related."

"Perfect. We can talk more about it later this week. What day did you say you were free?"

"I didn't, but how about Wednesday? It'll give me two days to get caught up."

"Want to go to Sawyers again?"

"How about I make the plans this time? I'll text you the details by midday Tuesday."

"You're going to keep me in suspense?" He dragged out the words.

"That's the plan." A moment of silence lingered and became somewhat awkward. "I'll let you go then," she said.

"I'm already looking forward to Wednesday. But before you go, I wanted to tell you how much I enjoyed yesterday."

"I had fun too." It was a good thing he couldn't see her, as she knew her face was a deep shade of pink. Not from embarrassment but pleasure because he liked her and they had plans to see each other. They said their goodbyes and Anna wandered through the house.

She could hear his soft, husky laugh over and over in her head. His voice was smooth, which caused her pulse to quicken. Liza would be thrilled to know that all was well on the man front. She texted her sister. *Mystery solved. It was his sister. Ttyl*

It didn't matter that Liza didn't respond. Anna sat up in her chair. She needed a plan for Wednesday, but first a quick check of the weather. Maybe they could go on Jack's boat. Did Colin even like boats? Better play it safe. A picnic in the park? Nah. Too cliché. She needed to give this more thought and come up with something fun that would show him the date was important to her too.

And that's when it hit her. There was a car show downtown Wednesday night, where gearheads put their hot rods on display. That would be fun, and there was a companion fundraiser earmarked for the teen project in town. Besides, Anna had a special fondness for smoking-hot cars, all thanks to Leo. She and her younger brother had spent a couple of summers working on his hot rod and although she had no desire to be covered with grease, she loved the feel of a powerful car in her control.

Hey, if Colin couldn't deal with her love of fast cars, she'd rather know now before they went any further in this relationship. But who wouldn't love walking around, seeing all the cars on display and the owners ready to share every last detail about the restoration? Usually there were photo albums of the process.

Should she ask him or let it be a surprise? She picked up her phone and hesitated. Part of her really wanted to just let it happen. Talking to herself, she jotted off a text. *I'll pick you up at five on Wednesday. Just let me know your address*. She hit send. If nothing else, she was having a good time.

Her phone beeped and she glanced at it with a smile. "Hmm, that's interesting. He didn't even ask where we're going."

Colin read Anna's text. His curiosity was piqued. She didn't give him any details, but she was picking him up. He checked the time. His sister would still be awake. He dialed.

"Colin, I didn't expect to hear from you tonight. What's up?"

"Remember today I told you about the woman I had coffee with yesterday?"

With a laugh, she said, "You mean the coffee date that turned into dinner and dessert? Yes."

"We're going out on Wednesday and she's picking me up but didn't say where we're going."

"How fun."

"It's cool that Anna is making plans for us. It's only our second date, so she must be interested, right?"

"You need to stop with your old-fashioned ideas. We live in the twenty-first century. A girl is perfectly capable of planning and picking up her date."

"It's just that I thought she was quiet and shy and this side of her is quite the opposite."

"Does it bother you, the potential shift in her personality? After all, you've only talked to her when her dad was in the hospital and for one date. It's not like you know who she really is below the surface."

"I hear what you're saying."

"Do you want advice from your sister or did you just call to talk?"

He sat down on the arm of the chair. "I'm listening."

"Go out and have fun. If she wants to take you skydiving, maybe you could decline when you get to the airstrip, or not. Enjoy yourself. After all the years you've spent going to school, and then screwing around with Daphne and her three-thousand-mile long-distance relationship that was a sham, it's good to see you've taken a real interest in a woman."

He could hear the controlled laughter in her voice, but it didn't piss him off. "You know how that turned out, and that makes me sound like a loser."

"No. You're a guy who's been out of circulation for a long time. Now let go of your preconceived notions and have fun. Ya never know what might happen along the way. Heck, you might even fall in love."

"Stop pushing, sis. I know you'd love for me to find a great girl."

"You deserve to have someone special in your life and if Anna's not the girl, you can still have fun."

He would count himself lucky if he'd find someone to fill the space he had reserved in his heart for love. "Night, Marie." He set the phone on the table. She was right and he knew better than most that life was short.

11

Anna put the top down on her car, tied her hair back with a scarf, and cruised down the road. She was excited to be going to the car show with Colin. His address was plugged into the GPS and she knew of the area but had never been in his development. She slowed as she clicked off house numbers on his street. These weren't merely houses; she'd describe them as luxury homes. Maybe he came from money.

His house sat at the end of a cul-de-sac. She couldn't help but notice it was set back and thick woods bordered the backyard.

"Very nice," she murmured to herself as she parked in the driveway.

Before she turned off the car, the front door opened and Colin came down the wide stone steps. He smiled as he approached.

"Hey." He gave a low appreciative whistle. "Sweet ride, a Benz."

She cocked her head and smiled. "My indulgence."

"I would have taken you for an SUV kind of lady."

"Up until a few months ago, you would have been correct.

But this year, I promised myself I'd stop waiting for my life to start"—she tapped the dashboard—"and this little baby was a kick start for new adventures."

Colin eased into the low-slung passenger seat and clicked his seat belt. He gave her a wide smile. "Where are we off to?"

She flashed a grin at him. "You'll see."

She eased out of the drive and drove slowly down the wide street. "Have you lived here long?"

"About two years. I bought the last house in the development, and it was a good deal, as a family backed out at the last minute. I guess it was too basic for them. I've been making upgrades and making it my own and if I decide to flip, it has gone up in value, considerably."

"So, you like to do house projects?"

"I do." He nodded. "Where do you live?"

"I have a place south of town."

"You're out in the country then?"

"I bought an old farmhouse a couple of years ago and have been renovating it ever since. There's not much left to do." She tucked a wave of hair under her scarf as it teased her nose. "It's peaceful."

"It sounds nice."

"My family thinks I'm nuts to be out there by myself, but after working with the family, I need some space."

"Do you have animals?"

"Not yet. I'd like to get a couple of dogs. They'd be good companions and with the contractors just about wrapped up, the timing will work."

"I had a black lab, Charlie, and he was my shadow. I lost him a couple of months ago. He used to greet me after a shift at the hospital and I miss him."

"I'm sorry about your fur-baby. They leave a huge hole in our hearts." Anna downshifted and slowed the car as they approached Main Street. There were signs for parking and she pulled into the first lot and took a space in the last row.

She was hopeful no one would park next to her, but who knew for sure.

"The car show? This will be a first for me."

"I thought it'd be fun to get out and walk around. I've wanted to go the last couple of years but haven't made the time."

Colin beamed. "I've either been in school or working and missed it. Rumor has it the cars will knock your socks off."

Anna gave a low chuckle. "You have no idea."

He took her hand and their fingers intertwined as they strolled through the parking area. "Is this okay?"

She smiled. "Yeah." She liked how their hands fit together.

They crossed the police barricade to Main Street, which was lined with every make and model of hot rod imaginable, along with late model muscle cars and sports cars. Anna's smile grew broader with each passing step.

Colin gave her a sidelong look. "You're really excited."

She tugged him down the right side of the street. "Come on. Leo should be down here with his latest project car." Her steps slowed when she noticed the lineup of vintage Camaros.

"This one here." She pointed to a sleek black convertible. "It's an SS and has a three-fifty engine, four-speed manual transmission. A blast to drive." She gave him a lopsided grin. "I have a weakness for the '69."

They continued to examine each car and she relayed the best features of each one. At last, she saw her brother.

Speaking softly, she said, "That's a very rare Buick Grand National; only one hundred and twelve were made. Leo found it in a barn in Ohio and he's taken over a year to restore it." She could hear the pride in her voice.

"Is there anything you don't know about cars?"

"They are a weakness, but Leo is the genius when it comes to any classic car." She gave him a searching look. "Am I boring you?"

"Not at all. I'm impressed. I would never have guessed you were passionate about cars."

They drew closer to Leo's car. He walked toward them.

"Hey, guys. When did you get here?" He kissed his sister's cheek and shook Colin's hand.

Anna ran her fingertips over the hood. "A little while ago. This is the first row we've been down."

Leo stepped to his car. "Colin, wanna check out my baby?"

"Sure. Anna was just telling me you found it in an old barn."

Leo beamed. "I did. It was under some old oilskin tarp and I wasn't sure what I'd find when I'd tear the engine down." He gave a one-shouldered shrug and ran his hand over the fender. "The mice had made a few nests in the seats and engine compartment, so I took it down to the frame and rebuilt it. All with matching numbers."

Colin looked at Anna and then Leo. "Sorry, new to the classic car scene. What do you mean by matching numbers?"

Anna explained, "They're factory parts. Not aftermarket. The car is more valuable if you rebuild it with factory parts. Sometimes you can get parts from people you know or at a swap meet." He looked at her with an appreciation—or maybe he thought she was nuts and she was misreading the look.

Leo straightened and smiled at a pretty girl who was passing by. He said hello but she kept on walking. His gaze followed her until she stepped into the emergency medical tent and out of his view. Without looking at Anna, he asked, "Any idea who that cute blonde was?"

"No, but if you want to find out, we'll hang by the car and you could go to the medical tent and ask for a Band-Aid." Anna grinned at Colin.

"Go for it," Colin said. "We'll hang out and take the credit for the car. And since Anna is well versed in cars, we can pull it off."

Leo gave a short snort. "This from the guy who just learned about matching numbers." He turned back to the crowd. "I'm good."

Anna wanted to encourage Leo, but if she said any more, he'd consider her to be pushy and take a huge step back. As the youngest brother, he was the least confident when it came to the opposite sex.

"Are you guys going to hang around long?" Leo smiled. "Maybe we could catch a drink when the show shuts down."

Anna turned to Colin. "I'm not sure, but maybe we can catch up with you some other time." If she were being honest, she wanted to keep some personal distance between Colin and her family for a little longer.

"Sure. Sounds like fun." Colin took her hand. "Besides, I'm on call as of midnight tonight, so no drinking for me."

"You should have said something. We didn't need to come out tonight."

He gave her a warm smile and applied gentle pressure to her hand in his. "I've got plenty of time."

She flashed a grin in Leo's direction. "We're going to take off, but see you at some point."

"Yeah. Are you going to dinner at Mom and Dad's on Friday?"

"Wouldn't miss it. Dad has something up his sleeve. The last time he pulled us together like this, Don and Kate moved back and took over the winery."

"Since there are no apparent major changes, it really shouldn't be anything other than just getting together." He gave Colin a quizzical look. "Are you coming?"

He got a deer in the headlights look. Anna stepped in to rescue him.

"I don't think I should subject Colin to a family dinner just yet. Even if everything is normal when we all gather, it's beyond chaotic. With kids and adults." She grinned. "Under the best of circumstances, it's something a person has to ease into." She wanted to laugh when the look of fear still lingered on his face, but she didn't.

After saying goodbye to Leo, they strolled away, hands linked.

He swung her hand with his. "You seem to be in your element while I'm a little uninformed."

"We all have our hobbies." She gave a short laugh. "When we hit the driving range, I'm going to be the one on the other side of the knowledge base and skill."

"Speaking of golf, are we doing nine holes?"

"I thought we had planned the driving range first, then if all goes well, we'll hit the links."

"You're right. I'll book a range time."

"Great. Just tell me when and I can meet you there if you'd like."

He held her arm tight against his side. "I'll pick you up." He looked up and down the street. "If you could choose any car here, what would you drive home in?"

"Hmm." Her gaze roamed Main Street. "We need to go down South Street and Oak before I can decide."

"Then we'd better get walking." He made a turn onto Oak Street.

Colin was enjoying walking around town with Anna. She was easy to be with and so very knowledgeable about vintage cars that he felt out of touch. While he liked looking at cars, the truth was that he didn't care what he, personally, drove as long as it started when he needed it to and got him from point A to point B.

"After tonight, I have an entirely new appreciation for cars."

"They're so entwined in our history. From the time Henry Ford rolled out the Model T, it changed everything, and even way back then, people wanted choices." She swept her hand in a three-sixty. "This is what happened from that humble beginning."

"Why didn't you do something with cars, like an engineer or something?"

He watched as her face transformed into a mask. "My entire life, I knew my place was with CLW. It wasn't optional."

Confused, he said, "But Leo and Liza don't work for the business."

"I think by the time they came around, most of the positions Dad needed to have filled with family were already in the works. We were groomed for our roles." She released his hand and stuck her hands in her capris.

"Don was going to be president. Jack loved the land. Tessa's business acumen was apparent from the time she opened her first lemonade stand, and I was passionate about science." She gave a small shrug. "There was always room for the twins, but it wasn't critical. However, it would have been the cherry on top of the sundae for Dad."

"Would you leave if you could?" He kind of felt sorry for Anna. It sounded as if she felt trapped.

She shook her head. "We're family. It's been drilled into us from the time we were kids. My parents firmly believe we're stronger together, and that includes the family business."

He dropped his voice so they wouldn't be overheard in the crowd. "I don't disagree with the logic, but you have the right to be happy, Anna."

She gave him a bright smile that didn't reach her eyes. "Who says I'm not?"

"Are you?"

Looking straight ahead, she said softly, "I'm working on it.

In fact, Liza and I are doing a bike ride tomorrow night with a club in town. That should be fun."

He pulled her into his arms and held her close. "I can't wait to hear all about it."

She relaxed against his body. Her breath caressed his cheek. "I thought you wanted me to pick out my favorite car." She brushed her lips against his cheek. "And I'm going to see how much you've retained from our adventure."

He slipped his arm around her shoulders as they strolled down the street. "Maybe I'll pick one out and you can quiz me to see if I paid close attention to what you've been teaching me."

She took a step closer so every part of their bodies was very close. "That smile on your face makes me think you've had fun."

"This was interesting and not that I want tonight to end, but I'm already looking forward to our next date."

12

Anna hesitated with the phone in her hand. She and Colin had a fun time a couple of nights ago at the car show. Was it too soon to see him again? Who said there had to be rules? She dialed the phone. On the third ring, he picked up.

"Hey, Colin, I was wondering if you wanted to have lunch with me."

"Hi, Anna. This is a surprise. I'm working today but if you wanted to come to the hospital, we could have lunch at the picnic tables."

"That's sounds great, if you can take a break."

"For you, of course. Meet me by the duck pond at noon and I'll grab sandwiches from the cafeteria."

"That's okay. I'll bring lunch. See you soon." There, she had asked him out for lunch. Who said she couldn't step out of her comfort zone? Now all she needed to do was run down to the bistro and see if there was something she could pack for a picnic.

. . .

Anna was setting out lunch when she heard someone whistling a tune behind her. She turned. Colin was striding toward her with a smile on his face. He looked handsome in light-green scrubs and the person who said scrubs were boring never saw the way they made the green in his eyes stand out.

"Hi there." He leaned in and placed a chaste kiss on her cheek. He surveyed the containers, paper plates, and plastic forks on the table. "This is quite a spread."

The smell of the hospital clung to him even outside but for a change, it didn't make her nerves jump into overdrive. "I wasn't sure what to bring so I packed a little of everything that looked good." Little did he know she agonized over each item she chose, wondering if he would enjoy it.

"Everything looks delicious." He gave her a smile. "You look beautiful too."

They sat across from each other as the light breeze teased her hair. She tucked the lock behind her ear. "Thank you."

"So did you and Liza have fun on your bike ride?" He scooped up some salad and sliced chicken onto his plate and handed Anna the containers.

"We did, but I had no idea how popular this group was. There were a of ton people, but I felt like we were back in high school. It was kind of cliquey. And Liza, being the mom, was ready for anything. She had a checklist of things she wanted us to bring and she even picked up padded seat cushions since we haven't done any serious riding in years. Even though it was our first time, we looked the part. Unfortunately, we didn't think we could act the part, so we decided to bring up the rear. That way, we wouldn't slow anyone down. We just enjoyed the scenery and the experience."

"It sounds like you and your sister had a good time."

She leaned forward and groaned for dramatic effect. "The hill was *huge* and it took forever to get to the top."

He chuckled. "But you can say you did it."

She pulled out her cell and showed him a couple of selfies they took. "I thought we might need proof we actually made it to the top of the falls." She grinned. "You should come with us sometime. It'd be fun."

"It might be. When I was in my ER rotation, I saw a few nasty bike accidents, mostly from people who didn't wear a helmet." He gave her a quizzical look.

She held up a hand. "Yes, before you ask, we both had on brand-new helmets. You can't preach safety to the younger set if we don't follow the same rules."

"Good, glad to hear it. I have some doctor friends who ride. Who knows, maybe if we find it's one of our things, we could go with them sometime."

"Not that I don't want to meet your friends but maybe we could try a different activity. I'm going to be sore for days." She rubbed her backside. "I don't think cycling will be my activity of choice unless the ride is a lot shorter."

"Maybe it'll be golf; there are no helmets or padded seats necessary." He reached across the table and gently wiped her cheek with his napkin. "Dressing."

"Thank you." Her heart fluttered but her eyes never left his. "Tell me about your day. Why did you decide to become a nurse practitioner?"

Colin was enjoying this impromptu lunch. Anna was so different from other women he had dated, which said more about the type of women he had been attracted to than her. She was genuine and funny and smart; she was beautiful but that it came from within was the real attraction for him.

"I'm sure your real question is why I didn't become a doctor."

She shook her head. "Never crossed my mind. I think we

all find the path that works for us, but I'm curious. Why go back to school? From what I remember, you were a good nurse."

"I did like being a nurse, but I realized being an NP gave me more influence over a patient's treatment plan and I wanted to be able to spend more time with my patients. As a nurse in the hospital, they came and went. The only way I found out how people were doing after they had been discharged was if they either were readmitted or I happened to see them around the area. I wasn't satisfied with just helping during a crisis. I wanted to be a part of their good health all the time."

"That makes a lot of sense." She had her hands folded on top of the table and was listening to every word. "So what is a normal day like?"

"There isn't a typical day; with cardiac patients, I have to be on my toes. Like your dad, for example. He was doing all the right things and had been feeling well, but there was something more going on and the heart attack was the indicator we needed to fix it. Or I could have a patient in rehab doing great, losing weight, exercising, watching what they're eating, and when they get off the treadmill or bike, they might get dizzy or pass out."

Her eyes widened. "Why would that happen, and could it happen to Dad?"

"Usually it's a medication adjustment; blood pressure is coming down, but that's why we do the cardiac rehab—to monitor these changes and get them corrected quickly." He placed a hand on hers and caressed it tenderly. "Please don't worry. It's rare that something like that happens. But that is what I mean when I say nothing is predictable."

"You love it."

He wiped his mouth with the napkin and said, "I do. There's nothing like it and I wouldn't trade my job for anything. What about you? Do you love what you do?"

"I guess. Once my dad realized I was good at math and science, he encouraged me to get a degree in chemistry, and here I am today."

This was curious. Anna didn't look like a woman who was passionate about her career choice. "If you could do something different, what would it be?"

"No one has ever asked me that before." She stacked containers in a soft-sided cooler. "Maybe a teacher. So many kids get overwhelmed by the math and sciences. I'd love to excite someone about all the cool things those subjects touch."

"Why don't you?" He checked his watch. It was time to go back inside, but this was an important conversation to have. He could hear the longing in her voice.

Anna stood up and finished packing the cooler. "I have a career and I can't make a change now."

"What about volunteering as a tutor or something?"

She lifted her eyes and he could almost see the light bulb go off above her head. "There was a STEM program at my old high school. Maybe I could help."

He took the cooler from her hands as they strolled across the grass to her car.

"You should check into that." He stowed the cooler on the floor of the car and kissed her cheek. "Thanks again for lunch."

"I'm glad you could get away."

"I'll call you later? My shift gets over around nine tonight. I need to fill in for someone."

"I have dinner at my parents, but I'll be home later." She slipped behind the wheel and he watched as she left the parking lot. *Anna Price, you are an amazing woman.*

When Anna got back to CLW, she popped her head into Liza's office.

"What's going on here?"

Liza looked up from her computer screen. "I stopped by your office earlier. Coming in late today?"

"No, I was here, and then I had lunch with Colin."

Liza grinned. "That sounds promising. Things are heating up, huh?"

"Maybe. Hey, while we were talking, I had an idea. What do you think if I were to volunteer

at the high school? I know there used to be an after-school program for the girls' STEM team. Maybe I could get involved." She tipped her head from side to side. "Give me something to focus on where I'd make a real difference."

"That's a great idea. You would be amazing." Liza grinned from ear to ear. "They'll be lucky to have you. Just realize you'll need to have a background check and a bunch of other stuff before they let you participate."

"Good to know but I'm not saying I'm going to do it, just that it's something to think about."

"Since you're here and we have time before dinner, do you want to head over to Gear Up and see what other adventure clubs are available?"

"Maybe there's kayaking or something. After all, we're trying to get out of our comfort zone." Anna pulled her phone out of her bag. "First, we should check that app I overheard one of the guys talking about on the bike ride, Happenings. It's supposed to have active clubs in the area. Biking was fun, but if we're going to push the envelope, I'd like to try something a little more challenging: rock climbing, bungee jumping, or whitewater rafting."

Liza shook her head vigorously. "I'm not jumping off a bridge, tethered to an elastic band. I'm a single parent with responsibilities. What about horseback riding?"

"Maybe, but that is less of a group activity and our goal was to meet people."

With a soft laugh, Liza said, "The last group wasn't overly

social and we did try. I said hi to at least five people with barely a smile back."

"We can't assume the next group of people will be as standoffish." Anna hopped up and held out her hand to her sister. "Ready to go?"

Anna was aware of Liza's scrutiny as they drove out of the parking lot.

"Hey, you're awfully quiet."

"I was thinking about tonight."

"Are you worried?" Liza looked out over the sweeping views. "The last time, it was such a bombshell and we didn't feel all the effects until Tessa bought Sand Creek Winery."

"That turned out to be the best thing for her. She fell in love with Max and now they're married."

Liza clutched her heart. "So romantic."

"You're such a softy."

Liza pulled at a thread on the hem of her shirt. "Dad's already talked about the next generation running the business. I want my boys to have choices, and if they decide they want to be in the wine business, it will be their decision. They need to see that being independent is a good thing but also honoring the family's business, able to work together or apart makes us stronger."

"That's a long way off, but it makes sense. Don't forget Don and Jack are happy with their roles at CLW. It doesn't have to be a burden."

"Jack didn't always feel that way. Remember, he spent almost eight years in California."

Anna tipped her head. "He did, but he wanted to see how other wineries worked in order to help us grow." She felt bad, thinking that part of Liza's concern was a direct result of her complaining. She needed to fix this. "Can I tell you something I've never said to anyone?"

Liza's eyes opened wide. "You can always confide in me."

"I never told Mom or Dad that I didn't want to follow the path they laid out for me. I went along with it and never said a word. I made my decision a long time ago. Just like Jack and Don. We're lifers."

"People change the course of their lives all the time."

"This is going to sound cocky, but I'm instrumental in creating the future of Crescent Lake Winery. I actually create wine formulations, and the only other person in our family who can do that is Dad. I'll spend my career at CLW, and I'm okay with it."

"There are other people capable of doing exactly the same thing." Liza gave her a playful shove. "Other wineries prove it, year in and year out."

Anna forced a bright smile. "I'm doing my part to secure the family legacy."

"What are you going to do so that you're happy?"

"With your help, I'm going to become a thrill seeker. I want to physically challenge myself and who knows? Maybe the volunteer thing will work out."

Liza said. "It will. I just know it."

With a laugh, she asked, "The adrenaline junkie or potential volunteer gig?"

Liza released her. "The school gig, of course."

"And the adventure part of my plan?"

She shook her head. "I don't like the idea you're going to become addicted to an adrenaline rush."

Anna parked in front of the store. "I promise we'll be careful while we take risks." With a laugh, she added, "But not too careful."

13

Anna sat in the car, looking at the house she grew up in, reluctant to be the first one inside, not because she didn't want to see her parents but because she was nervous about what was so important that the entire family had been summoned for dinner. Nothing good ever seemed to come from this kind of command performance.

Don's large SUV pulled in next to her car, and Jack's truck parked on the other side. Reinforcements. She pushed open the door and walked around the front of Jack's truck. Kate got out of the SUV and joined her.

"Hey." She held up a covered glass pan. "I brought cookies."

"By any chance are those triple chocolate Romeos?" Anna smacked her lips. "Those are my favorites."

She nodded. "Your mom wouldn't let me cook anything for tonight, so at least I'm contributing something." She leaned forward and winked. "There's a dozen on my seat for you to take home."

"Thanks. Why do I deserve special treatment?"

"Two reasons. One, you love them and two, you don't bake."

"True statements. I can barely cook anything but pasta."

As they approached the front steps, three more cars drove up. Kate said, "There's the rest of the family."

Anna nodded. "Let the games begin."

Once again, the adults were gathered around the table, sipping wine or coffee, and the kids were happily playing a board game on a square table at the other end of the room. This scene was exactly the same as when Tessa had dropped her bomb that she had bought a vineyard.

Anna wondered when Dad would fill them in on the reason they were all here. She glanced at her siblings and their spouses. The tension was beginning to be palpable.

She said, "Dad, you look good. How are you feeling?"

"Like I have a new lease on life." Dad took Mom's hand. She gave him an encouraging smile.

"I'm glad we could get together tonight. I'm sure you're curious as to what's on my mind. After we've had two family dinners where we've talked about major changes, this will be the third." He slowly looked around the table. "I'm so lucky to be the father to six of the most amazing and talented people I've ever had the pleasure to work with and spend time with. However, since my recent heart surgery, I've been reminded I have an expiration date." He dropped his gaze. "We all do."

Mom gave his hand a squeeze. "Sam, tell them the rest."

"It has become apparent that I may, with having the best of intentions, put a lot of pressure on each of you regarding your career choices. I won't apologize for doing what I thought was best for the family and our business, as it was expected of me to join the business when I was a young man." There was a catch in his voice. "Mom and I want you to know that if any of you would like to leave your current positions, you can with no hard feelings. You need to follow your hearts, pursue your dreams, and live a life that makes you happy."

Anna held her breath. What exactly did that mean for CLW?

Don sat straight up in his chair. "Dad. Do you want to sell the winery?"

"No. I have no intention of selling or shutting down. But if any of you wishes to make a change, you can."

Anna slumped in the chair. She could leave CLW, no repercussions? She leaned forward. "Dad, are you firing us?"

"No." He clasped his hands on the table. "I had time to think when I was lying in the hospital and around the house. I remembered my father grooming me to assume control. As an only child, I never even thought about doing anything different. The winery has grown beyond even my expectations. Jack." His face was drawn into an unreadable expression. "What do you think?"

Jack didn't look at anyone. "We've had our differences, but I've never wanted to do anything else. I've always wanted to work the land, our land. Nurturing the vines, watching the weather and holding my breath each season—will it be too dry, hot, wet, or whatever. I'm happy here and someday I want to raise my family here."

Sam nodded. "Don, I put a lot of pressure on you and Kate. I assumed that giving Kate the opportunity to have her own bistro was the way to get you both to do what I needed." He looked at Tessa.

She opened her mouth and then snapped it closed.

"Tessa, I didn't give you enough credit for being able to run the business. After seeing what you've done with Sand Creek, I now understand CLW would have been in very capable hands."

She said, "We already cleared the air, Dad. We're good."

He gave a half nod and returned his attention to Don and

Kate. "Give it some thought. If you want to go back to Loudon, I would understand. Kate misses her family."

Kate said, "Don and I are happy here. I'll admit it took me a while to stop being angry at your coercion, but that's the past. This is our home now."

Don's eyes shone with pride at his wife's statement. He leaned over and kissed her cheek.

"Anna, other than Leo and Liza, who serve on the board of directors, you are the one who may want a change. I'll understand if you're ready to move on."

"Dad. I—" She paused. "I don't know what to say."

Liza said, "Yes, you do." Anna swiveled in her chair. She wanted to ask what she was doing, but not in front of everyone.

Anna couldn't believe her younger sister was meddling in her life. Liza gave her an encouraging look.

Dad's eyes bore into hers. "Anna, is there something you'd like to do?"

She swallowed hard and steeled her nerves. "I'm going to talk with a guidance counselor at the high school to see if there is a girls STEM program. I have the time to do it, but I don't have teaching credentials. Maybe I'm not qualified." She shifted uncomfortably in her chair. She hated being the center of attention within her family.

"That is an incredible idea." Dad beamed. "Do you want to pursue a teaching degree; would that make you happy?"

"What makes you think I'm not happy?"

Dad made a circle in the air. "That beautiful, sweet face cannot hide anything from your mom and me."

"Dad." She wanted to cry. She had felt sad for a long time. She had longed for a change and now that it was being presented to her, what should she do?

"You don't need to make any decisions tonight, Anna. We want you to know that we think you are talented at what you do and would hate to see you leave, but even more important than CLW is your personal happiness. And now that you're dating Colin, well, it's been good to see a new sparkle in your eyes."

She nodded, unable to speak.

"We can talk about what your future looks like at a later date. But you know where we stand. I'm really stepping back from the business. I'll be a board member and I won't be coming to the office every day." He clasped Mom's hand and smiled broadly. "We're going to take a long overdue vacation as soon as I'm cleared to travel."

Mom beamed. "You don't need to worry. We won't miss any important events such as babies being born, birthdays, and school events."

Everyone started talking at once, expressing their surprise and joy at the direction things had turned. Anna was still in shock that she had just been given a choice about the direction for her future. Now, what was she going to do with it—and for that matter, how was Colin going to fit into her new options? Dating him was like rediscovering a part of herself that she missed. It was then it dawned on her that she was having fun.

Anna sat in the middle of her bed with her journal open on her lap. Tonight had not gone the way she had expected. Suddenly, her future was wide open. Dad was giving her a choice to live a different life. But was that what she wanted? She loved what she did at the winery, but there was a difference now that he was finally asking her if that was what she really wanted. She tapped the pen on the paper. When facing big decisions, she found it helped to clear her thoughts to make a pro and con list.

Pro Con

ChangeLeave fam

IndependentPotential harm winery

See worldFinancial uncertainty

Leave freedom/control

Leave Colin!!!!!

She mused. Well, it seemed on the first pass that the cons outweighed the benefits. She closed the journal and shut off the light. Her phone pinged. She picked it up to read the text. It was from Colin. She smiled, but thought he was going to call.

Still at work but wanted you to know I was thinking about you. How did everything go?

She hesitated. How could she explain? *Just some changes within the business and M/D going to travel when able. Thanks for asking. See you tomorrow?*

She set the phone aside. It pinged again. *Yes… I'll call and we'll make plans for the driving range. Sleep well.*

She sent him a sleepy face. There would be time enough to talk tomorrow.

She slipped under the blankets and turned out the lights. Just when she thought she knew what to expect, things had gone wonky. She lay in the dark, willing herself to sleep. The hands were in triple slow motion on the clock face. Giving up, she flipped back the covers, pulled on a lightweight robe, and slipped her cell in the pocket. She padded down the stairs. The cool wood floors against her feet soothed her.

She wandered in the darkness. The moonlight bathed her sunroom in a soft glow. She really could use someone to talk to. Liza might still be awake.

Are you awake?

In response to her text, her phone buzzed.

"Hi."

"I wondered when you'd call." Liza's voice was a whisper. The boys must be asleep in her bed again.

"All I can think about is what Dad said. That he was

giving us all an out, to change our lives and do something we might really want to do."

"Have you made your list yet?"

Anna smiled in the glow of the moonlight. "You know me so well. Of course I have."

"And how did it turn out?"

"For many reasons, leaving is not the right thing to do."

"What is your heart telling you?"

Anna sighed. "I'm going to talk to Dad tomorrow, but your idea was spot on. If I get some time to volunteer and maintain my position at CLW, I'll have the best of both worlds. I know Don will be supportive, but I want Dad to understand too."

Liza gave a small soft laugh. "I knew it, and Colin?"

"I want to give this relationship a real chance. He's a great guy and I'd be a fool to just walk away from him."

"I'm glad you've finally opened your eyes to see this amazing man standing right in front of you. I know from experience life is too short."

"Thanks, sis, for having my back. I don't think I would have brought it up if you hadn't prodded me."

"You'd have done the same for me."

A little voice said, "Mommy, you're talking too loud."

Before Liza could say anything more, Anna said, "We'll talk tomorrow. Night, sis."

Liza whispered, "Sweet dreams."

Anna put her cell into her robe pocket. She stared into the shadows. It was blissfully quiet. She yawned. Time to call it a day.

14

Anna strode into the winery the next afternoon and took the stairs two at a time. She was going to see Don and then run over to her parents' house.

She rapped her knuckles on the doorjamb and stuck her head in the office. "Do you have a minute?" It was too bad he was working on a Saturday and she knew where to find him.

Don looked up from a stack of papers.

"Come on in. I'm reviewing invoices for the last shipment of bottles. The glamourous life of the president."

She eased down into the buttery soft leather chair across from him. "Why don't you have the accountant do that?"

"Randomly I pull invoices just to keep eyes on the more mundane aspects of our company. I'm not surprised to see you." Don set his reading glasses aside and rubbed his eyes.

"Interesting dinner last night." She crossed her legs and waited for Don to pick up the thread she dangled. "Did you have any idea what was coming?"

"I guessed Pop's mortality had him reevaluate a few things. I'll tell you, I was shocked when he admitted that he basically forced me and Kate to move home." He watched her closely. "And then when he said if you wanted to leave the company, he would support you, I was really surprised. No, that's not right, either. I was stunned." He leaned back in his chair. "Thankfully, he wasn't planning on dismantling the business for the family without talking to me."

"You had no idea what he was up to?"

With a slow shake of his head, Don said, "No. I was glad to hear Jack is happy in his role, and we have good people like Peyton in the tasting room."

"She's good. We're lucky to have her running things. But I'm worried about Dad. Do you think his health is worse than we've been told?"

"You're dating Colin. Has he said anything?"

"No. He can't. There are privacy laws and I don't want to put him in that position and ask about something that is confidential."

Don pushed back from the desk and paced the length of the oversized office. Anna kept a close eye on him. "I'm worried about him."

"We all are. This time was much worse than the first heart attack." She gave a brisk nod. "Which is why I'm going to the house after I leave here and ask him straight out about his health and the business."

"I like that. When you ask him directly, you can see how both he and Mom react. If there is anything wrong, you'll know." He leaned against the window, attempting to appear casual with the expansive view of the vineyard as a backdrop. "What have you decided? Do you want to leave?"

"No. I'll be right here, waving my magic wand in the lab."

He visibly relaxed. "Good."

"Did you think I would?" She figured after last night, everyone thought she was a sure bet to leave.

"I'm sure you've felt tethered to the winery and when Tessa left, it may have crossed your mind that there were opportunities elsewhere for someone with your skill set."

"Is that your way of saying I'm valuable to the organization?" Don had never given her a compliment regarding her work without someone else being around.

"Are you kidding?" His eyes grew wide. "We can hire someone to market, run the fields—hell, even do my job—but each season, you just know how to extract the best from every harvest. That's not something you can teach. It's innate, an intangible sense of how to blend effectively."

She looked out the window, taken aback by his compliment. "Everything I know, I learned from Dad."

"And Dad learned from Grandpa. You're the lynchpin for CLW." His face softened. "You had no idea, did you?"

She squirmed in her seat. "You never said anything. For the last two years, you've been sitting in this office and you've neglected to come to my lab and tell me I was doing a good job." Her voice cracked. Didn't anyone realize how that might have made her feel?

"Anna, I'm very sorry. I figured you knew."

She wanted to be mad at him, but he really hadn't thought about it. Don was like Mom in some ways but in others, he was more like Dad.

"Can I give you some sisterly advice?"

"Yeah." He leaned forward.

"Think about what Dad said last night and the mistakes he's made with us kids. You're a good man, but don't make those same mistakes with your kids. If someone does something good, tell them. Don't assume they'll know." She rose. "It would be a shame in twenty-five years if your kids are having a similar conversation about you." She crossed the room and gave him a kiss on the cheek. "Now go home and spend time with your wife and son. No one should be working seven days a week. Not even you."

"Thanks, sis." He turned away but not before she saw his emotion-racked face. He heard her message. Now it was up to him to make some changes in his life. She left the room. Time to face Mom and Dad.

She opened up the front door and listened. She could hear the television in the family room. It was reporting the weather at full volume, which meant they were in Dad's office at the other end of the hall. She stopped and clicked off the TV. "Mom? Dad?"

"In the office, Anna," Mom called to her.

She poked her head inside. Dad was sitting on the corner of his desk and Mom was in front of the computer.

"What are you two looking at?" Anna came around the side of the desk and placed a hand on Mom's shoulder. "Cruises? You're serious about traveling. Good for you."

Mom looked up from the screen. "We're thinking about the fall. Dad should be ready to travel. I want to go to the Virgin Islands."

"Sounds nice."

Dad came around the side of the desk and sat on a small leather sofa. He patted the other cushion. "You didn't come to hear about our travel plans. I'm assuming you've come to a decision about your future."

She sat next to Dad and looked at Mom, who gave Anna an encouraging smile.

"I made a list," she announced.

Dad didn't make a comment, so she continued. "You know, the whole pro and con thing."

"And what did you come up with?" Mom asked.

"Well," she stalled. "I want to stay in my current capacity at the winery but take some time each week for volunteering at the high school. When Liza and I talked about it, she mentioned I was a good teacher. It got me to thinking about girls who may not have the same advantages I had. I'm going to call Ms. Kelley, my old teacher, and see if it's possible. Otherwise, it's a big waste of everyone's time."

Dad tapped his hand against the arm of his chair. "There

is still a business that will need your attention, and Don needs to know he can count on you."

"That's out of line. And I talked to Don, and he's supportive of the idea." Her temper began to simmer. "I've never shirked my responsibilities. Ever."

"That isn't what Dad is saying."

"For a change, Mom, don't jump in and defend him."

"I wasn't. It's, just, the two of you can be oil and water."

"Sherry, she's right. If we're going to kick off the next phase of our lives, I want our children to know that I'm listening to them. I haven't done enough of that while they've been growing up and it's time I change."

Shocked, Anna said, "Okay, you're scaring me. What has the cardiologist told you that you haven't told us. Are you dying?"

With a small smile, he said, "We all are, Anna."

"Are you thinking your expiration date is sooner than later?" Fear clutched her heart. She wasn't ready to lose her father.

"To ease the concern I see written on your face, no. The doctor hasn't said anything that would make me think the clock is winding down." He patted her hand. "But I do want to make up for what I may have done to bruise your spirit."

"I appreciate that."

"Now that you've made a decision, you should let Ms. Kelley know your schedule and maybe they can structure special events around the harvest."

"I'll talk to her, but no micromanaging. I can handle my life." Anna grinned. "This may sound backward, but in a way, I'm glad you had the heart attack."

Mom cried, "Anna, that's a terrible thing to say."

Sam chuckled. "Dear, think about what our daughter has said in context with the last twenty-four hours."

Mom's face scrunched up. "I guess I'm missing something."

"If Dad didn't have his heart attack, he might never have realized that things were skewed and you wouldn't be ready to travel the world." As Anna spoke, she watched as the truth of her words dawned on Mom.

"I'm sorry, Anna. The strain of all the changes we've been facing has me frazzled."

"It's okay." Anna stood up. "I'm going to head back to the lab and make a few phone calls."

Mom said, "Good luck with the school."

"Before you go, how are things going with Colin?" Dad eased himself off the sofa. "I do like him."

She dropped a kiss on Dad's cheek. "That makes two of us."

"Bring him by for dinner soon," Mom called after her as she left the house.

"We'll see."

She closed the front door and paused on the wide porch to pull out her cell. There was a voicemail from Colin. "Hey, got called into work so I'll need a rain check for the driving range but how about dinner instead?"

She dialed his number and waited for his voicemail. "Hey, Colin, give me a call when you can. I'm done with family stuff and dinner sounds good." Feeling as if a weight had been lifted from her shoulders, she skipped down the steps and to her car.

When Anna got back to her lab, her phone rang. It was Colin. When he said hello, she swore she could see him smile through the phone.

"Hi, I'm so glad you called. What time do you want to get together tonight?" She doodled with the pen on the scrap paper on her desk.

"That's why I'm calling. I'm going to be stuck at work. A

couple of people got food poisoning and the unit is short-handed and full so I'm going to help out." He waited half a beat. "I'm really sorry."

"It's okay. Can I ask for a rain check?" She was disappointed but she appreciated his dedication to his patients and if it was Dad lying in a bed, she'd want to know he was getting good care.

"I'll do you one better. Not only will I give you a rain check, but some night when you least expect it, I'll pick you up and whisk you away on an adventure."

She chuckled. "That would nice. If you want, give me a call later."

"Sounds like a plan."

Liza hovered in the doorway to Anna's lab, waiting until she finished her phone call.

"Sis, what brings you to my neck of the woods?" She gave her a warm smile.

Liza sank to the wooden stool in the corner of the room. "I am meeting clients to go over plans for a wedding in October and had some time to kill. And of course, I was dying to know what happened with Mom and Dad earlier."

"It went better than I had hoped." She pushed the chair back from her counter-height desk. "Dad is being supportive."

Irritation flashed over Liza's face. "Did you ask him for permission?"

"No. I told them what I was planning. After what happened with Tessa and his health, Dad has a new outlook. I've thought about it a lot and I think he appreciated the courtesy when I shared my plan. After all, there isn't one person in this family who doesn't take their job very seriously." Her tone was firm.

"You don't need to convince me. I'm on your side, remember? What else did they have to say?"

Anna slid from her high-backed chair. "I was wondering

why he was really stepping back and had it in my mind that he might be sicker than we all knew. So I asked."

Liza's face paled. "What did he say?"

"I think he's had an epiphany. Dad's spent his entire marriage to Mom putting her second after the winery, and time is slipping away. She's stood by his side, worked the business, raised a family, and made life easy for him. All Dad had to do was concentrate on the winery, and it's paid off for all of us. Now he's going to give her the travel experiences she's longed for."

Anna could see her own outlook had changed over the last twenty-four hours. She was feeling more confident. She brightened. "I left Colin a message to see if he had plans for tonight, but he's been called into work. Do you want to tag along when we go to the driving range?"

Liza's face fell and she looked at the floor. For a split second, she felt a deep sense of loneliness from her.

"Thanks, but no. Maybe I'll go at some point, but you're just getting to know each other and you need to spend time alone with him."

"Oh, that leads me to the last point. Mom asked me to invite him for dinner."

"Good heavens, I hope it's just the four of you. I want this guy to stick around so you'll keep smiling." Liza glanced at her watch and stood up. "My clients should be here soon, but do you want to come to the house for dinner? I'm going to swing by and get the boys from Mom's when I'm done here, and we're going to eat around six."

"Since my plans have changed, I'll do you one better. I'll pick up the boys and we can have dinner at my place. Just come out when you're done here. And no rush. I'd like some quality time with those two little hellions." Anna waved her out of the office. "I'll take care of everything else."

When Anna got to her parents' house later that afternoon to pick up the boys, there was a Jaguar parked in the driveway. After taking the front steps two at a time, she walked in, curious about the visitor. The sounds of cartoons drifted out from the family room and she discovered Johnny and George glued to the screen. On the back deck, her mom and dad were talking to a blond-haired man. She couldn't see his face but he seemed to be overdressed in a suit coat. Curious, she took one final look at the boys and stepped onto the deck.

Dad looked up and said, "David, here's Anna now."

She looked between her parents and the handsome blonde. He was the kind of man who walked by on the street and was so good-looking, a person was compelled to watch him.

He stood and extended his hand. "David Marchand. It is a pleasure to meet you."

His accent was unmistakably French. She clasped his hand with a firm grip. Her radar pinged. Why did his name sound familiar?

"Will you join us? I'm in the country on holiday and when my father Henri told me about Sam's heart attack, he asked me to make a stop and express his good wishes." His words sounded sincere, as was the smile on his face, but his gray eyes were guarded.

"It's a pleasure to meet you." She walked around her parents and took a seat opposite him. "Dad, you didn't tell me you were expecting company."

David clasped his hands on the tabletop. "I only called a short time ago. I wasn't sure of my schedule prior to this morning and your parents have graciously asked me to stay for dinner. Will you be joining us?"

"No, I'm sorry. I'm here to pick up my nephews, but maybe next time."

"Crescent Lake is lovely, so I plan to stay a few days, and Sam has offered to give me a tour of the winery tomorrow. Perhaps I'll see you then. I understand you're the talent behind the wine."

That was an interesting way to phrase it. "You're planning on staying a few days?"

"Yes. I've never had the opportunity to tour wineries in the States in the spring. Your climate is different than ours, so I'm intrigued to see the variety of grapes that grow here."

"I'd be happy to give you a tasting."

David said, "I'd like that very much." He tipped his head to the side. "*Merci.*"

"Would you be able to meet me around noon tomorrow? I'll arrange the tasting over a light lunch."

Dad said, "That's an excellent idea and I'll make sure we've wrapped up our tour by then."

She pushed her chair back. "Mom, I'm going to take the boys home."

David stood and shook her hand. "Until tomorrow."

A shiver raced over her, and not the good kind either. Call it being overly cautious, but David Marchand didn't just happen to be in the area, and she was going to find out what he really wanted.

15

Anna put her feet up on the leather upholstered footstool, holding the most recent release from her favorite mystery author. It was a special treat to have time to cozy up in her sunroom. She was reading when her cell phone rang. Her heart lifted when she saw who was calling.

"Hi, Colin."

"Hi. Hectic day at work."

"Tell me about it."

"A patient was brought in and we thought she was stable and then everything went sideways. She coded not once but twice. We worked hard the first time to stabilize her, and then when she coded again, I didn't think we'd be able to save her. But she was stronger than I expected and her heart went back into rhythm. I've never seen anything it. She actually opened her eyes and smiled at us and then thanked us for taking care of her."

"Whoa. It has to make you feel good to know that you saved her." She knew what that family would be feeling, and her dad hadn't been that bad by comparison.

"Tell me about your day." She could hear the smile in his voice.

"Not nearly as exciting as yours. I had my sister's boys over for dinner, and they left a while ago. We constructed forts with sofa cushions and blankets and strung fairy lights off the chairs to create a magical forest. It was a blast but man, I'm tired. I don't know how my sister makes it look so easy."

"That sounds like fun. I haven't made blanket forts in forever."

"Wait till you hear this. When I picked the boys up, there was a French man at my parents' house. David Marchand. He just showed up out of the blue. There was something about him I just didn't like."

"Did he say something?"

His voice smoothed her jagged nerves when she thought of the man again.

"No, but he basically finagled a tour from Dad for tomorrow and then we're going to have lunch."

"Go in with an open mind, but you're sharp. Trust your instincts. If you think there's something suspicious, keep your eyes open."

She was pleased at his compliment. "Want to come for lunch and meet David?"

"Thanks for the invitation, but I'll pass. On another topic, if you're still up for swinging clubs, I checked the weather and tomorrow night looks like it'll be clear and cool."

"Did you ask your sister if I can borrow her old clubs?"

"I did, and she said she'll give them to you." With a laugh, he said, "You have to know my sister. She hates clutter. She calls herself a minimalist so if she hasn't used something in six months, she either gives it to someone she knows or donates it."

"That's very generous and might get expensive." She could picture him lounging on a sofa with a smile and maybe a beer in his hand even though she hadn't seen the inside of his house.

"I'm not sure if she'd replace an identical item, but I'd hazard a guess that she has."

"Please tell Marie I'm happy to buy the clubs. Just let me know what she'd like for them."

"I'll ask, but don't count on it. I think she's just happy I'm cultivating a new golf partner."

Anna let that sink in. It sounded really nice. "Does she like wine?"

"She does. Why?"

"I'll put together a variety case and you can give it to her as a thank you."

"Anna, that really isn't necessary. She's happy someone will use them."

"I would like to do something; one kind gesture deserves one in return. And, Colin? You won't change my mind."

With a chuckle, he said, "I give. If you want to have the case ready, we could drop it off after the driving range and you could meet her."

Was she ready to meet his sister? Now she was being stupid. He knew her entire family and it was fine.

"Anna, are you still there?"

"Yes. I was just thinking about what wines I'll put in the case." Silently, she apologized for the white lie.

"I can pick you up when you get out of work. And just in case you're free, I'm off Wednesday too."

"That's nice, to have a midweek day all to yourself. I'll get out a little early and we could have some fun."

"It is, but I'm on call next weekend. Midweek days off give me time to gear up for what is typically a crazy couple of days."

She could hear the pause and the click of glass on a table before he continued. "Did you know that most people put off going to the doctor when they're having issues? They don't want to face the potential of what might be happening.

Wham, then it's off to the emergency room and they'll end up in the cardiac unit."

"Like my dad."

"I'm sorry. I didn't mean anything by that."

She could hear the chagrin in his voice.

"But it's true. Dad put off going to the doctor because of Tessa's wedding and he figured he could wait until the doctor's office opened on Monday."

"I'm glad for your dad's sake he came in when he did. It avoided additional damage to his heart."

"Would Dad have died?"

She heard him take a deep breath. "There is no way to tell for sure, but it's never a good idea to ignore symptoms of a heart attack."

She was nodding even though he couldn't see her agreeing with him.

"How's your dad feeling? I know he has a follow-up scheduled."

"He's good. I saw him and Mom this morning and they're planning a cruise as soon as he's released to travel."

"Good for them."

"Now, back to our date." It gave her a thrill to use that word in conjunction with Colin.

"Yes?" He drew the word out.

"Is there a dress code? I read something about having to wear a collared shirt?"

He started to chuckle.

"I'm serious. Are shorts and a t-shirt okay or I should go buy the golf outfit I saw last week at the store?"

"Whoa there. No need to go shopping." He laughed again. "Unless of course you want to. But shorts, a comfortable shirt with a collar, and sneakers will be just fine. You might want to bring a sweater in case it's chilly; the wind tends to whip up the hill at the range. But the main thing is comfort first."

"Okay then." She tried to stifle a yawn and hoped he didn't hear her.

"You sound tired and I'm going to let you go. I can't wait for Wednesday."

"Me too. Thanks for calling."

"Sleep well, Anna."

The phone clicked in her ear. She set it down and wondered if she should look up how to golf on the internet. Just in case.

The back door banged open the next day as Anna finished setting a table in the bistro with wine-glasses and the selection of wines she was going to have David taste. She wanted to feature the best of what CLW offered. Kate rushed through the door carrying two canvas shopping bags.

"I picked up some salad things for a light lunch, and it's heart healthy, too, for Sam."

Anna eased back her sleeve and checked the time. It was almost an hour before Dad and David were due to arrive. "Can I help?" She took one of the bags and followed Kate into the kitchen and unloaded it onto the counter. "Have you heard of David Marchand before?"

"No, but Don's mentioned Henri. I was surprised David showed up out of the blue."

"Me too." She pursed her lips. "After the tasting, I'm sure he'll be on his way."

Kate gave her a sidelong glance. "I hear that tone in your voice."

Anna folded her arms over her midsection. "I don't believe in coincidence or that David just is being nice. And I don't think he wants a change of scene and would like to work for CLW like Jack did when he went to the West Coast after graduation. There's no reason for him to want to see the vineyard in the spring. He's up to something and I intend on keeping my eyes and ears open."

"Why don't you go back to the lab and I'll finish up here." Kate's eyes held a hint of laughter. "You can plan your line of questioning like in one of your mystery novels and discover his true agenda."

"Is that your way of getting me out of your kitchen?"

Kate shrugged. "Not really, but you're better at making a plan when you're not distracted, and I agree something is off about this surprise visit."

Forty-five minutes later, Anna's cell phone pinged with a text from Dad. He and David were waiting for her in the bistro. She hit a few keys and locked her computer before slipping her dark-gray blazer over her pale-green blouse. She was ready to spend a couple of hours with Dad and his guest.

When she walked into the bistro, David crossed the room, took her hand, and kissed both of her cheeks. That was way too familiar, having only met once, but she gave him a pass since it was customary in France and their families were friendly.

"Hello, Anna. It's very nice to see you again."

"Hi. Did you enjoy the tour?"

"I was highly impressed with the size of the winery. Our two wineries are very similar, and Crescent Lake reminds me of home."

"Hey, Dad." She gestured to the table. "Please make yourself comfortable and we can enjoy lunch." She couldn't help but notice her father's eyes. Something had upset him and she wouldn't get the chance to ask what until after David left.

She entered the kitchen, where Kate had left three plates of salad with grilled chicken. Fresh-baked bread was sliced in a covered basket. Placing everything on a tray, she carried it into the dining room. David got up and took it from her hands.

"Please allow me to help."

She set the plates and basket on the table and noticed there was a bowl with dressing already in the center. "Thank you."

Dad was sitting at the table, his gaze sharp. He was totally focused on what David was saying while he poured the Marechal Foch and Cabernet so they could breathe. Next, he uncorked the Cayuga and Pinot Grigio, setting them into chilled sleeves.

David held Anna's chair and she murmured her thanks.

As she sat down, she looked up and a smile spread across her face. "Colin."

He crossed the room and lightly kissed her cheek A smile danced in his eyes. "I had a change of plans so I hope you don't mind I decided to join you for lunch after all."

Smooth as a fine merlot, she said, "I'm so glad. Please slide a chair over and I'll get another plate. I know Kate has more food in the kitchen; she always makes plenty."

Dad put a hand out to stop her. "I'll take care of it. Introduce Colin to our guest."

Colin extended his hand to David. "Colin Grant and you must be David Marchand." They shook hands. "It's a pleasure to meet you." He slid his arm around the back of Anna's chair.

She held in her grin but was happy he was by her side.

"It is a pleasure, Colin." He sat on the other side of Anna and turned his attention back to her. "As I was saying, Anna, which of these wines is your favorite?" He took a seat next to her.

With a laugh, she said, "That's like asking my mom which one of her kids is her favorite."

She poured the Pinot Grigio. "Let's start with this and

enjoy our lunch, and you can taste what we have. These four are a good representation of the CLW line."

David held up his glass. "*À votre santé,* to your good health."

Sam, Colin, and Anna tapped his glass. "To good health."

Anna looped her arm through Colin's after Dad and David had left the bistro.

"I am so glad you came today. You should have seen the look on David's face when you swooped in."

"It was fun and the best part was that I got to see my girl in action. I even learned a little bit about wine."

She kissed his cheek. "So, does that mean you're my guy?"

"I like how that sounds." He took her in his arms and lightly kissed her lips. "Ready to head over to CL Driving Range and give golf a swing?"

"Give me a few minutes to change, and then we can head out. I'll meet you outside the tasting room." She stood on tiptoes and kissed his cheek. Today was turning out to be full of surprises. Who knew, maybe she'd be able to hit the ball too.

With a wink and a chuckle, he said, "I'll pull the getaway car up to the door."

Anna pulled her ponytail through the back of her dark-gray baseball cap. It sported the logo of Tessa's winery, Sand Creek. And just to be sure she wasn't accused of bias, she had tucked a dark-green cap for Colin in her bag. It bore the CLW logo.

She had selected gray shorts, a bright pink-and-white-striped golf shirt, and a pink sweater. Based on what she had seen online, if she couldn't hit the ball, she'd look the part. In her tote bag, she stashed her purse, bottled water, and a brand-new pair of spikeless golf shoes that she found on sale. She figured the minimal investment was worthwhile.

When she heard a toot from the parking lot, she grabbed the bag and pulled the tasting room door closed behind her. Colin got out of his Subaru sedan and opened the passenger door for her. She couldn't remember the last time a man had been so gracious, and she was definitely flattered. He stowed her bag in the back seat.

"Hey." She got in and buckled her seat belt as he went around to the driver's side.

He brushed her cheek with his lips. "You look like a golfer."

"Thanks."

Dark sunglasses covered his hazel eyes but his green polo shirt would complement them. She glanced at his slacks.

"Should I have worn pants?"

"No, you look great. I just thought I should wear pants to lunch."

"Do you want to change before we take off?"

"No, I'm comfortable. So, tell me. Did David bring his family on this mystery trip?"

"No, just him." She adjusted the seat belt. "I was surprised he didn't ask about my new formulation for a summer wine, which is another blend."

"I didn't think wineries developed new wines every year." He sped up when they reached the main road.

"This one might never be commercialized, but I love to play around and see if I can come up with the next big buzz in the industry. It jazzes me up for the regular work."

"Which is?"

"Each season, the juice is different. We have a guideline of how we'll blend to make every variety, but there is usually some tweaking involved to maintain consistency from year to year for the standards like the cab or Cayuga. I always need to pay close attention to how the different juices will work with others."

"Huh. I never realized it was that complex. I thought you take juice, put it in silver vats and wait a while, then put it in bottles."

She clapped her hands together with a hoot of laughter. "On your next day off, you should come by the winery and I'll give you the full behind the scenes tour, including a tasting. That will give you a much better idea of what I do."

He wiggled his eyebrows. "This means we have at least two more dates planned. Playing golf and now the winery."

She felt a slow smile spread over her face. Her heart skipped a beat and she met his eyes. "I guess it does."

He took her hand and their fingers interlaced. She noticed his were long and slender, but strong. She couldn't help but let her mind wander as to how they would feel as they slipped over her skin. She shivered.

"Are you cold? I can close the sunroof."

"I like the fresh air."

His smile warmed her body and soul. She wondered what his flaw was and if it was fatal. She had spent enough time dating guys who turned out to be losers, overly possessive, thought she had deep pockets they could tap or, worse, had a child they didn't take care of but she could. Was Colin a nice guy whom other girls decided he was too nice to date?

She gave him a side-glance. "Do you have any deep, dark secrets I should know about?"

He gave a half shrug. "I was engaged once."

"I'm sorry. What happened?" She waved her hand. "You don't need to answer that."

"It's fine. We just grew apart and had different dreams of what our futures would look like. She moved to the West Coast and thought a long-distance relationship could work. I wanted to live here, sink in some roots, and raise a family."

"I'm sorry."

"Thanks. We wished each other well and parted company. What about you?"

"I've dated off and on, but nothing has really clicked." She licked her lips. "Yet. I may need more than two more dates to decide." Part of her was anxious to see where they were headed and the other side of her was enjoying living in the moment and reveling in all the new experiences.

16

When they got to the driving range, Anna slung the bag of golf clubs Colin's sister had loaned her over her shoulder. She was sporting her new golf shoes and she slipped on her pink sweater. A slight breeze teased her ponytail and the afternoon was perfect, not a cloud in the royal blue sky.

"Do we need to go to the clubhouse?"

"No. I'm a member so I called and prepaid." Colin finished tying his golf shoes.

She chewed her bottom lip and looked out over the range. "Did I tell you I watched a bunch of tutorials online? I think I've got the hang of it."

He laughed. "This is more of a hands-on sport. But you get a point for initiative."

They walked down a short flight of stone stairs and followed the signs that stated *CL Driving Range*. She noticed there were stands for a dozen golf bags. In front of them, the ground had a steep decline, and she guessed the balls dropped onto that grassy area. Huge signs indicated the footage markers. They were the only people at the range so she didn't feel the need to keep her voice low, as was customary golf etiquette, something else she had learned online.

A flash of nerves washed over her. "How long have you been golfing again?"

"Since I was a kid, but that never matters in golf. You can have a good, great, or horrible day from one round to the next."

This sounded weird. If you didn't steadily improve, what was the point? "Then why do you keep coming back?"

"Because you just never know when you'll make that hole in one or birdie a putt. There are so many factors out of your control, how the greens are kept, the wind, how the ball lands and if it bounces or not."

She could hear the sincerity in his voice. "You really do enjoy the game."

"I do and I hope you do too."

She set her bag in one of the stands and pulled out a random club. "Do we use our own balls?" She was confused. "Then how do we get them back?" She frowned and shoved the club back in the bag.

He grabbed her hand. "Come on. We need to get a bucket of balls." He held up a swipe card and pointed to a short, squat metal box at the edge of the range. "Over there." They strolled over the perfectly manicured grass.

She took in their surroundings. "The grounds are stunning."

"Some of the best landscaping I've seen is on a golf course. Someone is always doing something." He slowed his steps. "My mom always said a good walk around the course is spoiled by having to actually hit the ball."

Her steps slowed. "Is that a warning?"

"Nah. Mom's an amazing golfer, but I do think she likes the scenery the best."

They grabbed two empty wire-coated buckets and placed one under the chute. Then Colin swiped what looked like a debit card and hit the button. She gave him a questioning look.

"It's a card the club provides so we can get range balls."

"Clever idea. Is it all it's good for?"

Balls thunked into the first bucket and he handed it to her. He filled another bucket.

"No. We can use it at the nineteenth hole too."

"I'm confused. I thought there are only eighteen."

His grin split his cheeks. "That's the bar where you go after a round."

"Are we skipping everything and going straight to nineteen tonight?"

He gave her a quick look. "It depends on how you do at the range."

She replied with a "Hmm" and pretended to stalk back to her clubs, deliberately making her ponytail swing.

"Anna," he called after her, "I was joking."

She flashed him a wicked grin over her shoulder. "I plan to dazzle you with my skill." She set down the bucket and looked at her clubs. She grabbed one with a flat metal head. "It's says it's a seven. What does that mean?"

His eyes grew wide and mischief made them sparkle. "Missed that in the online tutorial, did you?" He pulled out a long club with a fat, round head. "The higher the number on a club, the shorter the distance. This is your driver. Let's start with this one."

"Okay, but how do I know it's the driver?" She took the club from his hands and gripped it like she had seen online. Hand over hand.

"It typically doesn't have a number but sometimes it's labeled as ONE." He gave a soft laugh. "I know you're determined to knock my socks off, but would it be okay if I gave you a few tips?"

She propped her hand on her hip. "It would be rude to

refuse." Once she had the club in her hands, she wasn't sure what she should do next.

He came around behind her and slipped his arms over hers. His hands repositioned her fingers and he said, "Interlock the pinky on your right hand with your left index finger and grip the shaft firmly but don't squeeze."

Her heart knocked against her chest wall. He was so close to her that his warm breath caressed her cheek. How was she going to be able to pay attention to his directions if her mind was racing with different ideas? It was his fault because of his choice of words.

"Now, I want you to take a deep breath in and slowly exhale. As you do, I want you to really concentrate on the ground in front of you and keep your head down."

"Ball?" She was definitely having trouble forming a coherent sentence.

"We're practicing."

His breath tickled her neck. Inwardly, she groaned. Did they really need to practice? Silently, she admonished herself to focus. This was a golf lesson, not a seduction.

"Now keep your head down. We're going to swing your arms back slowly in an arch and your hands will be about shoulder height. Then, with more speed, you're going to bring the club down, and you want to graze the grass in front of you. That's where you'll connect with the ball. You want to follow through and the ball will go forward."

She looked over her shoulder and brushed the dimple in his chin with her lips. "This is fun," she murmured. Her pulse kicked up. She liked the little kisses here and there and was looking forward to when they took them to the next level.

She could feel his body rise and fall with silent laughter. "We'll do one without the ball together and then you can give it a try, with a ball."

Good heavens. All the innuendos she could make, and would, if she knew him better. She stifled a laugh.

"Alright. So I hold the club firmly, but not too tight."

"Yes."

She shifted slightly in her stance, which brought her closer to him as she lifted her arms up and back as he instructed. She paused as the club hung in the air.

"Now I bring it down and try to hit the grass," she said.

"Yes. This way, you'll give the ball lift."

Slowly, she swung the club head down. It whiffed the air.

"What did I do wrong?"

"You picked your head up and you need more speed on the descent. Try it again, but this time when you address the ball, keep your eyes glued to it on the ground and keep your arms straight until you get up to ninety degrees when you cross your body. You don't need to look at anything but when the head of the club meets the ball, and don't forget to follow through."

He stepped away from her. Which, as far as Anna was concerned, was too bad.

He selected a ball and walked over to the defined area of grass. Sticking up from the center was what looked like a short PVC straw. He balanced the ball on it.

"Ready?"

She came over and stood in front of him.

"Do you want me to help you get into position?"

"No. I'm all set." *But I'd like to watch you swing a club.* She definitely needed to focus.

"Take your time. There's no need to rush."

She exhaled and dropped her shoulders and eyes as Colin had said. The head of the club rested to the right of the tee. She totally focused on the ball. She took another deep breath and swung the club back and then brought it down with a rush. Clumps of grass flew up and she looked down the range, scanning the area for her ball.

"Where did it go?" she exclaimed.

With a soft chuckle, Colin said, "Look down."

Sitting on a tuft of sod was her ball. Her shoulders slumped. "How did I do that?"

"You hit the ground before you hit the ball. When you brought the club down, it was more of a chopping motion and less of a graceful swing."

With a laugh, she said, "I'm going to try again." She plopped the ball on the little plastic tee and did the exact same thing again. She looked out of the corner of her eye. He was watching her with a serious expression.

"Am I doing this wrong?"

"Not at all."

She straightened and leaned against the club. "Care to show me how it's done? It might help to see it in person and not on the screen."

He gave her a wink and grabbed a club from his bag, along with a range ball from the bucket.

She said, "Everything is better when you use the personal touch."

His eyebrow shot up. "True." He set the ball on the tee. "See how I hold the club and how my head and shoulders are relaxed?"

"Uh-huh."

With a slow, deliberate swing, the club arched up and behind his shoulder and accelerated in speed on the way down. It connected with the ball, which flew over the grass in a perfect arch. Then Colin struck the golfer's classic pose she had seen online and she watched him while he watched his ball.

"That was spectacular."

He dropped the club into his bag. "Your turn."

"I don't think I'll ever be able to do that or look like that."

"It takes practice, but you'll get there. Remember, we all start in the same place."

If only she could. But he was right. Everyone had to start at the beginning of the learning curve. She followed his instructions exactly. Set the ball in place, hold the club with fingers interlaced. After several deep breaths with her eyes locked on the ball, willing it to fly through the air as cleanly as Colin's did, her mantra repeated over and over. *I can do this. I can do this.* She swung the club back. Without hesitation, she brought the club down, her eyes on the dimples in the ball. She felt it connect as she followed through in a full arc.

She didn't want to look down. Would the ball still be sitting there? No, she had felt it fly.

"Anna. It went one hundred yards. Look!"

"Where?" She scanned the area in front of her.

He slipped an arm around her waist and extended the other for her to follow out to the range.

"Do you see that little white lump to the left of the one hundred sign?"

"That's mine?" She was shocked. She had done it. She turned toward him and, with one hand on his shirt, pulled him close. "I did it." Anna claimed his mouth with hers and kissed him long and hard. The club slipped to the ground.

When he pulled back, he looked deep into her eyes. "I'm guessing you like this game after all?"

"You have no idea." She pecked his lips. "I'm going to do that again."

"What, hit the ball or kiss me?" Colin didn't release her.

She snaked her arms around his neck and stepped closer to his body. She murmured, "I really like this part of golf."

17

Anna smiled as she sorted through the stack of mail on her desk at the office, remembering how much fun the driving range had been the night before. She noticed a thick cream envelope. She turned it over. The return address was from the Director of the London Wine Fair. It was a prestigious event, but why were they sending her a letter? She ripped it open and pulled out several pages. She scanned the contents and leaned back in her chair as she reread the letter again.

Dear Ms. Price,

As you may know, the London Wine Fair is in a few weeks, but we have an unexpected vacancy in our master class schedule. Would you be interested in presenting a lecture on red wines?

I've attached the summary of several other presentations to give you the flavor of what would be expected. We will gladly pay for your travel arrangements and hotel accommodations while you are in London. I look forward to hearing from you.

Sincerely,

Lisette Bishop, Executive Director

Anna was dumbfounded. Why on earth would one of the premier organizations in the world want her to speak on red wines? She set the pages aside and turned on her computer. While she waited for it, she walked down the hall to the efficiency kitchen and fixed herself a cup of strong black coffee. She hoped to be back in her lab before Don got in.

"Good morning, Anna."

Don's deep voice caused her to jump, sloshing the hot coffee over the rim of the mug and onto the floor.

"Don, you startled me."

He grabbed some paper towels and wiped up the floor. "Sorry. I didn't mean to. I guess your mind was someplace else."

She could hear the playful tone in his voice. "I was thinking about a letter I received today, from the London Wine Fair."

He gave a low whistle. "What did they want?" He tossed the paper towels in the trash.

"They offered me an opportunity to present on red wine, but I think talking about the blending process for innovative wines based on the grapes is a better topic."

"Agreed, and it's a sweet opportunity. So you're going to do it?"

"I'm not sure, but it's something to think about. CLW hasn't exhibited in a while. Why not?"

He leaned against the counter. "It's been a few years and probably something we need to think about. If you go, you could check it out for us and let us know if we should try and get space next year."

"I can do that." She gave him a gentle shove. "For now, I have samples to gather from the tanks and testing to do. We're getting close to bottling the shiraz from last year's harvest."

"Good. Let me know what you find out and when we're going to schedule a run. I'll bring in some people to get the line ready to go."

"Right." Anna was going to head back to her lab when she said, "Don?"

He grabbed a carton of cream from the fridge. "Yeah?"

"When you went to the wine fair in London, were there a ton of people there?" She wondered how many people might attend her presentation.

He sipped his coffee. "I went my first year as president. It was packed and I made some great contacts, had some fun in London, but it was exhausting. Most of my time was at the convention hall. The presentations were popular. Why?"

"It might be interesting to go. Any timing issues that you could think of?"

"No. We can work it out. Especially once we get the shiraz bottling organized."

"Dad's feeling good too."

"It's a true statement. You should go; your instincts on harvesting and blending are the best I've ever seen. Even Max said he wished he had your intuition."

This was the second time in a short period he had given her a compliment; maybe he had taken what she'd said to heart. "Thanks. See you later." She hurried down the hall and, once she got inside her haven, closed the door behind her. The lab was immaculate. Everything had a place and that was the way she liked it. She reread the letter from Ms. Bishop. *The only reason they asked is they're desperate.*

She set it aside and picked up her notebook and a pen and set them back down. Going to London would be a good change of pace, and it did say her expenses would be paid. Heck, a paid vacation—that was worth considering. She'd swing by her parents' after her meeting about the STEM program and bounce the idea off them. She folded the letter and stuck it in her bag.

It was time to get down to business. She flipped open the notebook and made a few notes. They were close to bottling this batch, and then it would age for another six months. If all went well, it'd be ready in time for the holiday sale.

The next afternoon, Anna entered her old high school. Her heels clicked on the dull linoleum floor. The long corridor was lined with metal lockers, and overhead lights shone bright as she looked for the math department. Things hadn't changed since she had been a student here. The familiar smell of pine cleaner filled the air. Kids had gone home for the day and most of the classrooms she passed were dark.

The math and science rooms were down on the left. They used to overlook a grassy field but from her observation outside, it was now a large greenhouse.

At last she found Room 122. She tapped on the glass side panel and poked her head inside. An older woman sat at the desk. She looked up from the stack of papers in front of her and gave Anna a warm smile.

"Anna Price. How nice to see you again." Her former teacher, Karen Kelley, welcomed her into the classroom.

"Ms. Kelley, it's good to see you."

"Karen, please." She gestured to a small round table off to one side. "Have a seat and tell me how things are at the winery."

She pulled out a chair and sat down. Karen took the chair across from her. She really did look as Anna remembered. She had pale-blue eyes, a quick and easy smile, and a splash of freckles. Her reddish hair had a few strands of gray and she must be nearing retirement after all these years. Ms. Kelley had taught all of her sisters and brothers.

"Things are good. I became an enologist." She saw the confusion fall over Karen's face. It wasn't unusual for her to get this reaction when she told someone what she did. "It's a fancy way of saying I'm in charge of winemaking at the vineyard. I work with Jack to keep the vines healthy, and I blend all the varieties we make and follow up until it's ready for sale. So basically, I'm from vine to table." She gave her a smile.

"It sounds like a pretty important job." Karen crossed her arms over her midsection. "Do your sisters and brothers work there?"

"Tessa owns Sand Creek Winery with her husband."

"I went there for a tasting when some friends were in town a few weeks ago. It was nice, but I didn't know she owned it."

"She took ownership about eighteen months ago."

"And the twins?"

"Leo is a mechanic, but he's moved into classic car restoration now, and Liza has become an event planner. She does some events at CLW, but she can work at any venue. But Don and Jack work with me."

"A nice family business." She gave an approving nod. "I was surprised to get your phone call the other day."

"Really? Why is that?"

"Not in a bad way. I'm thrilled you want to volunteer with us."

"I think it would be rewarding and I remember we had a good STEM program here. Is it still active?"

"I couldn't agree more. And you would be an excellent role model. You always were in the top of your class in school."

"Thank you." Anna really wanted to find out when she could get into the classroom with the kids. The small talk was driving her buggy.

"But the program you're referring to ended a few years ago from lack of money, and we would need community leaders to support its relaunch. I've talked with the other teachers in the science and technology departments, and we all agree starting an after-school club for girls would be a wonderful opportunity. Sadly, we'd need funding and approval from the school board and both of these will take time."

Anna sat up straighter in the chair. She felt her bubble burst.

"The most successful programs are carefully planned, wouldn't you agree?"

Anna understood. "You're right. It makes the most sense to have a sound plan before presenting this to the board."

"I'm glad you understand. I'd be interested to see an outline of your ideas." Karen stood up and walked to the desk. "Please stay in touch."

"I will." She picked up her bag from the table.

"Anna, I love your enthusiasm for this project." Karen extended her hand.

Giving it a firm shake, Anna said, "Thank you for your time today and we'll be talking very soon."

Anna left the school pleased with how things had gone despite it being slower than she had hoped. She texted Colin. *Dinner? I'd love to tell you about my exciting day.*

Before she pulled out of the parking space, she got a *YES!!!* in return.

Meet me at Anthony's at six?

He responded, *Looking forward to it.*

Her next stop was to see her parents and show them the letter from the wine fair. What could Dad share about her presentation topic or who she might meet in London? She laughed to herself. Her mind was made up and she was going.

Once she got behind the wheel, she pushed the hands-free option to call her parents.

Mom answered on the third ring. She was slightly out of breath.

"Hey, Mom."

"Anna, this is a nice surprise."

"What are you doing?" She eased out of the parking space and drove slowly through the lot. Looking right and left, she pulled out onto the quiet two-lane road.

"I was just pulling out some old luggage from the storage room."

"That's exciting. Do you mind if I swing by?"

Mom laughed. "You don't have to call and ask. You know better. I'll brew some coffee for when you get here."

"That sounds good. I could use a boost of something. See you soon."

She disconnected the line and pushed a button on the steering wheel. Jazz filled the car. Her thoughts turned to Colin. Maybe he'd want to go with her to Europe. They could rent a car and hit the open road. Now that sounded appealing, and she could ask him over dinner.

18

Anna drove slowly down her parents' drive and parked in front of the garage. Her parents were sitting on the porch glider and appeared to be deep in conversation when she walked up the wide, shallow steps.

"Hey, Mom, Dad."

Before either of them could respond, she held up her hand as Mom started to get up. "I can get coffee, or would you prefer wine?"

Mom said, "Coffee, please."

Anna set about the task. After she returned with steaming mugs of coffee, she settled herself on the wicker chair and asked, "You're done sorting luggage?"

"We will need to buy a few new pieces. What we have is older than you."

Dad said, "What brings you by today?" Mom tapped his leg and he smiled. "Not that we're not happy to see you."

"First, I wanted to ask you why you were angry with David the other day at lunch."

"He offered to purchase CLW for a paltry sum of money, said he was helping out an old family friend who needed to retire." His lips pressed together, and then he took a deep breath. "I reminded him that we are a family-run business and it takes all of us to be successful."

"Wow, he was bold."

He wiggled his eyebrows. "It was nice to see Colin."

"It was, and we're not talking about Colin, but David."

He shook his head. "Let's not dwell on David. I set him straight and he's headed back to France. But what else did you want to talk about?"

She pulled the oversized envelope from her bag and passed it to him. "I got this in the mail and wondered what you thought."

He took his time reading the cover letter and subsequent pages before he handed it to Mom and gave her a thoughtful look. "What do you think of this opportunity?"

She noticed he didn't give his opinion but was waiting for her to respond. "Well, on the one hand, I'm honored they contacted me, but on the other, I feel like I'm just a last-ditch effort to fill in for someone better. However, I want to go."

He nodded as she spoke. Measuring his words carefully, he said, "I can tell you that being on this list is very prestigious. I believe you were to be invited next year and pulled up with this vacancy."

"Why would you think that?"

"I submitted your name"—he held up his hand—"and before you get mad, I want you to have the recognition you deserve and maybe I should have told you, but in my defense, I didn't want you to start worrying about it."

She had to admit she hadn't thought of it in those terms. "Interesting perspective."

Mom handed her the envelope. "It's exciting."

"To be honest, when I first got it, I thought about saying no. But an all-expenses paid trip? That's hard to walk away from. And now, Dad, the idea that you submitted my name to them and they agreed with you gives it more significance. I'm definitely in." She took the letter and jammed it into her bag.

"But I'm just a part of the family business. I'm not a great world-renowned enologist."

Dad sat up straight in his chain and beamed. "Anna, you sell yourself short. You're very talented and the recognition you'd get from attending the convention would be good for both you and CLW."

She sat up. "Over dinner, I'm going to ask Colin to go with me."

Mom grinned. "Take a few extra days and do some sight-seeing. How long has it been since you've been to Europe?"

"A couple of years, and I do love England."

"Give the queen our regards." Mom sipped her coffee.

"But of course." She smiled. "Dad, I can't figure out David's angle. Why do you think he really came here?"

"Henri and I talk occasionally, and we've always had a friendly rivalry even though we have an ocean between us. He's never mentioned an interest in purchasing CLW, not that it would be for sale. Just bizarre." He looked over the rim of his mug. "You did a good job with the wine selections. He enjoyed them and we really put our best glass forward."

"We have good wine, so it was easy." Her gaze slid over the greenery of vines, the leaves dancing in the soft breeze. "We have good growth this year, and the new field is almost ready for Don to plant his new variety."

"It took him a while after living in Loudon for so long, but now he and Kate are home and ready to get started on their own blend." Mom took Dad's hand. "I'm glad they're going to carry on your grandfather's tradition of each married couple planting a section of the land to ensure the future of the family."

Anna said, "Do you think Tessa and Max will plant a field at Sand Creek or here?"

Dad stood up. "There are acres put aside for them on CLW land so I hope they do, but I understand if they want to start their own tradition."

He excused himself, and Mom watched him with a tender smile on her lips. "Checking the weather is something he's done his entire life. I guess some habits are hard to change." When he was out of earshot, she said, "It still stings, what happened with Tessa. He understands why she walked away from CLW, but there are things like the new vine tradition he never thought would end for any of our children."

"Maybe they'll plant in both wineries." Anna leaned forward and took her mom's hand. "How is Dad really?"

"He has an appointment with the nutritionist for a follow-up and blood work. We'll know next week how things are going."

"I'm curious. Did you talk about traveling after the first heart attack?"

"We did but never took action. We kept putting it off, saying there was plenty of time." Mom looked into her eyes. "He slowed down the number of hours he worked, but he never really walked away from the business, just like Grandfather Donald, who died too young." There was a catch in her throat. "I want you to live an amazing, full life. What do you want? Do you see Colin in your future?"

"I've been thinking about my future and Colin a lot lately." She shrugged. "I do know I don't want to be alone anymore and I'm willing to take chances and explore new opportunities, but I love my job at CLW, and that will never change."

"I've been worried about you for a while. Find what makes you happy and live your best life."

"Thanks." She gave Mom a one-armed squeeze. "I'm going to take off; I'm having dinner with Colin."

Mom gave her a quick hug. "Have fun tonight."

Anna was waiting for Colin when he got to the restaurant. She looked up and gave him a wide smile. He leaned in and lightly kissed her lips before sitting down.

"I'm so glad you texted. Seeing my favorite person is a great way to wrap up a very long but hectic day."

"I hope it's okay I ordered you a beer."

He loved a woman who was confident, and Anna certainly exuded that every time they were together. "That will hit the spot," he said and looked up just as the waiter set down a glass of red wine for Anna and beer in front of him. He left the menus and said he'd be back for their order.

"Before we talk about medical stuff, tell me all about your day. Your eyes are shining like you're bursting to tell me all good stuff."

She picked up her glass and tapped his bottle. "I got invited to attend and present at one of the premier wine events in Europe."

He could feel his eyes grow wide. "That's great. When and where?"

"In three weeks." She lifted a shoulder, trying to act nonchalant. "I talked to Don and my dad and it's a pretty big deal. So, I'm going to go."

"That's awesome. Do you know what you're going to talk about yet and what kinds of people you will be presenting to —wine drinkers, vineyard owners, or other enologists?"

"I'm not sure. I plan on preparing two versions of the same lecture so I can read the room and tailor it to them. I love to over-prepare. And I'm excited about spending five days in London, three onsite at the convention and taking an extra day or two and doing a little sightseeing. I've always wanted to go to the port village of Folkestone and spend a night or two in a charming little inn. It's supposed to have wonderful views of the English Channel, and I've heard there are stone pathways along the ocean and the Cliffs of Dover." She set her glass aside and leaned across the table. "Which brings me to my question. How would you like to go with me?"

Without a moment of hesitation, he said, "I would love to go to England with you. In the morning, I'll check the schedule to make sure I can get the days off." He kissed her lips and lingered there. "We are going to have so much fun. After you're done wowing the wine world, that is."

She tipped her head back and laughed. "I love your high opinion of me." She cupped his cheek and kissed him again. "Now I'm really looking forward to England."

19

Two days later, Colin strode into the Crescent Lake Winery tasting room. He was on a mission—to see if he could get Anna to play hooky with him for the afternoon. He looked around, curious. Since this was his first time in the main building, he had no idea where her office was. Scanning the room, he wondered if he should go back out and call her.

"Excuse me; can I help you?"

A petite brunette walked in his direction.

"Hi. I'm looking for Anna; I'm Colin Grant."

She gave him the once-over with a smile and stuck her hand out. "I'm Peyton Brien." She inclined her head to the bar. "I run the tasting room. Is Anna expecting you?"

"No, but do you know where I might find her?"

Her brown eyes twinkled. "I saw her go into the warehouse. Go on down."

He looked around and saw there were a couple of possible directions. "This is my first time here, so I'm not sure where to go."

She waved her hand in the direction of a brightly lit hallway "Come on. I'll take you to her."

Their footsteps clicked on the bright-green paint-covered cement floor.

"So you haven't had the grand tour yet?"

Colin shook his head. "I wasn't much of a wine drinker until I started seeing Anna; I'm more of a beer guy."

She gave him a side-look. "What have you thought of our wines?"

"They're good. I like the cabernet better than the white." Peyton's footsteps slowed as they approached a heavy steel door.

"Anna is in there. Go on in and if you ever want an official tasting, I'd be happy to set you up."

She left him standing in front of the door as he wondered how Anna would react when he just walked into her domain. He wasn't going to find out just standing in the hall. He pushed open the door and entered an enormous space with highly polished silver tanks lined up in rows the length of the room. He walked to the center aisle. At the end was another door, which logically would lead to another building of similar size if the exterior was any indication of the size of the space.

"Anna?" His voice echoed off the tanks. He heard a muffled response, but he wasn't sure if it was her or not. "Are you here?"

A minute later, she emerged from between tanks, carrying a small tray of vials. Her face lit up when she saw him. "Colin, what are you doing here?" She placed a tender kiss on his mouth. Her forehead wrinkled. "Did I forget we had plans?"

"We don't, but I was hoping to convince you to sneak out early."

She gave him a thoughtful look. "What do you have up your sleeve?"

His took a step closer and ran his hand down her arm. "Can you leave?"

"It just so happens I have a flexible schedule. Care to tell me where we're going?"

He had her interest piqued. "I discovered a place that holds trivia night once a month and I bought us tickets for tonight."

"Confident I'd say yes. What time does it start? I didn't know any place in town was doing that, but it sounds like fun."

"It's closer to Syracuse, so it'll take us about an hour to get there, and it starts at six."

She glanced at her watch and pointed to a back door. "Let me take these upstairs and I'll run my tests, and then we can leave. It should only take about a half hour, which will give us plenty of time to get there." She looked at him with a saucy grin. "Want to come with me and see a mad scientist at work?"

He laughed and pushed the door open for her so she could walk ahead of him. "That sounds like fun. Can I ask questions or do I need to sit quietly and observe?"

She gave him a solemn look. "Questions are always encouraged." Then she laughed. "This will give me a chance to practice for London."

He placed a hand over his heart. "I'm happy to be your guinea pig, Madame Mad Scientist."

In front of them was a set of stairs. She laughed again over her shoulder as he trailed behind her. He liked that he could make her smile and laugh frequently, and it was genuine too.

"Cowboy up, bucko." She entered a large, spacious room complete with a desk and computer on one side and what looked like a full lab setup on the other. "This is my office."

"Impressive." He walked around the space. "Important people get the big office, you know."

"You should see Don's if you want to be impressed. He's at the opposite end of the hall, and it's as wide as the building, with windows on three sides."

She set the tray on the counter and Colin pulled her into his arms. "Now for a proper hello." He kissed her tenderly.

She slipped her arms around his waist. "I love that you surprised me, but I wanted this visit to CLW to be the VIP experience."

"Not necessary, but I met Peyton when I came in and she offered to give me a tasting sometime."

Anna pecked his lips and eased from his arms. "If you'd prefer to do a tasting instead of hanging out in the lab, I understand. This can be kind of boring." She gave him an appraising look.

"I'd rather spend my time with you." He pulled back the cuff of his shirtsleeve and glanced at his watch. "I'm gonna hold you to that half hour. I'd like to be on the road as soon as you're done so we can take our time."

"You haven't told me where exactly we're going, other than trivia near Syracuse." She placed a legal pad on the tabletop and pulled a stool up to her workbench.

"I discovered a place that's not just a winery but brewery too, and the doors open at six. They do this trivia event, complete with a specialty burger and fried pickles that got a four-point-nine rating from customers. I thought it'd be fun to do something different tonight. You can taste wine and I'll drink beer."

"And what if I want to drink beer too?" She arched one eyebrow and crossed her arms over her midsection.

"Then I'll drink wine and you can drink beer. But how good are you at trivia? That's the most important question."

"Why, Colin." She batted her eyelashes and drawled, "You're looking at the family champ of every trivia game on the market."

"So you're saying you're the partner to have." His heart skittered in his chest. He loved spending time with her. She made him laugh and stop taking life so seriously.

"Now, that is an accurate statement." She pointed to a

chair across from her. "Have a seat and let me get busy so we can hit the open road. If you want, we can take my car and put the top down."

"Can I drive your baby?"

She winked. "If you promise to let me win, you can drive."

"But you're on my team…"

She put a finger over his lips. "The mad scientist has just taken over, so our banter will have to wait."

He leaned back against a counter to watch her work. He was having so much more fun than he had anticipated. Time spent with the beautiful Anna Price was the highlight of his day.

Anna and Colin walked through the large wooden door of the brewery into a throng of people. Happy hour was in full swing. He pointed to an empty table and they threaded their way through the crowd to claim it as home base for the evening.

"Looks like everyone's having fun." He held her chair out before signaling to a staff member.

"I didn't know anyone was doing trivia night, and definitely not in a combo brewery/winery. This is cool."

After ordering two pints of the Spring beer along with burgers and all the fixings, Anna rubbed her fingertips together as if they were tingling and, with a grin, said, "I'm ready to start slaying the trivia dragon." She leaned in closer. "Do you think there's a trophy or something for the winning team?"

"I like your confidence, but we might have stiff competition." His gaze roamed the room. "A good many of these people are wearing an expression similar to you. Out to win."

"But you have one thing they don't have." She gave an exaggerated wink. "Me."

He shook his head and grinned. "You're incorrigible."

"And you love me." She pressed her lips together as if she wanted to take it back. His eyes widened when she used the word love, even if it was in jest. At that moment, their drinks were delivered. He smiled and pecked her lips but before he could say anything, she raised her glass and tapped his. "Cheers."

The bartender stood up on the bar and tapped the microphone in his hand. The feedback got everyone's attention and he grinned.

"Don't you just love when that happens?"

A congenial laugh rolled over the patrons.

"Welcome to Tuesday Trivia. We'll get started in just a few minutes, but before we do, I wanted to remind everyone: Eat hearty, drink responsibly, and if you need a ride home as you've enjoyed a glass too many, we have arranged for Ubers to drop you at home—and it's on the house."

A round of applause filled the room and Anna wondered how many people would use the service. She knew she'd have just one and then turn to club soda.

Colin leaned close to her. "I'll change to soda after this beer, so feel free to enjoy the wine tonight."

"I was thinking the same thing." She took his hand. "You indulge. I've got you covered."

He lifted her hand to his lips and grazed them over her wrist. A shiver ran up her arm and straight to her heart. She leaned in for a kiss.

"The things you do to me."

His eyes were deep pools of green and gold and she felt like falling into them even farther. "Have I told you I think you're terrific?"

"No, but I guessed you kind of liked me since you have

gone out with me several times." He caressed her cheek. "I have a confession to make."

"Do tell?" She leaned into his hand. She liked the feel of it on her face.

"Do you remember the first time we met a few years ago? Your dad was in the hospital for a heart attack and you were lying across his bed and I came in to tell your family to bring the decibels down since there were other patients."

Her eyes grew wide. "You remember that?"

"It was the night my life changed. I wanted to ask you out then, but I had only been single for a few months and I thought it was too soon. I didn't want to bring any baggage into a new relationship. And then Sam was discharged and I never had the opportunity to ask for your number."

"You were interested in me even then?" She had remembered meeting him, but this was a new twist.

"I thought you were so beautiful and I loved that you were a bit quieter than the rest of your family. But your smile did me in." He lightly tapped the end of her nose. "It still does, and now I get to see that smile and hear you laugh all the time. You're a very special woman, Anna."

She was bowled over, not just by his words but the look in his eye, which made her heart pound like a bass drum in her chest. Her lips tingled. She licked them and he leaned in. His mouth brushed hers.

He searched her eyes. "You're unforgettable."

"Colin, why didn't you ever look me up at the winery? There is only one Price family in town."

"I didn't want to seem like a stalker. I had faith we'd bump into each other at some point and even though it wasn't under the circumstances I had hoped, here we are today in a meaningful relationship."

"Are we exclusive?"

"Are you asking if you want to be or if I think we are?"

She smiled. "Both?"

"We are exclusive, and that's the way I want it to be. And you?"

She brushed her hand over his well-trimmed beard. "That is exactly what I wanted to hear. I'm crazy about you and there isn't anyone else I'd rather spend time with."

"Good. Now that we know exactly where we stand, let's get ready to play some trivia and have a great evening." He gave her one last lingering kiss. "You're the only woman for me, Anna Price."

20

Anna was packed for England and waiting on her front porch for Colin. The last few weeks had been amazing as they spent more and more of their free time together. She gave him a kiss and he took her suitcase.

"You look great." He slipped an arm around her waist and pulled her into his chest to kiss her again.

Her pulse quickened and she wanted to linger right where they were. "Thanks."

He put her suitcase in the trunk. "For the kiss or the compliment?"

Giving him a saucy look, she said, "Guess."

He cocked his head and pulled her closer. He watched her until her eyes closed as he lowered his mouth to hers. Her breath caught and she leaned into him. The kiss was soft at first and grew in intensity. Between kisses, he murmured, "I'm going to miss you." He pulled back. "Oh, wait, I'm going with you."

"Ten days with just you and me." She pecked his lips. "Can you believe it?" She gave him one last lingering kiss.

"As fast as the weeks flew, our time together in England will go even faster." His finger trailed the side of her face.

"Let's hit the road. It might take a while to get through customs."

Anna sat in the middle seat as the second flight climbed through white puffy clouds before they reached the deep blue sky. Colin snoozed in the seat next to her and she knew she should do the same, especially since the trip so far had been uneventful, but when she closed her eyes, all she could think about was spending all this time with this wonderful man. They had agreed to get separate rooms, and she was hoping the hotel was able to make them adjoining. As much as she wanted to be with him, she wasn't quite ready to be intimate with him. Not that she hadn't thought about it. She had, but she wasn't quite ready yet and he seemed to get it.

She opened her laptop to look over her presentation. She wondered how many people would ask questions, or would she be at the podium staring into vacant faces or, worse, no faces at all? Was that even possible? Surely someone would have to come. She pushed that thought aside. The committee must have thought she had something worthwhile to share or they wouldn't have invited her to speak. She needed to shake off the nerves and self-doubt or it would show up in her lecture.

She was going to present how to determine what juices to blend for an original red wine and how she used the taste of the grape, market demands, and sales figures to project what might be the next trend. She had to admit she had been pretty lucky in her career. The blends she created always sold well. Some better than others, but that was to be expected.

Satisfied with her speech, she shut down the computer and pulled out a paperback. It had been some time since she had enjoyed the simple pleasure of reading a romance novel.

She opened the book and after reading the first sentence was swept up in the story.

Sometime later, the older gentleman sitting next to her complied with the request to put his seatback up as they prepared to land. He gave her a warm smile. "Is this your first time in London?"

He had a quaint French accent, a well-trimmed gray mustache, short hair, and was dressed in a pair of dark blue jeans, a pale-blue shirt, and a black V-neck sweater. He reminded her of her late grandfather.

She spoke softly to not disturb Colin. "No. But the city gives me a thrill. So much history everywhere you look."

"You're an American." He didn't ask a question but made a statement. "Business or pleasure?"

"I'm a speaker at a wine conference." She felt as if she was confessing a secret to a complete stranger.

"Ah, what a coincidence. I'm also here for the wine conference." He gave her his hand. "Henri Marchand."

"Anna Price." She shook his hand. "Are you related to David Marchand?"

"It is a pleasure to meet you, Mademoiselle Price. And yes, he is my son. Do you know of him?"

"He visited my father's winery a few weeks ago."

Henri looked as if he was about to say something else when the jet wheels touched the tarmac.

"To me, it is rare that we have a smooth landing. But all is well, no?"

"Yes, we're on the ground."

Colin stirred. "I'm sorry for sleeping the entire trip."

She touched his hand. "I'd rather have you sleep now than fall asleep while we're taking in the sights."

He brushed the hair from her cheek. "Now that we're on the ground, you have my undivided attention."

The plane eventually glided to a stop and the seat belt sign went off. People scrambled to gather their belongings.

Henri stepped into the aisle and waited for Anna and Colin to join him.

"Thank you." They eased down the aisle and then out of the plane, onto the jet bridge. She half turned. "Henri, enjoy the conference and maybe we'll run into each other."

"Perhaps." He gave her a courtly bow. "I hope you both enjoy your visit."

They were swept into the throng of people all moving in the same direction. Baggage claim and rental car signs were overhead, guiding them forward. She had lost sight of Henri in the crowds. It was nice to meet him. She turned her attention to the handsome man holding her hand.

"Do you want breakfast as soon as we get to the hotel or do you want to get cleaned up first?"

"Shower, change clothes, and then a huge breakfast." He kissed her cheek. "I'm starving."

Despite losing her luggage, Anna was ready to conquer London with Colin by her side. They stood on the hotel's stone steps and looked over the busy street. Horns honked and the traffic created a hum.

The concierge asked, "May I help you?"

"We want to walk to the convention hall for the London Wine Fair."

"It's a nice walk, but long. It would be quicker if you took the Tube." He gave them simple directions for both options.

They set off at a leisurely pace, strolling arm in arm. The air was warm, with the sun playing peek-a-boo with the clouds. Who cared if it rained; she was having a blast. Chic boutiques that would need further investigation before they left were only a blip on her radar.

"Colin, look. There's a sign for the Sherlock Holmes Museum; that would be fun to do."

"I do love a good mystery, and Arthur Conan Doyle was a master." He pointed to the Tube entrance up ahead. "We should take it to the convention hall and then later we'll have more time to wander."

"I hope you don't mind that we stayed farther away from the convention. I want us to have as much time alone as possible, and chatting with people I don't know isn't my thing."

The Tube was uneventful and when they exited the train, signs for the event were on billboards everywhere. Her steps quickened as excitement propelled her forward.

"Come on. People all seem to be headed inside, which is a good sign that attendance is high."

She might just have people at her talk after all. Surrounded by attendees, she listened to snippets of conversation about wine. All sorts of different vineyards were mentioned, and Anna felt a pang that CLW hadn't attended recently. Maybe they'd been too focused on plant, grow, harvest, bottle, and repeat.

She approached the registration stand for her speaker ID badge and took a copy of the show guide, while Colin waited in the attendee line. She scanned the contents; there were over five hundred vendors, and taking a look up and down the aisles, she despaired ever finding any of the people Sam and Don had asked her to touch base with. The energy was palpable.

Some booths proudly displayed the country of origin as well as the vineyard name. When Colin was done, he joined her and they strolled down one aisle toward the French wines.

"I should see if I can find Henri." The crowd grew and he held her hand. "Are you ready to sample some wine?"

"Not yet."

"I adore the tradition of French winemaking."

"What makes it different from the States?"

"The history; the French have been making wine since the sixth century and they have a cooler climate that is perfect for growing grapes."

Her steps slowed as she approached the huge Marchand booth. That had been easy! She surveyed the wines and was pleased to see the extensive list of varieties. There was one label that drew her attention, as it was different from the standard Marchand brand.

It was very simple and contemporary, a cream-colored label with a butterfly seeming to float up from a nosegay of flowers. A D and M were intertwined. The simple beauty drew her in.

A deep male voice said, "Hello."

She looked up. A smile of recognition flashed over the man's face.

"Henri, this is a pleasant surprise."

"Anna, Colin." He leaned in and lightly kissed both of her cheeks and shook Colin's hand. "It is wonderful to see you both again." He gestured toward the bottle but his smile evaporated. "I see you have discovered the new wine. Would you like to try it?"

"Is this your wine? The label isn't familiar to me."

"Not really. It is an offshoot of Vineyard Marchand." Directing his attention to Colin, he continued. "My family has cared for the land and grapes for several hundred years."

A woman about Anna's age came over. "Perhaps you would care to share a glass with Henri so that you may relax and chat."

She didn't hesitate. "That would be lovely." Anna smiled her thanks at the woman and Henri.

He gestured to a small sitting area with bistro tables and chairs. "My daughter Sophia will bring it to us."

Anna took a seat and noticed that most vendors in the area didn't have tables and chairs in the booths. Henri sat across from her and Colin was at her side.

She said, “I had no idea it would be this busy already. The hall has only been open for less than an hour.”

“It is always this way.” His accent was melodic. “Did you have any trouble finding your hotel?”

“No. We’ve checked in and freshened up from the trip, but my luggage has been delayed.” She flashed a smile at Colin. “But someone who shall remain nameless didn’t have the same issue.”

Henri said, “I’m sorry to hear that. Did they say when you could expect your bag?”

Sophia placed three glasses on the table along with the open bottle.

Anna shrugged. “I’m all set until tomorrow and as long as I get my bags before my presentation, I’ll be fine.” She wanted to appear relaxed, but she was anxious about her suitcase not arriving. For today, there was nothing she could do about it.

Sophia smiled. “I am happy to go shopping with you. It would be an excellent excuse to cause my credit card to weep.”

Anna gave her a smile. “That is an excellent description. If you can sneak away for a few hours, I’d love to go shopping.” She looked at Colin.

He waved a hand. “If you ladies need someone to carry bags, I’m happy to join you. If not, I can find something to keep myself occupied.”

“Papi, would you mind if I accompanied Anna to a few shops?”

He gave his daughter an indulgent smile. “Of course not, Sophia. If you’d like, David is coming in, so you could go this afternoon.”

Anna said, “What time should we stop back?”

“In about two hours. That will get us past the midday crowd.”

Henri nodded and looked away from Sophia and concentrated on Anna and Colin. “Now, let’s get back to the wine.”

She left Henri to pour. "This is our pinot noir blend. Something our winemaker thought would be of interest. I'm curious to hear what you think of it."

Anna took the glass and swirled the wine. She studied the color and the bouquet. Henri watched her intently. Colin mimicked her motions.

"Would you like to share your thoughts?" she asked Henri.

He tipped his head. "No. I prefer to have your unbiased opinion."

"I will have to say personally, I love the label—but marketing is not my forte. However, it's whimsical and fresh, which attracted me to stop. Also, the balance of subtle colors didn't detract from the illustration. From a purely aesthetic point of view, well done."

He gave her a half nod. "Go on."

She picked up the glass again, closed her eyes, and inhaled. She could feel Colin watching her, but she was in her element. "The nose is excellent." She gave him a small smile and took a taste, holding it on her tongue. It was wonderful. "Velvety ambrosia."

He raised an eyebrow. "I don't think anyone has compared this wine before to something immortal." He looked at Colin. "What do you think?"

"Unlike Anna, I have an uneducated palate."

"All the more reason I would appreciate your opinion." Henri gestured to his glass. "Please."

Colin sipped some of the wine and looked at Anna. She placed her hand on his leg.

"I like it and would actually want to buy a bottle." He drank a little more.

Anna followed up. "It's wonderful and I predict once people discover it, you'll have a best seller on your hands." She drank a little more. "But I suspect you didn't need me to tell you that. You've been in this business many years."

"You've grown up in it and your reputation proceeds you."

She hoped she masked her surprise at his compliment, pleased to hear that Henri knew of her work.

"Your father and grandfather have been my friends for many years. Both are exceptional winemakers and excellent stewards of the business."

"True. My dad taught me everything I know."

His smile included Colin. "And like all children, you have surpassed his knowledge to acquire your own." He waved his arm around the booth. "That is why you are here. To share with us your expertise." He clinked his glass to Anna's and then Colin's. "I, for one, cannot wait to attend your presentation."

"Thank you, Henri." She clasped Colin's hand and lightly squeezed it.

"It will be one of the highlights of this event." He gave them a warm smile. "*À votre santé.*"

"Cheers."

When Anna and Colin approached the Marchand booth two hours later, Sophia was waiting for her with her bag in hand. She kissed her father's cheeks and looped her arm through Anna's.

"We are headed to Sloane Street."

Anna didn't flinch when Sophia mentioned the high-end shopping area. She loved to browse and hadn't had the opportunity to go there on her last trip to London. This was going to be fun. Even though she didn't have Tessa's flair for fashion, she enjoyed indulging in a few designer outfits. By the way Sophia was dressed, it was easy to see she loved clothes; her outfit was straight from the racks of Chanel, her hair and makeup flawless.

Standing on the curb waiting to hail a cab, Colin said, "Drop me at the hotel and let's meet later for dinner."

"You don't mind?" Anna hugged his arm to her.

"Not at all. I'm going to see if I can track down your luggage and then maybe hit that charming bookstore next to the hotel while you're gone."

They got in the cab and told the driver the first stop was the hotel before settling back to enjoy the sights.

"What had you planned on wearing to present?"

Anna thought of her dark-gray suit and white blouse with a wine-colored scarf. "Just your basic suit and heels."

"After we are done, you will not look basic or ordinary." Sophia gave her a long look. "You are beautiful and you need to show off that gorgeous hair, and your skin is flawless."

"Thank you." She looked out the window. "What do you think I should wear? I've never attended this conference before, so I was playing it safe."

She patted Anna's hand. "We will be conservative and professional, but you will look stunning. More like a famous but hard-working duchess."

Anna chuckled. "My credit card might not recover."

Colin pulled out his wallet and handed her his card. "Consider this a congratulations present and your new outfit is on me."

"Thank you, but no." She laughed and handed him back his card. "You can buy dinner tonight. How's that?"

Sophia waved a hand through the air. "Papi said we should have a wonderful time today and I do not need to go back to the booth so we can have dinner together if you would like."

"That was very kind of Henri. Do you have a place in mind for dinner?"

With a musical laugh, she said, "One thing you will learn: I always have a plan."

Colin said, "That sounds good. Just text me the details."

Anna liked this side of Colin going with the flow; it was refreshing to see a man who was confident and sweet. She was enjoying Sophia's company. She shot Colin a grin.

A moment later, he kissed her cheek. "And don't rush. Enjoy yourselves."

Anna looked in the mirror. Her makeup was perfect and her hair was secured with a clip holding back her long auburn waves. Diamond stud earrings graced her ears. Her new tan jacket nipped at the waist and the matching high-waisted trousers were paired with a pale-lavender print silk blouse. She didn't care that her luggage had shown up; dressing in her new suit filled her with a sense of calm, and the confidence boost helped her relax. She stepped into nude pumps and picked up a matching leather bag. Sophia had been right; this was the perfect look. Time to go.

Colin was in the hallway when she came out. "I was just about to knock." He gave a low, appreciative whistle. "You look fantastic."

She took his hand. "We have a car waiting."

They stepped through the revolving door of the hotel. The car was a nice perk, compliments of the convention planner. The driver held the door open, and she slipped into the back with Colin behind her. The car merged with traffic as she checked her bag and confirmed the USB with her presentation was in a pocket.

She smiled. "I'm glad you're here with me."

"Me too. I've been having a great time and it's exciting to see how well known you are in the wine circles. I'm with a celebrity."

"That is so sweet." She wanted to say she wasn't, but being here had shown her that she was very well respected. "Are you ready to leave London tomorrow? We'll drive out of the city to that little town I told you about. I can't wait to get a lungful of crisp, salty air."

"It sounds like it will be wonderful. I'm looking forward to you showing me around. I've never been outside of the States, not even Canada."

"But you had a passport?"

"It's easier to fly in the US, and besides, you never know when a beautiful enologist is going to ask you to go to London with her."

She felt her cheeks almost split with happiness. "Our week is going by so fast and there's still so much to see. We'll have to plan on coming back again, and soon."

"I'm glad you're having fun despite working." He took her hand and brought it to his lips. "Next time let's just plan to be tourists."

Her heart soared. She loved making plans with him.

"I've got lots of places I want to see. What about you? Anything special you want to see while were here?"

The car was weaving through the streets of London and the familiar landmarks indicated they were close to the hall.

"I'll have to think about it, but for now I'm going to stop talking so that you can look at your notes one last time."

"You know me so well." She placed a protective hand over her bag. "You're going to be in the lecture hall with me, right?"

"I wouldn't miss it." He hesitated before saying, "In case you couldn't guess, I'm your biggest fan."

Her breath caught. "Oh, Colin, you say the sweetest things." The cab slowed. She squeezed his hand.

"You're going to knock 'em dead, sweetheart."

She smoothed the front of her jacket and picked up her bag. "I'm going to do my best."

• • •

Anna stood on the small dais. The wireless microphone was clipped to her lapel and she wandered across the stage, doing a sound check. She didn't plan on standing behind the podium, and she smiled at the technician. "I'm all set."

"Excellent. The doors will open in five minutes."

Now that she was in the throes of the event, her nerves had steadied and she was ready to rock the house. There were a lot of empty chairs in front of her, except for Colin who was sitting front and center. It gave her comfort to see his smiling face in a sea of unknowns. She moved to the side of the stage just as the doors opened and watched a line of people stream in to take seats near the front. Her hand quivered as she poured a glass of water.

Henri walked down the aisle and took a seat in the front row. Then she noticed Sophia and David choose seats behind Henri, who nodded when David placed a hand on his shoulder. She smoothed her blouse as the host introduced her and, to the welcoming sound of applause, she walked to the center of the stage.

"Good morning. I'm Anna Price, the enologist from Crescent Lake Winery located in the Finger Lakes region of New York State." She was bowled over to see the hall was almost full, with more people trickling in. She took a deep breath and exhaled the last of her nerves. With a smile, she said, "Let's talk about wine."

21

The sun peeked from behind a soft gray cloud as Anna and Colin motored through small, quaint villages on the drive to the coast.

"Can you believe how well my presentation went yesterday? The detailed questions people asked about the acidity of soils and how it effects the juice and fermentation process— I mean, some people were newbies, but everyone was engaged in the conversation. It was more like a group of friends gathering to discuss wine."

Colin laughed softly from the passenger seat. She was basking in the afterglow of the conference and she should. As the speaker, people had wanted her to share her expertise.

"Darlin', of course they wanted to pick your brain. You're Anna Price, one of the premier enologists in the business today."

She gave him a side-look. "Where did you come up with that?"

"I listened when people were talking. Everyone wanted to hear what you had to say, and you nailed it."

"Well, thanks. It was nice we got to see Henri and Sophia

before we left, but I didn't see David after the event. Did you?"

"No. As soon as it started to break up, he left."

"His agenda still puzzles me."

"Let's not think of David Marchand and instead focus on food. It's been hours since we've eaten."

She pulled up to the inn. "It's too early to check in. Instead, let's wander down the street to the art district and see if we can discover a charming café that's still serving breakfast."

The aroma of cinnamon and yeast teased his taste buds.

A sign said *Seat Yourself,* so they chose a table that overlooked the brick-lined street. A window box overflowed with trailing vines and colorful flowers.

A young woman crossed the wide-plank wooden floor. "Good morning." She handed them each a menu. "Would you like tea?"

Anna took the laminated card and said, "Yes, please." She looked at Colin. "Tea?"

He smiled. "Yes." He scanned the selections and set the menu aside. "Want to share the full English breakfast? I saw one yesterday and it's an insanely huge amount of food."

Before Anna could respond, the girl returned with a tea pot and mugs. "Have you decided?"

"May we have the full English breakfast with poached eggs, but is it possible to share it?"

The scent of cinnamon called to him. "What is that wonderful smell?"

"Fresh baked cinnamon buns." She gave them a sunny smile. "I could add one or two to your order if you'd like."

"That sounds wonderful."

With a laugh, Anna said, "You've twisted my arm about the bun."

"If you would like to read today's news, there are a few

copies on the window ledge." The waitress gestured to the area next to the door. "Help yourself."

"Thank you."

She moved away and Anna picked the paper up. He hadn't read any news in days and wondered what might be happening in the world, but he didn't care. He poured the steaming, fragrant tea into their mug and added a splash of milk to both. He knew it was just the way she liked it.

"I don't need to read the paper when I have you sitting across from me." She gave him a wide smile. "What's been your favorite part of the trip so far?"

"You mean other than being with you?"

Her heart fluttered. His gaze was intense, and she wondered if he wanted to kiss her as much as she wanted to be kissed. "Be serious."

"I am but if I have to pick something else, it would be what's to come: walking through this quaint town, holding your hand, and a few long walks on the beach so we can explore."

She had to admit that sounded like heaven. "I'm looking forward to that too. The last five days have been so hectic, it'll be nice to unwind."

"I also plan on kissing you as often as I can. I'm not going to let this opportunity go to waste."

She could feel color flood her cheeks. The waitress came and set down an oversized plate and a smaller one with the bun overhanging the sides. Anna thanked her.

"I'm surprised the table is still in one piece with all this food." She laughed. "You did say you were starving."

"Together we can conquer our breakfast and then"—he pointed outside the café—"the world."

After they finished most of the food, they strolled through

the town and took the path that rimmed the shoreline. She stopped on the small stone-covered beach. "Let's sit."

Seagulls swooped in. The wind swept away the cobwebs that lingered and the air was fresh and crisp. The sun warmed her face and arms. But again, the overwhelming feeling of happiness washed over her like the warm waves sliding against the beach.

"You didn't say what your favorite part of our trip has been." Colin had his arm around her shoulders and held her close.

"I don't think I could choose just one thing because the two of us being together has made every moment special and this will be a trip I remember for the rest of my life." She pulled a scarf from her bag and tied her hair back. "Walk with me?"

Colin pulled her up from the bench and against his chest. "I'll go anywhere with you." He cupped her cheek and tilted her lips up to meet his and she melted into him.

She and Colin watched the ocean as they roamed the cliffs of Dover. The ocean was a stunning blue-green and the breeze tugged at her scarf. She tilted her face to the sun and inhaled the brisk, salty breeze.

"Anna, is that you?"

She looked over and squinted against the sun. The silhouette of a man was in front of her. "Excuse me?"

"Anna Price, David Marchand. We met at your winery several weeks ago and I saw you speak at the wine convention."

His French accent was still charming, but what was he doing here? "David, I recognize you, but this is a surprise."

He nodded to Colin. "May I join you both?" He gestured to a nearby bench.

She took a seat at the opposite end and Colin stood behind her, his hand on her shoulder. "Yes, of course."

He looked out over the ocean. "It is beautiful here, yes?"

"It's lovely. I find the ocean to be calming." She glanced his way. "I'm surprised to see you here."

"I must confess I wanted to speak with you at the event, but I had many meetings. I talked with my father and he mentioned you and Colin had come to Folkestone. I took it upon myself to come here in hopes of having an opportunity to speak with you. Would you join me for dinner?"

Colin applied gentle pressure to her shoulder but he didn't interject.

"Anna." David turned on the bench to face her. "I would like it very much if you would both agree to have dinner with me this evening."

"I know you spent time with my father at our winery, and he made it very clear we are a family-run business."

"I wish you would consider dinner. I have a business proposition that I would like to talk with you about."

Colin said, "Out of courtesy for Henri, Anna and I will meet you for drinks at our hotel at six."

Anna sat up a little straighter. She liked that Colin had her back and she was curious to know what David's business proposition was. Colin was right. Better to take control and find out.

He tipped his head. "Excellent. I'll meet you at six o'clock? I think you'll agree after we talk that my idea has merit."

"You have piqued my curiosity." She studied him carefully.

He rose. "Enjoy the rest of your afternoon." He shook her hand and nodded again to Colin. "*Au revoir*."

She waited until he was far enough away before pulling out her cell. "I need to call Dad and fill him in on this development, and then we'll get back to just us."

Colin sat down next to her. "That man is obnoxious. I'm glad you don't have to meet him alone."

"That makes two of us."

Anna and Colin waited in the bar at a table. She glanced at her watch and David walked in. At least he was punctual.

"Hello." He tipped his head, a habit which Anna found annoying.

He took his seat. "Shall we order wine?"

Anna gave him a polite smile. "I took the liberty of ordering; I hope a white is agreeable."

"Certainly, let us wait for our wine. Then we can discuss business."

As if on cue, the waitress returned with the bottle. She offered the label to Anna, who smiled and gestured for her to pour a sample. She nodded her approval. Only then did the waitress add some to Colin and David's glasses and move away.

The cat and mouse game needed to end. He had a few minutes to spill it or drinks would be over.

"My father and I were very sorry to hear about Sam's recent health issue, and it caused me to think about how we might come together and create a larger and stronger company."

Her heart slowed. That was not how it sounded. "You want to partner with CLW?"

He gestured with his hands, palms up. "Not exactly. Your marketing director left the business; your brothers left the business for a few years and are back, and your father's health is precarious. You are the only constant, with fourteen years on the job."

Colin took her hand under the table and applied a reassuring touch. She had an idea where he was headed, but he'd have to be specific.

He paused, not for nerves, as he didn't look like they would ever afflict him, but for effect for whatever his plan was.

"Crescent Lake Winery has been a family business for over seventy-five years. The Marchand family has been making wine for several hundred years. Both companies have achieved great success, but what is lacking is a company which can produce an excellent wine that will bridge a new clientele."

Colin asked, "Are you looking to expand by importing French wines?"

David folded his hands together and rested them on the top of the table while he leaned forward. "I'd like to make wine in France and New York and sell what is produced regionally there, eliminating the need to import or export any finished product, which can be costly." He swirled the wine in his glass. "Anna, your father is the force behind your family and therefore the force behind CLW. With his plans to retire and travel, I assumed that he'd entertain an offer."

Anna's temper flared. To have a stranger dilute her family's life work and her nephews' future with little regard for what their plans might be was disturbing.

"The family business is stronger than one person. What did my father say when you broached the idea?"

"I did not mention this when I met with your parents. I wanted to tour the operation and get a feel for it without the pressure of trying to discuss terms."

Well, that cleared up one thing. He wasn't to be trusted. "If you didn't talk to them, why are you broaching the subject with me?"

"I thought as this generation of winemakers, and with the idea of a wider variety of grapes with which to showcase your talents, we could discuss the particulars."

There it was. He wanted her to sell out her family and hitch her wagon to his horse. She was stunned.

"I can promise you," he continued, "the Price family will be well compensated for the land and all the buildings and, of course, everyone currently employed at the winery would be kept on, maybe not in the same capacity, but they would have a job." He reached out to place his hand on hers and he looked at Colin and withdrew it and said, "However, I can assure you nothing would change with your position. You are key to the success of this new venture."

She knew about takeovers. People lost their jobs. She put her hand under the table. "Don is the CEO of the winery, and you should be having this conversation with him, not me. But the notion of you trying to convince me to help you has left me speechless. I'm not sure what else to say."

"I thought with your support, Don and Sam could be persuaded to sell, especially if you think the proposal is solid. We should continue to discuss this opportunity over dinner."

With a slow shake of her head, Anna pushed back her chair. "If you'll excuse us, we have plans."

Colin stood beside her and took her hand.

They had taken a few steps when David said, "Wait."

She gave him a hard look. "Goodbye, David." She strode from the bar.

When she and Colin walked out to the street, she said, "How am I going to tell my father this person is determined to go after our business?"

"Do you think your family would contemplate selling the winery?"

"No. Absolutely not."

He gave her a hug. "Then you just give him the facts. Don and Sam will know how to handle Marchand."

22

Colin would have liked nothing better than to stand in that airport parking lot and continue to kiss the woman he loved. Their trip was over far too quickly, but now they could get back to day-to-day living and maybe even think about their next big adventure together.

"Are you happy to be home?" With her free hand, her fingers trailed down his arm.

"Yes and no. Our trip made one thing clear. I love spending time with you and I hope the real world doesn't intrude on us continuing to do that."

She touched his cheek. "We won't let it."

"Speaking of time together, I got a text from my parents and they'll be in town for a visit next week. I was hoping you'd have dinner with us. I'd love for you to meet them, and my sister too. We could have dinner at my place. Wine from CLW, and Marie would make one of her amazing cheesecakes."

"Ah." She gave him a small smile, but her eyes betrayed her suppressed laughter. "You're ready for me to meet your family and just in case they don't like me, I can ply them with delicious wine?"

"Something like that, and I figure it's fair. I've met yours." He brought her hand to his lips. "And you're important to me, so I want them to get to know you."

"I'd love to meet them."

"Would it be possible to recommend a few wines I should pick up? That is out of my area of expertise and I want to show off your skills to them."

"Tell me what you're having and I'll supply the wine." She gave him a smile.

"I wasn't asking you to bring it."

"You didn't ask. I offered." They were driving through the center of town. "Any chance we can swing by the market so I can pick up a few things?"

"That's all taken care of. I texted Liza and asked if she'd stock your refrigerator and we even have a cold dinner waiting for us and one other surprise." He glanced her way. "I hope it's okay I asked her to help me?"

"I appreciate your thoughtfulness." Her eyes twinkled. "And dinner sounds like heaven."

"Then it's settled." His car picked up speed as they headed out of town. As he drove toward her place, their hands were clasped together and his heart was filled with a sense of peace.

Her farmhouse came into view and when the car stopped, Anna hopped out and stretched her arms overhead. So much had happened while she was gone, and Dorothy was right; there was no place like home.

Colin unloaded her bags and met her at the front door. She turned the knob and he said, "Wait."

She quickly withdrew her hand. "Why?"

"Remember? I said I have a surprise for you. Close your eyes."

She did as he asked. He opened the door and walked her

over the threshold. She was excited to see what was next. He guided her through the front hall and turned in the direction of the living room. "Open your eyes."

On the hall table was a large vase of flowers. A riot of colors and scents filled the space.

"I wasn't sure what your favorite flowers are, so I ordered all different kinds."

Anna whirled around and threw her arms around his neck, kissing him thoroughly. "Thank you," she breathed between kisses, "for doing this for me."

He cupped her cheeks in his hands. "Anna, I'm crazy about you."

She pulled away. "I can do you one better." She searched his eyes and said, "Spending the last ten days with you, I discovered I'm completely in love with you."

He kissed her again. "I love you too."

After dinner, they sat on the sofa. She toyed with his fingers. "I'm sorry we didn't get to the Sherlock Holmes Museum, but when we take a trip back to Europe, it has to be on the to-do list."

"I can't wait to play tourist with you again. Are you up for a movie or ready to call it a day?"

"Rain check on the movie? I'm exhausted and now that I'm full, it's really hitting me."

He kissed her lips. "Say no more. We'll talk tomorrow? And then Sunday, my parents are in town."

"Of course. I'm looking forward to meeting them."

He pulled her up from the chair. "Walk me to the door before your eyes close for the night."

His arm encircled her waist and at the front door, he gave her a long, lingering kiss. "Sleep well, my love."

She stood on her tiptoes and looked deep into his eyes. "Thanks for dinner and the flowers. It was a nice way to wrap up our trip."

With one last kiss, Colin was out the door and she

watched him drive away. She turned off the lights as she walked through the house. One of these nights soon, she was asking him to stay.

Sunday had arrived. Anna peered through the windshield; there wasn't a cloud in the bright blue sky as she drove to Colin's place, ready to meet his parents. The tote bag on the passenger seat held six bottles of wine: two bottles of Picnic Basket from Sand Creek, a cabernet, and three bottles of the Cayuga she knew Colin liked. Who knew what they would like? Hopefully she had her bases covered and for good measure, she stopped at a local brewery and picked up a couple of growlers of Colin's favorite beer.

Anna had dressed carefully in a blue floral skirt, matching short-sleeve blue top, and leather sandals. She wanted to make a good impression on his family but also didn't want to appear as if she were trying too hard. Thank heavens her wavy hair was behaving and the humidity wasn't bad so it was under control.

She tapped the brakes as she pulled onto Colin's street and drove through his subdivision. All of these houses were too close together; it wasn't her idea of living, but it seemed to suit him. There were two cars parked in front of the garage: a silver sedan and the other a vintage black Mustang. *I wouldn't mind taking that car for a spin.* It was easy to guess the sedan's owner, but she didn't think Marie was a Mustang-driving woman. She parked on the street and grabbed the tote bag. Surprisingly enough, she was only a little nervous. If his family was like hers, they'd get along just fine.

The front door opened and Colin came out of the house barefoot, wearing navy shorts and a light-blue striped polo shirt. His smile was the only greeting she needed to feel welcome. He met her at the bottom of the front steps and took the bag from her hand while slipping an arm around her waist and pulling her in for a kiss.

"Right on time."

She savored his woodsy cologne. "I hate being late." She wiped a smudge of lipstick from his lips. "Pink isn't your shade."

He chuckled. "You look beautiful. Come in and meet the folks." He dropped his head. "Marie brought a couple of good friends with her."

"The more, the merrier." That explained the Mustang.

He kissed her temple. "They're going to love you."

They climbed the short flight of steps and entered the cool, air-conditioned house. "Everyone's on the back patio."

She nodded. "You'll need to put the Cayuga and Picnic Basket on ice and the cab needs to breathe."

He cupped her face. "I've got this." He peered into the tote. "Six bottles should be enough."

"Oh, wait. I have something else in the car. Be right back." She hurried through the house and ran down the steps to retrieve the growlers from the floor of the passenger side. Colin was waiting in the doorway and he broke into a grin when he saw what was in her hands.

"You stopped at the brewery too?"

"I did. Do you have someplace to keep them cold?" He met her halfway down the steps and she handed the jugs to him.

"We'll make room. Now come on in and meet everyone."

A young woman with dark hair but Colin's eyes burst out of the kitchen into the foyer. She gave Anna a broad grin. "Anna, it is so good to meet you. I've heard so much about you and don't worry; it's all good things."

Confused at first, Anna remembered that the woman she had seen Colin with had blond hair. "I thought she'd be blond like you."

He said, "Marie changes her hair color frequently. She was recently a blonde, then a redhead, and now a brunette."

Marie pulled Anna into a warm hug. "It's my rebellious nature."

"It's nice to meet you." She hugged Marie and appreciated the warm welcome.

"And to take the heat off today, I brought one of my parents' favorite people, Ginny, and my good friend Drew."

Colin set the jugs on the counter next to the bottles of wine. "That's a lot of information in one gush."

Marie laughed. "Just bringing your girl up to speed." She grabbed Anna's hand. "Let's go meet the parents."

"I'll do the introductions, sis."

"Um." Anna looked over her shoulder as Marie ushered her to the sliding door. "I should help Colin with the wine."

"Plenty of time for that in a minute." She urged her forward and whispered in Anna's ear, "They already love you because we all can see how happy you make my brother."

He was behind them as she was led through the sliding door onto the brick patio. An older version of Colin stood up. He graciously held out a hand to a woman as she came to her feet. She clasped Anna's hands before Colin could do the introductions.

"Hello, Anna, I'm Addie and this is my husband Walt. We're thrilled to meet you."

They instantly put her at ease. "It's nice to meet you as well, Mrs. Grant. Did you have a pleasant trip here?"

"Call me Addie, and we did. Let's sit and get acquainted."

Addie directed her to the table and chairs under the large yellow-striped umbrella. Anna took a seat and flashed an inquisitive look at Colin.

"I'll take care of the wine and be right out."

He quickly reappeared with a tray of lemonade and glasses. He gave her a wink.

"Marie volunteered for KP duty."

Another man about Marie's age walked across the backyard with a woman she guessed was Ginny.

"Hey, I'm Drew. Nice to meet you." He stuck out his hand and gave it a firm shake.

He looked vaguely familiar to Anna. Then it dawned on her. She had seen Drew's picture in the paper. His family was very wealthy and personally, he spent a great deal of his time working with several well-established children's charities, including one for juvenile diabetes.

"Drew, it's a pleasure to meet you." She returned his firm handshake. "I believe we have some common friends."

His brow arched and he gave her a curious look. "Perhaps."

She turned to Ginny, who gave Anna a friendly hug. She was tall and slender with long black hair and deep blue eyes.

"It's nice to meet you, Anna. Colin has told us all about you."

"It's great to meet all of you." She had questions for Colin later, like what exactly he had said, but everyone was welcoming so she guessed it really didn't matter.

Addie watched the exchange with interest.

"I'll go and give Marie a hand." Drew crossed the patio and disappeared inside.

Addie dismissed Drew's departure and turned her attention to Anna. "Colin tells us your family owns a winery in The Valley. We'd love to hear all about it, and he mentioned you're going to be mentoring a group of girls in the fall for an after-school program. That's very exciting."

Colin said, "Mom, please don't interrogate Anna about every minute aspect of her life. We should enjoy conversation and food. Okay?"

She pursed her lips. "I'm sure Anna wouldn't mind telling us more about herself."

"Not at all, Addie. My life is an open book." Over her

shoulder, she flashed Colin a reassuring smile but for now, she was on the proverbial hot seat.

"How was London and the wine conference?" Addie asked.

Anna said, "It was wonderful. I gave a lecture on blending specific types of juice and how to measure the success—other than sales, of course." She sipped her lemonade.

Addie beamed. "That sounds very exciting. Is it a big event?"

"It's actually the largest wine event this year."

"Mom, you don't need to drill her."

"Not drilling, Colin. Just interested in what Anna does."

"Why don't you come to the winery tomorrow and I can give you the behind-the-scenes tour and we'll do a tasting. I can even arrange for us to have dinner in the gazebo." She looked at Marie, Ginny, and Drew, who had returned with a tray of appetizers. "You should come too."

"That sounds like fun. What time should we be there?" Addie asked.

Anna looked at Colin. "You are out of work at four, so we can do the tour at two. Colin can meet us at the winery, and then we'll all enjoy a nice dinner."

He leaned in and kissed her cheek while whispering in her ear, "Thanks."

She looked around the table. "Dinner for seven?"

Colin's family nodded an enthusiastic yes.

"Then it's settled. You'll see behind the scenes and tour the entire operation, so wear comfortable shoes. We'll be wandering in the fields too."

Addie said, "We've never done a winery tour so this will be very interesting. Thank you, Anna."

"You're welcome." She winked at Colin and grinned.

23

Anna relaxed in a lounge chair with her legs stretched out. Liza's deck overlooked the backyard, where Johnny and George were wrestling in the grass.

"It went well with Colin's parents on Sunday and yesterday?" Liza asked.

"Yeah, it did. They're all very nice."

"Relationships are easier when the family likes you. I was lucky that Steve's family and I got along well."

She sipped on iced tea with her eyes closed against the bright sun. "Marie had a couple of friends over for the picnic."

"Anyone I'd know?"

"Her friend Ginny and Andrew Cameron."

Liza sat up in her chair. "Drew? Marie knows Drew Cameron?"

"Do you know him?"

"Are you kidding? He is a benefactor of that new children's clinic they want to build and just last year, he donated all new equipment to the park, right down to the protective cushion under it."

"I heard he did a lot of good work but had no idea it was so close to home."

"He's done amazing things for the area." Liza sipped her tea and yelled for the boys to be careful. "Do you think Marie knows who he *is*?"

"I would say yes." She gave her sister a side-eye.

"You should find out what the deal is with him."

"Liza, you're being a little nosy, don't you think?"

She chuckled. "Hey, when a nice and good-looking guy like Drew is involved, I'd really like to know if he's a jerk or upholds my image of him."

"Colin and I are going to meet Marie for lunch on Sunday. I'll let you know what I find out and fill you in on all the details. Now, when does Dad go back to the doctor again? I know Mom is itching to book their trip."

"In a couple of weeks, and he finishes cardiac rehab next month. I'm going to guess they're cleared to go late summer or early fall."

Anna nodded. "I never got a chance to tell you about London and meeting the most charming man."

"Does Colin know?"

Anna couldn't hold back her laugh. "Henri knew Gramps and is roughly the same age. I hardly think he's competition for Colin."

"Henri who?"

"Marchand. We happened to sit together on the plane, and then I was exploring the convention before I had to speak and we shared one of his newest wines—well, I think it was his. He acted kind of funny when we talked about it. Which was amazing. And then from there, he came to my lecture and sat in the front row. It was great to have him close by, a friendly face and all."

"Dad knows him too, right?"

"Yes, and he's been to the Marchand vineyard in France. It is one of the older estates. Henri said if I ever wanted to spend some time there to just let him know. I have an open invitation." She smacked her hand on the arm of the chair. "But wait until you hear this! Remember David Marchand who dropped in on Dad after his surgery?"

"I didn't meet him, but Mom told me about it. By the look on your face, you must have bumped into him too."

"Better. He followed us to Folkestone and invited Colin and me to have drinks with him all under the guise that he had a phenomenal idea. It turns out he wanted me to convince the family to sell CLW to him so he can expand his enterprise as an offshoot of Marchand. David thinks our family business is the perfect solution to expanding his company."

Liza frowned and tapped her nail on the side table. "Did you tell Dad and Don?"

"Of course. Dad brushed it off as no big deal. I guess this happens from time to time, where different wineries want to expand geographically so they buy up successful businesses when owners are ready to retire. Usually it's because the family is ready to get out of the business, but in this case, we're not. I also called Tessa just to give her a heads-up too. Who knows, maybe he's just got an ax to grind against the Price family."

"How did you handle David? Did you cut him off at the knees?"

"I think I did pretty good and it didn't hurt to have Colin by my side."

"Do you think he's lost interest?"

"I hope so. He should be able to find another winery that fills his needs. But enough about David Marchand."

Liza took the hint. "I heard from Don that you did a kick-ass job with your speech, which I, for one, never doubted."

"It was interesting. It appears that I am better known in the industry than I realized. After the lecture, I spent a long time talking with people, and the questions were very specific. I could probably make a comfortable living consulting if I decided to leave CLW." Making this trip had shown her that she had made a difference. Not just at CLW, but her methods for winemaking were something that people wanted her to share.

"Do you think you'll be asked back to the convention next year?"

"I'm not sure. But if they did, I would be honored to go. Especially now that I know what it's like. In fact, I want to talk to Don and Tessa about a booth. You could go too. We'd have a blast, sightseeing, dining, and shopping. We might even be able to eke out a side trip to France."

"Now that sounds like fun, but we'd have to make sure Mom and Dad were around. Now that they've almost gotten the green light for travel, I won't have anyone to watch the boys."

"Leo would take them, and he's really good with them. He's the male version of you. Or Jack too."

"Just because Leo and I are twins doesn't mean we're interchangeable."

"The boys respect Leo and even more, they listen to him. I've seen it. When they're wearing you down"—she pointed to them, still wrestling on the lawn—"all Leo has to do is say *Boys…* and they behave like normal kids again."

"It's only going to get harder as they get older." Liza's face fell. "Steve was a good dad and we made a good team."

"And you miss your husband." Anna's tone was gentle. She couldn't imagine what it was like for Liza to have lost her husband when both boys were under the age of five. Did they remember Steve other than the pictures they saw scattered around the house?

"I miss him like crazy and it hasn't gotten any easier."

She considered her next question, but it was something the family had discussed when Liza wasn't around. "Have you thought about dating?"

She shrugged and her eyes locked on her sons. "What would they think about their mother spending time with a man other than their father?"

"Iz. You deserve a life too. If you talked about it in a positive light, I'm sure they'd be fine with it."

"I don't think I'm ready." She turned away from Anna but she could still see Liza's scrunched-up face.

"There's no rush for you to do anything and until then, we'll continue to have lots of exciting adventures. Like a rafting trip, or maybe now I could talk you into skydiving?"

George cried out, causing Liza to flip her head in their direction. She hopped up and stalked to the deck railing. "John! George! I would strongly suggest you find a new game before one of you gets seriously hurt!"

Anna watched in amazement as her sister went from vulnerable to powerhouse in seconds. It was even more inspiring when the boys stood up, twigs and grass sticking out of their hair, faces smudged with dirt, looking angelic.

"Okay, Mom," Johnny said.

George nodded in agreement and grinned.

"It's easy to get sucked into those little faces."

Liza returned to her chair. "You have no idea." She slumped down. "There are times I want to laugh but to do that is to let them know I actually think they're funny. Then life would be over. I'd lose control of the asylum I call home."

"If you ever need backup, call in the troops. We're here."

"Appreciate that, sis."

"I'm going to head home and call my handsome guy to see what his work schedule is. Maybe we can sneak away for dinner or something later."

"Does his schedule bother you? I know he works odd hours and weekends."

"Not at all. I've adjusted my schedule to be more flexible so we can spend time together. Unless we're in the middle of the crush, I don't have to be at the winery on a nine-to-five schedule. A benefit for sure." She gave Liza a hug and ran down the steps. "Toodles."

Unable to connect with Colin after leaving her sister's last night, she was counting the hours until she would see him tonight. With feet up on her desk, Anna leaned back as far as she could, stretching her arms overhead. The chair creaked as it crashed backward, taking her along for the ride. As she lay on the floor, holding her head where it had met the wood, she heard the sound of pounding feet coming down the hallway.

Dad popped his head in. "Anna, are you okay?"

She groaned and rubbed the back of her head. Damn, that hurt. "Hey, Dad. When did you get here?"

"I was talking with Don and heard you go head over teakettle and thought I'd check on you."

"I've tilted this chair back so many times, I've learned how to fall. I still managed to hit my head harder than I'd like." She stood and righted the chair.

Dad made himself comfortable in her other chair. "Why don't you buy a new chair that actually leans back? Less chance of gravity taking control."

"And lose the challenge of defying it? Not a chance." She sat down and rubbed her head again. "What were you and Don talking about?"

"I filled him in on my follow-up call to David Marchand and told him again that CLW wasn't for sale."

"Is Don concerned? What if David tries to do something underhanded?"

Dad thought for a half second and gave her a wink. "You've been reading too many thriller books. No one is going to try to do a hostile takeover of CLW."

She gave her head a shake and winced. "Dad, be serious. Is there anything David can do?"

"Not a thing. Financially, we're solid. And I think Henri might persuade him to think differently."

"If you say so." She wasn't convinced Dad was correct in his assessment, but she would defer to his expertise.

"Mom and I are planning a cruise in late September. At least that's what we're shooting for if the trip we want isn't sold out."

"A good time of year to travel, and you'll have fun."

"We're looking forward to it." He eased back in the chair and seemed to have something more on his mind.

"Do you want coffee?"

He shook his head. "Speaking of the Marchand family, Henri called me this morning. He said you gave an excellent lecture and that he believes you're an even better enologist than I am."

"Dad, I don't know what to say." She could feel heat flush her cheeks. Praise from her father was rare and very much appreciated.

He gave her his trademark grin. "He's right. You're top in your field."

"That is certainly high praise, coming from you."

He nodded. "I'm not good at telling any of my children how proud I am of their accomplishments, but I'm trying to get better."

"I appreciate that. It was a good experience and thanks for encouraging me to go."

"Henri was impressed." Dad stopped there and Anna had the impression he wanted to say more but instead of continuing, he stood up. "I need to get to rehab. Stop over to the house for drinks tomorrow night. It's been too long, and bring Colin too."

"I'll see if he's free." She decided to walk Dad to his car.

"Thanks for telling me about your call with Henri. It means a lot that you think I'm pretty good at my job."

Dad gave her a sharp look. "It takes the entire family to make our business successful, and you're at the heart of that success."

She watched Dad drive away, then crossed the warehouse so she could take a few samples up to her lab. But first, she decided, before she went back up, she'd call Colin to see if he was up for drinks with her parents.

"Anna," Colin said when he answered, "this is a nice surprise. What's going on? Are we still on for tonight?"

"We are, but my parents invited us to have drinks with them tomorrow night. Interested?"

"Sounds like fun. What time? Six?"

"Perfect. I'll let Mom know," she said. "I was thinking about tonight. Are you up for a movie? There's one in the park on the green. I think they're playing a screwball comedy."

Before the word *comedy* was out of her mouth, he asked, "What time does it start?"

She laughed. "Since we're outside, the movie won't start until dark. We could meet at the entrance at seven. I'll bring chairs and a blanket if you want to bring snacks, and don't forget popcorn with extra butter."

He chuckled. "You got it. See you tonight, sweetheart."

She liked when he called her that. "I'm counting the minutes."

24

The next night, Anna and Colin strolled across her parents' front lawn. Before they reached the steps, he slipped his arm around her waist and pulled her close. She smiled softly and kissed him full on the mouth.

Anna asked, "Did you have fun last night?"

"Being with you is always great, but the movie in the park was a first for me. I had no idea those types of events still happened."

She placed her hand over his heart. "I haven't been in years." She pecked his lips. "It was fun having your family at the winery the other night, and I'm glad we were able to relax so I could get to know them better. I like your sister; she's got a great sense of humor and style."

"She does, and I meant to say thanks for being so nice. My parents can be pretty hard on her at times."

"They just want the best for you both."

"I know. All our parents want is for Marie to be happy." He kissed her again. "But I don't want to talk about our families." He ran a finger down the side of her face and tilted her chin up, then searched her eyes.

Her heart quickened and her breath caught. She didn't speak.

"Anna." His voice was soft while his finger grazed her lips. "I've fallen completely in love with you."

His smile helped her begin to breathe again. "Colin"—she kissed him hard—"I love you."

He caressed her cheek.

"Anna, are you two coming inside?" Mom called out, breaking the spell that had held them in a cocoon.

"Be right there, Mom." She laughed softly. "We got caught by a parent, just like teenagers."

"Let's go inside and later, when I take you home, we'll pick up where we left off."

She tipped her head. "Promise?"

"Most definitely."

Over drinks and appetizers, Dad cleared his throat. "We wanted to tell you the news."

Anna turned to look at him. "What news?"

"I've been cleared to take a fall cruise, so Mom is booking it tomorrow. It'll be our first vacation in years. There's a cruise to nowhere that departs from the Boston Harbor, and it lasts five days. Just enough to get our sea legs and if we like it, we'll book a winter cruise south."

"You'll have so much fun." She turned to Colin. "Why didn't you tell me?"

"Your father is my patient and there are confidential rules I have to follow even though we're in a relationship. You seemed to understand that before."

She crossed her arms over her chest. "If Dad were having a health crisis, you couldn't tell me?"

"If he asked me not to, no." His tone was unyielding. "It's the law."

She bristled. "He's my father and you're my boyfriend. You shouldn't plan on keeping secrets from me."

He shifted in his seat and leaned forward. "I'm asking you to respect my job." He softened his tone. "Ultimately, I can only tell you what he wants you to know."

She looked at her parents, hoping they'd back her up.

"Anna," Dad began, "Colin did the right thing, and I'm glad to know that he upholds his oath as a medical professional."

She looked at Mom, who said, "Honey, I have to agree with Dad and Colin."

She wasn't going to win this one, so she picked up her glass of wine and took a sip. She had to let this go. She knew he was right and had said something to this effect to Don months ago, but now was not the time to admit it.

"Why don't you tell us more about this cruise that basically drifts around the Atlantic for a few days? What will you do on board?"

Mom clasped Dad's hand. "Since we've never been on a ship, we checked to see what there is to do. It has everything the regular cruise has—amazing dining options, shows, there's even a casino—and, by going after school is back in session, it's less expensive."

"And if it's all we hope, I promised Mom we'll take a tropical cruise somewhere this winter."

Colin asked Anna, "Have you ever cruised before?"

"No. I'm not sure it would be fun to be stuck on a ship, waiting to get someplace. I like to fly, get off the plane, and start having fun."

"So you just like to get to your destination. But on a cruise, there would be fun things for us to do along the way: shows, the casino, lounging by the pool, and romantic walks under the moonlight before bed. Maybe we should try the same kind of cruise."

Anna quickly warmed to that idea. After all, it was a

floating hotel, and she liked he was making longer range plans for them.

"We should definitely check into it next week." Now, that put a time frame to it. She wondered if he'd balk at that.

Anna got up to clear the glasses. Her dad's face was starting to droop with exhaustion and Colin followed her eyes.

"Sam, how are you feeling?"

"I'm fine. Just tired. The days I go to rehab seem to wipe me out early." He stood up very slowly and seemed to sway before sitting back down.

Colin came around the side of the table and dropped to one knee. He took her dad's wrist in his hand to check his pulse. Mom's face paled.

"Sherry, I want you to breathe."

She nodded.

Anna set the dishes down. "Should I call nine-one-one?"

"Sam, we have to go to the hospital to get you checked out. Your heart rate is a little slow and I'd feel better if we did an EKG."

Colin gave a half nod. "Anna, can you get my car out front? No need to rush or panic. The situation's under control, so let's breathe and go one step at a time." He tossed her the keys and pulled his phone out of his pocket.

Anna hurried out the back door. She pulled the car in front, left it idling, and ran back inside.

"Mom, get your handbag. We have to go."

Moving in slow motion, Mom looked around. "I'm not sure where I put it."

"It's okay. I'll get it for you." Anna rushed down the hall to her parents' bedroom and grabbed the bag. When she got back to the dining room, Colin was walking her dad to the front door. Mom was holding it open. Anna slung the bag over her shoulder.

Once Dad was settled into the passenger seat, Colin got in

behind him and Mom sat beside him. "Anna, you should drive."

In record time, Anna got to the emergency room. Her heart thundered in her chest. Dad had remained quiet with his eyes closed since getting in the car. She was terrified he was going to die, but Colin was with them. If Dad had needed an ambulance, he would have called for one.

"Sam, I'm going to get a wheelchair."

Anna looked in the rearview mirror at Mom. Some color had returned to her face, but she still looked too pale.

Colin was back with a wheelchair and someone pushing it. He opened the door. "If you feel light-headed, let me know."

Dad eased out of the car and gingerly sat down in the wheelchair. He pulled Colin down so he could speak to him. Colin nodded and looked at Anna. "We'll see you inside."

Mom hadn't gotten out of the car but began to cry softly while Anna parked. She stashed the keys in her pocket and pulled open her mom's door.

"Come on, Mom. He's going to be fine. Colin will make sure of it." She took her mom's hand and pulled her from the car.

"I can't go through this again." Mom's voice quivered. "Not knowing if he'll make it through another surgery."

"He's in good hands. Walk with me."

They crossed the well-lit parking lot and through the automatic doors. The waiting room was on the right. They walked inside and approached the desk.

"Excuse me. Colin Grant just came in with my father, Sam Price."

"They're in an examination room and Colin asked that you take a seat. He'll be out when he can."

Anna thanked the desk clerk and helped Mom to a chair. She seemed to have aged before Anna's eyes. "I'm going to call Don and let him know what's going on. He can call everyone else."

Mom nodded and then placed a hand on her arm. "Tell them not to come, that you'll call when we know something."

"I'll be right back." She walked into the hall and called Don, her explanation of the situation coming out in a controlled sob.

"We'll be there as soon as we can."

Relief washed over her. She could use the support. "Thanks."

She took a few deep breaths. She needed to be strong for Mom. She returned to the waiting room to find Mom staring out the blackened window. Anna took the chair next to her and they waited, but as they did, Anna's impatience grew.

Colin came into the waiting room. He wore his poker face.

She rushed over to him, her mouth dry. "Is Dad—" She couldn't ask the question on her lips.

"He's resting." He walked over to Sherry. "He told me he's been having these episodes since he was discharged. He's lost weight and is exercising, so he needed an adjustment to his blood pressure medication. But to be safe, I'm admitting him overnight."

He patted her clasped hands. "I have to ask. Did Sam tell you he was having dizzy spells?"

She vehemently shook her head. "No."

Don and Jack burst through the door. Before Colin could continue, Don said, "I couldn't get ahold of the rest of the family and Kate's home with Ben. We can fill in everyone later."

Under her breath, Anna said, "Thank heavens part of the cavalry's here."

Mom shook her head. "You shouldn't have come. Colin was just filling me in, and your father's going to be fine."

Anna stood next to Colin. "Apparently, Dad's been having some issues and hasn't said anything. Once his meds are adjusted, he should be fine, and he's staying the night for observation." She looked at Colin. "Did I miss anything?"

He slipped his arm around her. "That sums it up."

She held up her hand. "Bottom line: We're all going home. And Mom, that includes you too."

She began to protest but Colin said, "Sherry, you should go home tonight and rest. Sam will be fine."

She looked at her sons and Anna and relented. "After I see him, I'll leave."

Anna kissed Colin's cheek and whispered, "We make a pretty good team."

"Darling, I've always got your back."

25

The rest of the week had been uneventful and Dad was home from the hospital. Anna checked her watch after shutting down her email and was pleased to see she had enough time to get changed before Colin picked her up. They were going to play nine holes of golf, her first on an actual course. He had told her all about where they were going, to a small, easy course with gentle hills. He explained it was a good beginner course, with the exception of the ninth. That one was a doozy. She had borrowed Marie's pull cart, but after using Marie's clubs and having fun, she bought a beginner set of clubs, her latest purchase for her more active life. Anna hadn't felt right just taking Marie's old set and she wouldn't take any money for them either so this way it was simpler.

She was dressed but searching for a water bottle to fit securely in her bag when she heard a tap on the door. She called out, "Come in."

"Anna?"

"In the kitchen."

Colin stepped into the sunny space. She waved two aluminum bottles in the air. "Do you need a water bottle?"

"Is that the kind of greeting I get today?" he teased. "I haven't seen you in two days."

She struck a casual pose, leaning against the granite counter, and crossed her arms over her midsection. Her brow shot up. "Are you saying I should leap into your arms the moment you walk into a room?" She held back the laughter that threatened to blow her fun.

In three long strides, he crossed the room and swept her close to his chest and covered her face and throat with kisses until she burst out in laughter.

"Stop! That tickles."

He rubbed his beard over her cheeks while she laughed.

In a nanosecond, things turned more heated. He let his lips soothe the light whisker burn he had inflicted. Her body melded to his and she inhaled his spicy cologne and savored each kiss. Lost in sensations, she slipped her arms around his neck. She could swear their hearts beat in sync.

Breathless, she pulled her lips from his. "I thought we had a tee time."

"We do." He nuzzled her neck. "I could cancel."

She faked a pout. "You promised." Looking up through her lashes for good measure, she batted them. She loved flirting with Colin because he always responded in the most interesting ways.

"I'm not going to forget where we stopped, and we'll pick up here later."

She liked how that sounded. "We can eat here later."

"Woman, I do love how that amazing brain of yours works." He kissed her again and then gave her a playful tap on the butt. "Put a wiggle on it."

She flipped him a saucy look over her shoulder as she turned to the water bubbler. "Be careful what you ask for; you might just get totally distracted."

"I'm counting on it. Later." He took the filled bottles from her and gave her one last, lingering kiss.

Standing on the first tee, Colin put the ball in the center of the tee box. When Anna started to get out her driver, Colin said, "Hold on. We'll walk to the ladies' tee when I'm done."

"I get an advantage?"

Her eyes were twinkling and the smile that graced her face made his knees weak. How on earth she had turned his world upside down in just a few months was beyond him.

He addressed the ball, swung with ease, and watched as it landed in the middle of the fairway.

She grabbed the handle on her cart. "Let's go, sparky."

"Sparky?"

She gave him a sidelong look and that killer smile. "When you hit the ball, I could imagine sparks shot out of it, like you're on fire."

"Hardly, but thank you for the compliment." They walked about twenty yards down the slope. "Now remember what I said. Keep your head down and your eye on the ball. I'll watch where it goes for you."

She held up a bright-yellow ball in a victorious salute. "I bought these to make sure you didn't mistake my ball for yours."

He silently chuckled as she set the yellow ball on the tee. She then wiped her hands on her shorts and adjusted the brim of her hat. Then she stepped away from the ball and looked at him.

With her hand propped on her hip, she asked, "What if I miss?"

"Then you swing again."

She looked behind them. He followed her gaze.

"If someone gets too close, we'll let them play through. We're in no hurry."

Her lush lips were kissable, but she had her game face on.

She was all business as she addressed the ball. Putting the club head down, she took a deep breath and exhaled, never lifting her head or eyes. With slow, deliberate purpose, she swung the club up. It arched over her back, and then she brought it down with speed. The face of the club connected with the ball and it sailed forward. But Anna wasn't watching the ball. She had her eyes closed as the club flew from her hands over her left shoulder.

"Oh no!" she cried.

Colin rushed forward and kissed her hard on the lips. "You did it! Your ball went about seventy yards."

"Really, it did?" She peered down the fairway. "I can't find it."

Colin pointed to a tiny yellow blip and she trained her eyes in that direction.

"That's me?"

"It is, and you did great." He retrieved her club. "Except for this." He tucked her club into the bag and they walked to her ball.

"Come on. I want to do it again. This is fun."

As they worked their way down the fairway, he helped her select each club as they drew closer to the green until it was time to putt.

"Now remember, this is a different feel. You're not going to drill this shot; this is about accuracy and finesse. It's like playing miniature golf."

She laughed. "I'm a shark at the Pirates Putt. Da-duh, da-duh." She whispered the first strains to the *Jaws* movie theme.

He pointed to the ball. "Ms. Shark, please putt this out."

She took out her putter and bent low.

"Hold on. Let's adjust your grip so you'll have more control." Who was he kidding? He wanted to be close to her, and this was a good reason to do it. He reached in from behind her, wrapping his arms around hers. He positioned her hands.

"Don't forget to interlock your fingers on the back side of the club." He could smell her shampoo. Coconut. "Now, in a pendulum motion, swing the club. Don't go for the big connect, but after you can see the line to the hole, tap it in."

She looked over her right shoulder into his eyes. Her dark-brown eyes held a smile. "You can step back now."

"Do I have to?"

"If you want to finish this hole so we can do it again, yes."

He gave her a peck on the cheek. "You win." He stepped away, missing the closeness of her against him. He wanted to be close, really close. He wasn't going to pressure her; when they became intimate was all in her control. But he was more than ready to take that step.

She bent low over the ball. He noticed she bit her lower lip. That was her tell as to when she had total concentration. Gently, she eased the putter back and with a soft smack, the ball rolled to the cup, perched on the edge, and after teetering, it dropped inside.

In a rush, she lifted her club into the air and jumped up. "Yes!" She threw her arms around him. "Did you see? It went in!"

"I was standing right here, and I promise I didn't miss a thing."

She squeezed him tight and then let go. "Let's play the next hole."

"Can I putt first?"

Her face broke into a wide grin. "Sure. I'll bet you a buck you don't get it in on the first try."

"Look who's gotten cocky." He debated if he should sink the putt or miss and give her a boost of confidence.

He addressed the ball and at the last second, she hiccupped. The ball fell short of its destination. He looked sideways and she grinned with a shrug.

"Sorry. I didn't mean it." She hiccupped again. "I need a drink of water."

He tapped the ball in and then scooped up the yellow and white balls.

"Come on, ace. Let's see how we do on the next hole."

Working their way around the course, Colin could see Anna was a natural. She didn't have a perfect hole each time, but for her first time on the course, she was amazing. He also was keeping one eye on the weather, as dark clouds were drifting in and the temperature had dropped. She pulled on a sweater but never once suggested they stop.

On the eighth hole, a few fat, cold raindrops landed on them as they finished putting.

"Do you want to call it a day?"

She took his hand as they walked up a steep slope. "Let's finish. I'm sweet, but I won't melt."

They stopped at the last tee box, and both of their balls went straight down the fairway. It was a short par three and the flag was sitting dead center at the bottom of a large hill.

He pointed to the crest. "We'll leave our clubs there and then finish the hole."

The slope was steeper than he remembered, but Anna kept pace with him. Once they grabbed their nine irons and putters, Colin paused before walking down to the green. "We should open our umbrellas to protect the bags. Just in case it really starts to rain."

"Alright." Anna did as he suggested and hooked the handle of the oversized umbrella on the bottom of the cart. Colin secured his umbrella the same way. The rain began to pick up in intensity, and they laughed like kids playing in the rain.

While they each took their second shot to the green, Anna's club slipped and it took two more times to get the ball in the cup. By now, the wind had picked up. She tapped the ball into the cup. Colin noticed the rain dripping from her nose. Even her ponytail had lost its bounce.

He quickly hit his putt and a gust of wind whipped up the

slope and caught the umbrellas. The carts tipped, teetering, and as they watched, everything slowed and the clubs and carts rolled over and bounced down the slope, landing in front of them.

Anna was laughing so hard, she was holding her midsection. He rushed over to right the carts and pick up the clubs, but she grabbed him and, with the rain coming down in sheets, kissed him full on the lips.

"As much fun as this was," she said, "it's time you drive me home so we can dry off and play indoor games."

She didn't have to make that suggestion twice. He grabbed both pull carts and kissed her one last time. "Let's go home."

26

Anna couldn't wait until she and Colin reached her place. Her pulse pounded in her veins like the rain on the windshield at the thought of Colin kissing her, touching her. She wanted the rest of their day to be romantic and unforgettable.

She held his hand as he drove. He kept glancing at her as if she might have changed her mind. She gave his hand a reassuring squeeze.

"I really had fun golfing today. We'll have to play again, and soon."

"You're a natural on the course."

She started to laugh when she thought of the bags and clubs sliding down the hill and the umbrellas tumbling end over end with the wind. "You should have seen your face when that gust came up and lifted your umbrella straight up. It looked like Mary Poppins might appear and float up into the clouds."

"Your face was priceless too. And then like it was no big deal with your hair and the back of your shirt drenched while water dripped from the tip of your little nose, you sunk that putt like a pro."

"What can I say? We had to finish." She grinned and took off her ball cap. "A memorable first time." If he caught what could be a double meaning, he didn't react.

"We'll have to lay the clubs out when we get to your house so they can dry." Colin eased the car around the circular driveway and stopped as close to the front steps as possible. "We're going to need to make a dash for it."

She looked at their clothes. "We can't get any wetter."

"True. If you get the door, I'll get the bags."

"We can each grab a bag; it'll make it easier and faster. Besides, I don't want you tripping up the stairs lugging two golf bags. No emergency room visit tonight."

He leaned across the console and cupped her cheek to pull her close for a passion-filled kiss.

A rumble of thunder caused Anna to jerk back. "We should go in." Her voice was soft and husky.

He seemed to be reluctant to leave the cocoon of the car. It was just the two of them against the elements.

"Pop the trunk." She pushed open the door and stepped into the driving rain. It chilled her heated skin. She moved to the back of the car and grabbed the strap on her bag. Colin waited for her to lift it out before pulling his out and slamming the lid firmly shut. With a few long strides, they were under cover of the porch roof. She withdrew her key and pushed open the door.

"I'll get some towels and we can let everything dry in the sunroom, out of the way."

He carried her bag through the living room while she went to get some old towels. As he made his way through the house, he looked around to see the best place to lay out the clubs and bags. He really liked this room. It wasn't overtly feminine; the furniture and décor were about comfort. Colors were muted, lighting was strategically placed, and the sofa reclined. There were also several overstuffed chairs and ottomans. It was a comfortable room. The sunroom, on the other hand, was all about light, color, and greenery. It was filled with plant stands, a wicker table, and two loungers. It was a great place to kick back and relax.

Anna returned with a stack of towels. "Why are we doing this?"

Colin took one and snapped it open; it fluttered over the tile floor. He took her clubs from the bag and dried them off one at a time with a smaller towel before laying them out. "It's best to make sure they really dry, and this is the best way to accomplish it."

Anna followed suit and together, they got the task done in a short amount of time. She shivered and rubbed her hands over the goose bumps on her arms.

"You're cold. Why don't you take a warm shower and get changed?"

"What about you?" She gave him the once-over. He was just as wet.

"I have sweats and a t-shirt in the car. I'll change and then we can relax, maybe watch a movie or something."

She felt a small smile begin. What was the *or something*?

"Are you hungry?"

His eyes grew a deeper shade of green and as he took a step closer, his finger trailed down her arm. Wherever he touched, fresh goose bumps appeared, and this time, they weren't from being cold.

"Yes." That one word made her breath catch in her throat. "We can"—her mouth went dry—"we can have an early dinner."

"Or we could have a snack. Save dinner and dessert for later."

Were they talking about food or something else?

"We can."

His eyes locked with hers. She felt his breath on her face.

She could take one step forward and be crushed against his chest. As much as she wanted to kiss him and make his blood run hot, it wasn't time. Not yet. Let the fire simmer until it was time to take what she wanted.

"Let me get you some towels."

She didn't move. She didn't want to break the spell that had been woven around them. As the storm raged outside, Anna felt a different kind of storm inside her. One that gave her a strong sense of who she was and what she wanted.

She blinked and sidestepped to the doorway.

Colin followed her through the living room. She turned on the lights in the first-floor bathroom and made sure there was soap and shampoo in the shower, along with thick, luxurious towels on the rack.

She waited until he came back in. "Take as long as you'd like." She turned toward the stairs, but he stopped her with a light touch on her hand.

"You are the most beautiful woman I've ever met."

She smoothed a hand over her rain-soaked hair. "You might need glasses. At the moment, I looked like a half-drowned version of myself."

He brought her hand to his lips. They lingered there, and his eyes were filled with longing. She knew this was one of the single most romantic moments she had experienced in her life.

Colin watched Anna disappear from his sight at the top of the stairs. This woman made him feel things and want things he hadn't thought were possible. She challenged him, teased him, and was sexy as hell but didn't realize it, which made him want her even more.

He wasn't going to waste time taking a long shower. If he hurried, he could fix them a plate to share while they curled up on the sofa and watched an old movie. He knew from their date in the park that she had a fondness for classic black-and-white flicks. He turned the water on hot and made short work of getting cleaned up and changed into dry clothes.

He moved around her tidy, well-laid-out kitchen. Opening and closing cabinets, he found a plate, crackers, and cheese, along with a bunch of grapes and an apple. Next, he took the liberty of opening a bottle of red wine from the rack. He was looking for glasses when he felt Anna watching him.

He turned slowly, and there she was, leaning against the doorjamb. She pointed to a cabinet. "To the left of the sink." A small smile played across her sensual lips. She was wearing a simple purple t-shirt with her hair twisted on top of her head. Her feet were bare on the dark wood floors, hot-pink toenails peeking out from black yoga pants.

"I hope you don't mind I made myself at home."

"I'm glad you did. I have trays standing on end next to the refrigerator." She crossed the room and pulled one out. "Will that help?"

He felt his gut tighten. She smelled of coconut and lime. He took the tray from her hands and set it on the counter. He wanted her. Now.

Was Colin's heart racing like hers? Did the blood in his veins feel like it was pulsating? She whispered his name.

His arms slid around her, crushing her to his chest, his kiss bringing her to her knees. It was different this time. Important. Demanding. Promising.

"Upstairs or down?" he asked as his lips nibbled down her neck.

She walked him to the stairs without releasing him. She didn't want to break their connection. She hesitated for a fraction of a second before Colin swept her off her feet and carried her up the stairs as if she weighed no more than a child. The door to her bedroom was open and he walked through it. He set her on the bed and knelt down. Bringing both her hands to his lips, he kissed them.

"If you say no, we'll go downstairs."

"And if I say yes?" She tilted her head back and their eyes met.

"Are you?"

She lifted her mouth to his and whispered, "Yes."

She pulled him to her and onto the bed and then took all that she had longed for.

He ran his hands down her arms, over her skin, electrifying it as he went. She melded into him. She wanted to feel his skin next to hers. She pulled his shirt off and tossed it aside. She then did the same with hers.

His breath caught when her fingers trailed down his back. His sweats and briefs and her yoga pants became a memory, and finally a slip of silk and lace.

There was nothing separating them. With all the time in the world, they explored the curves and planes of the other's body, not in a rush, luxuriating in each sensation. Time passed unnoticed as they discovered ways to make the other sigh with pleasure. Anna's breath quickened. She was ready for more.

"Colin," she whispered, "I want you now."

"I need..."

She pulled open the nightstand drawer. "I've been waiting for this moment." She handed him a small packet. "Will this work?"

He glanced at it. "Yes."

It was the first time but easy at the same time, like they had been doing this for years. She held him close and they moved together as one.

Afterward, they lay in each other's arms. With her head

resting on his chest, he twirled a lock of her now dry hair around his finger. At what point it had come tumbling down, she had no idea. Nor did she care.

"Do you always have protection in your nightstand drawer?" He looked down at her and kissed her forehead.

She shivered and he pulled the blanket over her shoulders. "Confession time?"

"Sure." It came out as a drawl.

"When I made up my mind that I wanted us to end up in this very spot, I stopped at the drugstore. A girl should always be prepared."

"I love a woman who knows what she wants."

She kissed his chin. "All I want is you."

He looked into her eyes. "I feel exactly the same way."

27

During dinner, Anna and Colin sat close and gazed into each other's eyes. He had gone all out in the romance department with tall tapered candles, a bottle of wine, and had taken over grilling the steak and veggies. He could have spent all night just lying next to her in bed; he just wanted, no needed, to be with her.

She topped off his glass with the last of the wine. "Thanks for cooking. It was delicious."

"I hope you liked your steak rare. I'm of the opinion that if you're going to have beef, it shouldn't be shoe leather."

"Other than missing sautéed mushrooms and onions, it was perfect."

"True."

"Next time"—she gave him a soft smile—"I'll cook. That is if you have a strong stomach."

The benign conversation about another home-cooked dinner brought a grin to his face and then it drooped.

"You frowned." She covered his hand with hers. "If something is bothering you, we should talk about it."

"It's nothing." He picked up his wineglass and swirled the ruby liquid in the clear glass goblet.

She cocked her head to one side. "If the shoe was on the other foot, would you want me to stay silent?"

He took a drink and set the glass down.

"Do you think we've moved too fast?"

Her face went scarlet. Her mouth dropped open and she snapped it shut. "Do you?"

"Not for a second, but we only get one chance at our first time and I was hoping I hadn't rushed you."

Anna laced their fingers together. "I couldn't have imagined a more perfect day. I wanted you." Her eyes twinkled. "Did you miss that?"

"You are very important to me and I'd never want to..." His voice trailed off as she placed a finger over his mouth.

"I'll always be honest with you if I don't like something or it makes me uncomfortable. All I ask is for the same in return."

"Let's make that a pact. We'll always be transparent with each other."

She leaned over the table. "Care to seal it with a kiss?"

He pulled her into his lap and slipped his arms around her. "Just one?"

She gave him a slow, seductive wink. "Play your cards right and you can get much more than that."

He nuzzled her neck. "I like how that sounds."

"Stay with me tonight?" She tenderly kissed his forehead and down his face, then nibbled on his earlobe.

Colin groaned. "I'm yours."

After a leisurely breakfast with Colin and a hot shower for two, he had gone back home. He had to get clothes, but they had plans for later. In the meantime, Anna was keyed up so she put on her sneakers to go for a run. She set an easy pace down the two-lane road. As her muscles warmed, she picked up the speed. Her spirits soared with each long stride. Music played in her earbuds and she kept thinking about last night. Lying in his arms, drifting off to sleep was something she could do every night. She was in love with a wonderful guy, and he loved her.

Thirty minutes later, she turned to head back home. Then the doubts crept in. How long would this relationship last? She didn't have a good track record with guys. Usually it was because she overlooked some fatal flaw. Did Colin have one? These thoughts consumed her as she made the final turn, surprised to see Liza's minivan parked in her driveway and her sister swaying on the porch glider. She waved, slowing to a walk so she could make the last few yards in cool down mode.

"I didn't expect to see you today." Anna walked through the front door. She called through the open window, "Water?"

"I'm all set."

Anna poured herself a large glass of water and kicked off her running shoes and socks. Padding barefoot, she went back to the front porch.

"Where are the boys?"

"They're fishing with Jack." Liza stretched her legs out in front of her. "I didn't hear from you since before the big date yesterday so I thought I'd drop by and get the scoop."

"It was a good day. I'm surprised how well I played and I'm starting to really like golf." She picked at a thread on her shorts. "You might want to try it. It's something we could do together."

Liza folded her arms over her chest. "Anna, I'm not asking about the golf game. And you know it."

She felt her face grow warm.

"I knew it!" Liza's fist-bumped the air. "Did you sleep with him?"

She gushed, "I did and it was amazing."

Nodding, Liza grinned. "By the look on your face, was it life-changing?"

"I have never felt this way before." She drained the glass of water. "Which is why I'm terrified." She gave Liza a serious look. "There's got to be something wrong with him. He can't be as wonderful as I think he is. Right?"

"He strikes me as the genuine article, and Dad likes him, and you remember how harsh he could be about some of the guys we brought home. He liked Steve. It took him no time to warm up to him and he was one of a kind, and now Colin. My guess, Dad has good radar when it comes to bull crud rolling off a guy's tongue."

"You might be right."

"How does he make you feel when you're with him?"

She didn't have to think about how to respond. "Special."

"I'm so happy for you. For the record, I happen to think he's a good man. I like how you smile when you talk about him." Liza pushed the swing again. "Where do you go from here?"

"We've agreed to always speak our mind and be honest with each other."

"That's good." Liza's face grew wistful.

"Are you thinking of Steve right now?"

"There are moments when I still think he'll walk in the door and this will just have been a nightmare." She blinked back tears. "I don't remember what he smelled like or how he would sound in the middle of the night when he rolled over, pulled me to his chest, and spoke in a soft, husky voice, telling me he loved me."

Anna jumped up and sat next to Liza. She put an arm around her. "Steve loved you very much."

A sharp edge came into Liza's voice. "I'm tired of sleeping alone. Doing the big and little things by myself. Stupid stuff like taking out the garbage and washing the car. I want to clean shaving cream and whiskers out of the sink again." Liza grasped Anna's hands. "I want you to have all of that with Colin. All the wonderful and crappy moments that a couple shares."

Anna gave a short laugh. "You paint quite an enticing picture for a committed relationship."

"There are so many awesome things about a relationship. Things you need to discover for yourself with Colin."

"We're having fun and now that we've"—she could feel the blush go from her neck to her hairline—"gone horizontal, I'm worried things will change between us."

"I hope they do." Liza stopped the swing. "Things are evolving into a new phase, and that's what you want. A relationship needs to grow and change with time. Otherwise, it fizzles out."

"I know I've said this before, but what's between me and Colin feels different. I can't explain it." She pulled Liza up. "I'm starving. Do you have time for brunch?"

"Of course. Like I said, our brother has the boys." She closed the screen door behind them. "For as hard and lonely as my life is at times, I'm pretty lucky to be a part of this family. Even without Steve, the boys and I will be okay."

"Was there ever a doubt?" They entered the kitchen and Anna flipped on the overhead lights.

"No, I guess not." She plucked a grape from the bowl and popped it into her mouth.

Anna placed a skillet on the stove, turned the coffee maker on, and began to pull items out of the refrigerator. "Omelet?"

"Extra cheese, please."

"Are you rushing me? I haven't even cracked the eggs," she said with a chuckle. "If you're that hungry, you can grate the darn cheese."

"I was sitting here looking around this beautiful home and wondering, do you want to have kids? You never talk about them, even in passing."

Anna cracked four eggs into a clear glass bowl and began

to whisk them with a fork. She glanced at the egg mixture, satisfied it was well mixed, and set it aside.

"There was a long time where I tried not to think about it. The last time it crossed my mind was when Ben was born and I got a case of baby lust."

"Holding that little boy in my arms made feelings wash over me that I didn't know I had." Liza began to grate a block of cheese onto a plate.

"I would love to hold my own baby in my arms someday, but my clock is ticking. I might be out of time."

"You still have time and you're healthy. Is Colin a dad kind of guy?"

Anna grew thoughtful. "He is a kind and caring man. I could see him with kids."

"If you really want a family, it's a discussion you'll need to have."

Anna frowned. "I don't think so. We haven't even talked about the future."

"Not now." Liza chuckled. "But when you do, and that topic will come up, trust me, you need to say you want to have kids someday. If he doesn't, then you have a decision to make. Because if he says no, chances are he'll never change his mind."

"Really?"

"When Steve and I first started to talk about getting married and having a family, I made it very clear the only place I wanted to live was right here. I didn't mind if he had to travel for work, but if he insisted we move, that was a deal-breaker and we'd have to go our separate ways."

"I never knew that." She dropped a couple pats of butter in the skillet and swirled it around to melt. "Was it hard to have that conversation?'

"No. It was actually easier than setting up a false expectation like I would move. It was the same when we talked about having kids. We agreed on three." Liza's face fell.

"You have two amazing boys. It really was the greatest gift Steve could have given you."

She brightened. "I'm going to live my life to the fullest with no regrets. And you need to do the same."

"How do you always know exactly what to say even though I'm the older sister?" She poured the eggs in the skillet. The mixture sizzled.

"Easy. My big sister taught me everything I needed to know about living an honest life."

"Hand me the cheese, and then we can eat."

Liza had made some excellent points and when the time was right, she would be upfront with Colin. Kids were nonnegotiable for her. But there were other things that might be. Time would tell.

28

The voicemail light was blinking on her phone when Anna got to the office the next afternoon. Colin had been called into work, so she had time on her hands. The message could wait. She secured her hair in a messy bun and picked up a divided wire basket that held small vials with snap-on lids. She slipped on a lab coat and checked the pockets for a Sharpie and a roll of masking tape. She had samples to collect.

She ran lightly down the stairs to the warehouse and then on to the tanks. She needed to check on one of last year's blends to see if it was time to bottle. She had a lot, personally, riding on this blush. She had taken some big chances, but they'd be worth if it was as good as she hoped. Especially because since the conference, she had been mulling over the idea of authoring a paper.

Her cell phone vibrated in her pocket and she ignored it. She went about writing on strips of masking tape and affixing them to lids. Her cell phone vibrated again. She pulled it out of her pocket and answered. "Hello."

"There you are." It was Dad. "I've been trying to reach you. Have you been to your office yet? I left you a message."

"Yes, but I had a ton of stuff to get done. Are you alright?"

"Well, of course I am." He sounded surprised at the question. "Can't your old dad just want to talk to you?"

She put the cap back on the marker and sat down on a bench. "Sure, but to leave a message and then keep calling my cell until I answer is a bit out of character, wouldn't you say?"

He chuckled. "Well, I just got off the phone with a mutual friend and I wanted to share some exciting news with you."

After an extended pause, she asked, "Are you going to keep me in suspense?"

"You remember Henri."

"Of course. He's a very nice man. I enjoyed talking with him and his daughter Sophia."

"He's going to be calling you at exactly two this afternoon."

Her father sounded almost giddy.

"Why?"

"He has an interesting proposition he'd like to discuss with you."

She rolled her eyes. She didn't have time for games. "Why don't you just clue me in since you obviously know what's going on."

"Nope. Not gonna happen."

She sighed. This was just like when she was a kid and he knew something she didn't. He'd be all cagey and think he was being funny by making her wait or work for the answer.

"Dad, then why did you bother to call? Just to annoy me?"

"I want to make sure that you are in your office at two. That's all."

She could almost see him grinning.

"I will be in my office by one fifty just to be on the safe side, if that will make you happy." She got up, ready to resume her work.

"Call me as soon as you hang up or better yet, I'll come down."

"Dad." Her voice was firm. "Stay home. I'll call you."

"You might want to talk with me right away. I'll see you soon." The line went silent.

She looked at it and shook her head. If it were anyone else, she'd call him back and give him a piece of her mind. A look at her watch showed she had thirty minutes, and at least one strong cup of coffee was in order. She couldn't imagine why Henri was calling her. Unless he wanted a copy of her presentation from the conference. But that wasn't a reason for Dad to be so mysterious.

Her voice echoed off the stainless-steel holding tanks. She checked each fermenting tank temperature and grabbed the logbook to record the readings for acidity. She hurried down the long cement walkway, making a quick detour past the kitchenette for a large cup of hot, strong coffee. As an afterthought, she poured a second cup. Dad was sure to show up right at two.

She settled in behind her desk and began to enter the numbers into a spreadsheet. As least this would keep her busy until the phone rang. Somewhere within the large, silent building, she heard a door slam. That would be her father.

Before she could investigate, her office phone rang.

"*Bonjour, Anna,*" she heard as she picked up the phone. "This is Henri; we met in London."

His French accent was more pronounced over the phone. "Hello, Henri. It's nice to hear from you. How have you been?"

"Very well. I trust you had an enjoyable time at the sea and an uneventful trip home."

"Actually, I ran into David in Folkestone. It was an uncomfortable exchange." Dad popped his head into her office, and she waved him to a seat and pointed to the mug of coffee. He sat down and nodded his thanks as she continued. "However, I did have the opportunity to relax. I intend to go back at some point and enjoy more of the sights."

"I am very sorry about David. He can be impulsive, and I hope that he did not cast a shadow over your holiday." He paused. "I trust all is well with your family?"

"Yes, everyone is in good health. Thank you for asking."

"*Très bien.*" There was a pause on the other end of the phone. "Have you spoken to your father about my call?"

"Dad told me to expect to hear from you, but nothing more."

"I was very impressed with your presentation."

So that was it. He wanted a copy.

"Thank you, and I'd be happy to send you my notes."

With a soft laugh, he said, "No, Anna. That is not what I was going to ask you, although that is very generous of you to offer."

Now she was confused, and Dad was grinning from ear to ear and nodding like a bobblehead doll on the dash of a car driving down a bumpy road.

"I'm confused. How can I help you?"

"I would like to offer you an opportunity to come to France, all expenses paid, of course, and spend a year working at Marchand Winery. I would like you to work, hands-on so to speak, with Sophia. You could provide her with a new perspective on winemaking."

"Henri, I'm not sure what to say. But I don't know what I can teach Sophia that she hasn't already learned from you. You've been in the business much longer than I have, and what about David? Why isn't he working with Sophia?"

"The talent you have is not something that I've ever seen before, especially in someone of your age. Most people acquire your skill after a lifetime of experience. I have discussed this with Sophia, and she was intrigued with the idea. She would very much like for you to give this serious consideration. Regarding David, he has a new idea he is pursuing."

She had to wonder what he was up to now, but maybe

Henri hadn't been in favor of him trying to buy CLW. "I'm flattered. But I don't think I can take a sabbatical from CLW. There isn't anyone to handle our harvest and..." She trailed off when she saw her father gesturing at her.

She mouthed, *What*?

Very softly, he said, "Tell Henri you want to think about it."

"But thank you for the invitation."

"Of course, there is a salary and you'll have a villa that will be exclusively for you."

"That is very generous. I'll need some time to think about it." This was an amazing opportunity. If only it wasn't happening now.

He named a figure, and she was thankful she was sitting down. She could hear him laugh.

"Anna, take all the time you need and if you have any questions, please email or call my cell phone number. You can reach me at any time." He rattled off his contact information.

She glanced at Dad, who was mouthing, *One week.*

"I will let you know my decision in a week's time."

"I will look forward to your call."

After she said goodbye, she set the phone back in the cradle, leaned back in the chair, and rubbed her eyes with her fingers. She could feel her father watching her. She had no idea what to say. Her first thought was of Colin. How could she leave him for a year? And CLW needed her here, not in France. There wasn't anyone who knew how to do her job other than Dad, and he had finally retired. But what an opportunity. Henri's vineyard's reputation was impeccable. How could she do anything to enhance their award-winning wines?

Dad cleared his throat. "Are we going to talk about this?"

She didn't look at him but kept her eyes shut. "It's an amazing opportunity."

"No. It's a once-in-a-lifetime offer."

She groaned. "I can't run off to France for a year. I have responsibilities here."

"Anna."

"Dad."

It was as if they were at a stalemate.

"You know I'm totally immersed in every aspect of this business," she said.

"And who taught you everything you know?" He sat back in the chair and crossed his leg over the opposite knee, waiting her out.

"You."

He gave a sharp nod. "I can handle things while you're in France, and we could arrange samples to be overnighted to you for testing. You'd still be heavily involved with Jack. I think there's a way to work this out, as I can be your eyes here. It can work, if you want to do this. Being hands-on in France would help CLW expand down the road. But ultimately it is your decision."

"I can't even begin to think about doing something like that. You just retired. Mom bought new luggage. Liza needs help with the boys. There is just way too much going on here." She threw her hands up in the air. "And there's Colin." He was definitely on her mind. His last serious relationship had crumbled under the pressure of long-distance. Could theirs survive?

"Colin could go with you, and the rest of your statements are excuses, Anna."

She pushed back from the desk and looked out the window. The view was one of her favorites. Vines as far as she could see. CLW vines. "I've never worked anywhere but here."

Dad crossed the room and gave her a one-armed hug. "The entire family will support you if you decide to do it."

She rested her head on his shoulder, just like she did when she was a girl.

"I have a lot to think about. Weigh the pros and cons." She pointed out the window. "That's my world out there. What if I fail in the alternate universe of France?"

"What if you reach new heights?"

"Do me a favor and don't tell anyone else about this. I need time to think, without any pressure one way or the other."

"I'm here if you want to talk, but, Anna, don't let your overly logical brain talk you out of it, either." He kissed her forehead. "I need to tell Mom so she knows we may need to be flexible in our travel arrangements."

With a small laugh, she said, "Swear her to secrecy."

"You know your Mom; wild horses couldn't drag a secret out of her."

Dad left her office. She could hear his retreating footsteps.

She called after him. "Dad, wait."

His footsteps slowed and he came back.

"Henri said David was on to a new project. Any idea what that might be?"

"Yes, but Henri and I agree, a joint venture of a single bottle of wine, a red that you will work on. In fact, David will be here tomorrow, and we'll discuss the path forward. If you'd like to join us for dinner tomorrow night, with Colin of course."

"I'll ask him and call Mom tomorrow."

He touched her hand. "Whatever you decide about France is fine with me."

He walked down the hall, whistling off-key and leaving Anna to mull over the idea of living in France for a year. For now, the only person on her mind was Colin. What would a year apart do to their relationship?

29

Anna had been thinking nonstop about Henri's call. Colin had worked last night so she had plenty of time to write her pro and con list, and she hoped taking a walk would give her clarity. Dad would support her whatever she chose, but it was a once-in-a-lifetime chance to live and work at one of the best and oldest wineries in Europe. These kinds of chances didn't come around every day. She was beginning to lean toward going, but leaving Colin weighed heavily on her. She wanted to talk to him about it in person.

As she began the return trip to her house, she came to a decision of sorts. Talking it out with Colin would help her gain clarity. They had plans to golf today with Marie and a friend. She wondered if it would be Drew. Tomorrow, she was going canoeing with Liza, but since dinner with David and her parents was tonight, she needed to have the conversation with Colin soon.

She turned the corner. In her driveway was Colin's car, the man himself leaning against the driver's door. No time like the present. She jogged across the dew-covered grass, unable to see his eyes. They were covered with dark sunglasses, but his smile said it all. He was happy to see her.

"Hey, you. You're early." She leaned in and gave him a lingering kiss.

"I hope it's okay I came over early." He slipped his arms around her and pulled her close while he brushed at the strands of hair that had escaped her ponytail. "I thought we could have coffee together before we meet up with Marie."

"Why don't you make coffee while I shower, and we can sit out back and have quiet time before we jump into the rest of the day." She stood on her toes and kissed him.

"I can do that."

Arm in arm, they walked up the wide front steps. It felt so natural and comfortable to just be in the moment. She'd bring up dinner with her parents and France over coffee.

She gave him a kiss on the cheek. "You know where everything is in the kitchen. I won't be long."

"Take your time. We don't tee off for a couple of hours."

She could feel him watching her as she climbed the stairs. Smiling, she closed the bedroom door behind her.

Colin shook his head as he watched Anna close the door to her bedroom. He would like to have followed her but there was a time for everything and besides, in his book, she hadn't given a clear indication that he was invited. Or was the flirty kiss and wink an invitation and he'd missed it?

He put together a small pot of coffee. No sense in brewing more than they'd drink. He selected two large mugs from the cabinet, set out the cream and sugar, and then turned on some soft jazz. From past experience, he knew the music could be heard in the rest of the house, including the back deck. Anna had done an amazing job with the remodel of her home. If they were to make their relationship permanent, could they start over in a place they purchased together, or settle here? He could see himself living here with Anna. His house had zero personality and it was too noisy. It was an investment instead of paying rent. *I'm getting ahead of myself. We're not ready to make long-term plans. At least, not yet, but the time will come. Of that, I'm certain.*

The sound of footsteps crossing the hall made him look up. His breath caught. Her hair was damp and falling around her face. She wore her usual touch of makeup, just enough to enhance her eyes and lips. His eyes trailed down the length of her. She wore a light-purple top with matching plaid shorts. Her feet were bare and today her toenails were a deep-lavender color.

"Coffee smells delicious."

He swallowed hard. "You look nice."

With a throaty laugh, she said, "Wow. Don't overwhelm me with flowery words like I look beautiful or great or hot."

In two long strides, he was in front of her. His mouth claimed hers. As his lips trailed down her neck, he murmured, "You're smoking."

This time, she laughed harder. Putting her hands on his shoulders, she put distance between them.

"If we start that, I won't want to go anywhere anytime soon and you promised Marie we'd meet her. Besides, there's something I need to talk to you about."

"I can see where making plans with Marie was a mistake."

She eased away from him. As she did, her finger trailed down his face and across his chest.

"You promised me coffee too."

"It just so happens I was waiting on you and now that you're here, I'll pour a mug and as promised, we can sit and plan our strategy for winning today against my sister."

Anna added a spoonful of sugar and a splash of cream to her mug and held it out for Colin to add the coffee.

"Is she bringing Drew?" She took a tiny sip.

"Doubtful. I don't think he plays often, and Ginny is pretty good, so my guess is she's our fourth."

They strolled out to the back deck. Anna ran a hand through her hair, fanning it out as it continued to dry.

They sat in the two cushioned lounge chairs.

"What a perfect day." She tilted her head back and let the sun wash over her face. "Hmm."

"Do you always have weekends off?"

She gave him a sidelong look. "Unless we're harvesting or it's crush time. There are weekends I help out in the tasting room or the café."

"Before me, did you spend more time at CLW on the weekends?" He was curious how much her life had changed since they started dating.

"More or less."

He looked at her over the rim of the mug. "I wouldn't mind helping out occasionally if you needed to be there."

She looked at him. He wasn't sure what was going on in her head. "Be careful what you volunteer to do. The winery is like a needy child sometimes. The more you give, the more it takes."

"It would be worth it to be with you." He set his coffee down on the table and got up. She moved her legs so he could sit on the edge of her chair.

"You have an important career and hanging out at the winery on your days off wouldn't give you any time to relax," she said. "How about we save trips to the winery for fun stuff only."

"I'm not saying I'd want to spend every free moment working at the winery, but I know how important the business is to you and your family. As long as we're doing it together"—he took her hand—"and you teach me everything you know"—he gave her a cheeky grin—"I'm happy to pitch in."

"You might be sorry you brought this subject up. Especially if you tell my folks. They thrive on turning people into wine nuts."

"I'll keep that in mind." He took her chin in his hand. His eyes twinkled. "I can promise you that I will never ask you to help out at the hospital."

Anna grinned and fanned herself with her hand. "Whew. I was getting kinda worried. I'm not really keen on the whole blood thing." She picked up her mug. "Speaking of which, do you see a lot of blood?"

"No, not really. I mean I'll look at incisions for healing but it's not like I'm in an operating room or the ER. I'm involved in looking at test results, working with patients on cardiac rehab, and the two doctors I work under are both top in their field and my case load is full."

She ran her hand over his well-trimmed beard. "I love your face."

He kissed the palm of her hand. "Thanks."

"There's something I need to talk to you about."

"Sure. What's on your mind?" He laced his fingers with hers.

She stalled.

Quietly, he said, "The best place to start is at the beginning."

"Do you remember Henri Marchand? We met him at the wine conference in London?"

"I do."

"He called me yesterday."

Colin waited for her to continue. His heart gave a thud in his chest.

"He asked if I'd be interested in going to his winery in France and working with his daughter, mentoring her in how to blend different juice into good wine."

He grinned. "That's great news. You get to go to France and work in a prestigious winery. How exciting is that?"

"It is. Apparently, Sophia's interested in working with me after she attended my lecture. She's grown up in the business like I have, but she could use a different perspective to really take charge of the winery. Sometimes it's hard being part of the family, especially if people don't take you seriously."

"You speak from experience."

"It was only recently I realized how far into our business I'm entrenched. I knew I was a part, but I had no idea, until I met people in London, how critical what I do is to the success of our wines. I've always dreamed of being recognized for my work, and going to London showed me that I was doing a good job. Dad said there is a way to work things out with my work here, but he firmly believes I must consider this opportunity, as it could benefit CLW as well as me."

His heart sunk in his chest and he pulled her into a one-armed hug. "I'm very proud of you." He swallowed the lump in his throat. "When do you leave?"

"I have to call Henri with my decision next week, and the gig is for a year."

His heart dropped to his feet and he took time to digest the information. "Yeah, we can make it work." His forehead wrinkled. "But an entire year." He shook his head.

"My parents asked us to dinner tonight. David will be there; would you mind if we went? I'd like to hear firsthand what his reaction is when Dad proposes a joint venture too."

His mouth gaped open. "Is this how the winery business works, with some subterfuge and keeping the enemy close?" He rubbed his hand over his face. He got up and crossed the deck.

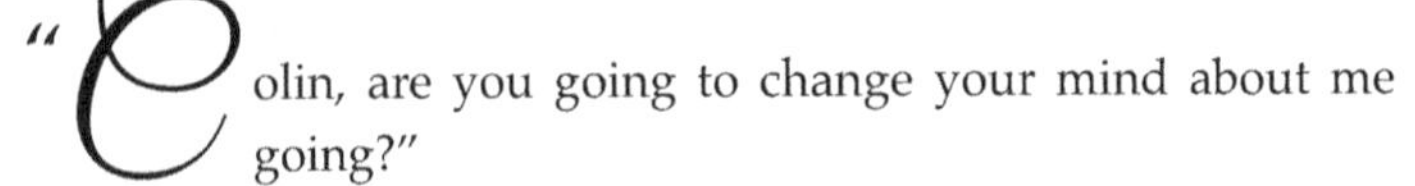

"Colin, are you going to change your mind about me going?"

"Not at all." He turned to her. "It's still an amazing opportunity and I know you've been searching for something to put your mark on. What about the after-school program?"

"I'll talk to Ms. Kelley."

"You've made up your mind to go." It wasn't a question but a statement. "Do you want us to break up?"

"No. I love you." She rushed to him. "And the last thing I want is to lose you."

He slid an arm around her waist. "I love you too. Our relationship can withstand a few thousand miles between us. But do you think it would be possible to carve out time every couple of months to meet someplace? We could see Europe together while you're there."

She slipped her arms around his neck and held him tight. "I'd love to explore the world with you." She kissed him full on the mouth. "A year isn't that long, either. But do you have enough vacation time to do that?"

He looked into her eyes as if he were trying to memorize the soft brown pools. "One good thing about working in a hospital is you bank vacation time for the hours you work. I've never been one to take a lot of time off, so I've got hours saved up."

She wrapped her arms around him, holding him tight. Her life couldn't be any better than it was at this moment. She had the man and now she was going to have an unbelievable career opportunity. "This will work. You'll see." Who was she trying to convince, Colin or herself?

He'd be content to spend all day right here on this deck with her in his arms.

"Then let's go play golf with Marie and tell her we'll have dinner with her tomorrow night. Loser is buying."

She lifted her head. "You know I intend to win, so you'd better bring your A game."

He stroked her hair away from her face. "I never plan on

losing, and you'll hold your own in this foursome." He pecked her lips. "Ready, champ?"

"Can we stay right where we are for five more minutes?"

He answered her by tilting up her face for a long, lingering kiss.

30

Anna waved to Marie and Ginny from the parking lot as they unloaded their golf clubs. "Hey there. We'll only be a minute."

"No rush; take your time. We're behind a couple of foursomes who are waiting to tee off." Marie leaned over the wheel in their cart. "And we're not in a rush."

Colin and Anna added the clubs to the back of their cart and Marie and Ginny walked over.

"Hi, Ginny," Anna said. "It's nice to see you again. I hope Marie told you I've only played once so far, and it was nine holes."

"Not to worry; we're playing best ball."

Anna's forehead wrinkled. "What's that?"

Colin said, "Whoever's ball lands closest to the pin is the ball we play for each hole."

"Well, then we'll be playing your ball."

Marie laughed. "That's not what I heard. You've got a nice swing and some ladies' tees have a huge advantage."

She wished the butterfly tornado in her stomach would settle down. "I hope I don't whiff the ball on the tee."

"You won't," Colin reassured her. "Do you want to drive?"

She wiggled her eyebrows and slightly tipped her head to one side. "Do I have a speed limit?"

"Yes. These little electric carts are fun to drive, and it's surprising how much gumption they have."

"Then yes. I'll drive." She slid across the bench seat behind the steering wheel. She patted the copilot spot and smiled at Marie and Ginny. "I hear there is a friendly wager on this round?"

Marie pointed to Colin. "Blame him. He's competitive."

"I'm a handicap for the poor guy."

Marie adjusted her hat and sunglasses. "From what I hear, you're a natural, but"—she glanced at Ginny, who nodded—"you can take all the mulligans you need."

"Huh?"

"Do-overs. Like if you whiff the ball or something, you can do it again with no penalty," Ginny explained.

"That's really nice, but it hardly seems fair."

"Don't worry, Anna. This is a friendly game, but my brother has the added pressure of winning against me." She wagged her finger at Colin. "I've got my eye on you, bro."

He nodded. "Right back at ya."

The two carts zipped to the first tee and they waited for the group in front of them to get off.

Anna placed a hand on Colin's thigh. "I don't want to be the reason you lose the bet."

He gave her hand a reassuring squeeze. "Win or lose, I'll buy dinner. It's just to keep Marie on her toes. She wants to play in a professional-amateur tournament at the end of the season and I've found this is the best way to keep her focused on her game."

"Does she know you have an ulterior motive?"

"I don't think so. But I'm guessing Ginny's figured it out. After I proposed the bet, she gave me a wink."

"She seems nice."

"She is, and she really cares about Marie. Which is all I want. I like my sister surrounded by good people."

Marie's cart inched ahead in front of them.

"You're a good brother, and I should know—I've got three of them, and they'd move heaven and earth for one of us girls."

"I knew you'd understand." He pointed toward the tee box. "Ready to get this party underway?"

"Ready as I'll ever be." She depressed the pedal and the cart lurched forward to park on the cart path. With a laugh, she said, "I hope I drive the ball better than I can drive the cart."

"Darlin', have fun. That's all that matters, and remember we're here to relax and forget about any decisions that have to be made. There's plenty of time for that later."

Anna and Colin made dinner plans with Marie and Ginny for another night, and now she was ready to get dinner with her parents over with. She was not looking forward to seeing David. He grated on her nerves.

As they arrived at her parents' house, Anna said, "I'm not sure what David's end game is, but Dad felt it was important to have dinner together." She looked at Colin when he turned the car off. "Ready?"

"I know you can't stand this guy, and frankly I can't either, but I'm curious why you would consider working with him. What he did, going around your father and trying to get you to support his idea, was underhanded since technically Sam's the owner."

"I won't be working with David but CLW and Marchand. My father can handle all the Davids of the world. He's very savvy."

The warm night air held a hint of rain and Anna looked at the sky. "Look at the clouds. If we get lucky, it'll rain all night. The land is a little dry for this time of year."

"Are you a storm watcher too?" He slung his arm around her shoulders as they walked to the back door.

"All part of the job." She stood on tiptoes and kissed his cheek.

When they walked into the house, David and her parents were on the back deck. The lush greenery gave her a flash of pride. She was a part of what was happening out there, and her heart was heavy just thinking of leaving.

"Hello, everyone. Sorry we didn't get here earlier, but Colin and I played golf today and the course was busy."

Mom gave them a welcoming smile. "You're just in time."

Anna knew that wasn't true since they were about fifteen minutes late.

Colin shook her dad's hand. "Hi, Sam. How are you feeling?"

"Better than ever." He returned the hearty shake and offered introductions.

Anna noticed David's surprise when Dad introduced Colin as her boyfriend.

He rose and kissed her cheeks and shook Colin's hand. "A pleasure to see you, Anna, and I had the pleasure of meeting Colin in England, but I thought you worked for CLW."

"That's right, you did. Colin is a nurse practitioner." Anna could swear she saw Dad's eyes twinkle. She gestured for David to take a seat and she and Colin got comfortable on the love seat. Mom handed them each a glass of pinot noir.

David raised his glass. "If I may make a toast."

Dad inclined his head for him to continue.

"To new friends and a bright future."

They tapped glasses around the group and Anna sipped the velvety wine. "This is the 2015?"

Dad beamed. "See, David. She knows her wine."

Colin casually draped his arm around her and said, "It is one of my favorites."

She smothered a grin. Tonight was going to be interesting.

"It is an excellent vintage, Anna, and my father was right to ask you to join Marchand temporarily and impart your technique to Sophia. My sister is good but under your tutelage, she can become even better."

"Thank you for the kind compliment. I hope Sophia does find some new nuggets in my process that will help her."

"Sam, I am curious. Did you ever have a moment's hesitation about selling me Crescent Lake?" David studied him with an intensity that Anna found off-putting. Was he hoping Dad would suddenly say he had changed his mind?

Sam smiled, and Anna knew that look in his eye. He was about to end this conversation quickly. "David, like your family business, Crescent Lake Winery will continue to grow with members of the Price family in control, just as it has for four generations. I'm confident it will still be here with a Price running it long after my grandchildren's children are gone."

"I see." David's brows knit together. "Then forgive me, but I am confused. Why did you agree to meet with me?"

"I may have recently retired, but my brain is much harder to convince and I still own CLW. Anna is considering the offer from Henri and Sophia, and of course, with you trying to conquer the wine world in your own right, your father and I have come to an arrangement."

David leaned forward and clasped his hands together. His sole focus was Sam. "I'm intrigued."

Sam slowly swirled the wine in his glass. "What if a new wine was created under a new label? A joint venture of possibly a white or red."

He nodded. "That is an interesting idea. And who will create the wine, as I'm assuming your intention is to each produce a wine which can export to the other country."

Anna knew where this was going. Henri and Dad had

effectively crushed David out of this venture. "David, if I can speak for my father, he may be thinking we could combine juice from grapes grown in each region to create a very special blend between CLW and Marchand, not between you and CLW."

Dad beamed. "Exactly. Two great wineries coming together. Henri agrees it is an excellent idea which will be supported with Anna working in France."

"Ah, now that is a fascinating idea. Of course, I'm disappointed you are suggesting working with my father and not me. However, I can see where Anna will be invaluable in this endeavor." He gave her a forced smile.

She took Colin's hand. "This would be an excellent opportunity to work with Sophia and demonstrate how we would take the best of our two great wineries and combine them into something new. It would be up to Don and our marketing manager, Beth, to create a joint label and develop the launch."

His eyes grew bright and his smile grew. "Are you making an announcement that you will come to France for a year?"

She put on her poker face. "I will be calling Henri with my decision. Until then, let's just agree to end the discussion for the balance of the evening and enjoy the delicious dinner my mother has prepared."

With that, Dad stood up. "We should move this dinner party inside."

"We can toast to the new joint venture between two great wineries." David gestured for Mom to go ahead of him.

Anna said, "We'll be right in." The door closed behind them for some privacy.

Colin asked, "Why didn't you tell David your decision?"

She could hear a different question in his words and see the worry in his eyes. "I will tell Henri." She cupped his cheek with her hand and pulled him in for a kiss. "And we have things to work out first." She kissed him again. "You have nothing to worry about."

He dropped his eyes. "I'm sorry."

"Cut yourself some slack. You found out this morning I was offered a wonderful opportunity, and we have something special between us that neither of us want to lose. But we"—she pecked his lips—"will have a plan, and a year from now, I'll be planning my return trip and we'll have had so many wonderful adventures that will make life in Crescent Lake look dull by comparison."

"Anna, no place is ever dull when you're around."

The door slid open, and Dad stood in the doorway. He gave them a wink. "You can stare deep into each other's eyes later. Dinner is served."

"Right behind you, Dad." Then to Colin, she whispered, "Give us three hours, tops, to have dinner and dessert and we can escape."

He whispered in her ear, "Make it two."

31

Over dinner with Marie and Ginny the following week, Anna laughed at all the funny stories Marie told about Colin.

"Did you all go to school together?" Anna poured more wine in her glass and offered to refill Ginny's. Colin and Marie, the dedicated drivers, declined.

Ginny said, "I met Colin and Drew when Marie and I were in college in Boston. Colin went to Northeastern. We used to hang out from time to time."

"Those were good times." Marie gave Ginny a poke on the arm and grinned. "We won't bore you with the details tonight. We'll save that for another time."

"Marie, you don't need to share the stupidity of my youth with my girlfriend."

Anna's heart skipped a beat. That sounded so good. Despite what she had said to Colin about France, she was a little worried about a potential strain on their relationship.

After Colin paid the check, the couples went their separate ways with the promise of a rematch before she left for Europe if time permitted. She and Colin strolled hand in hand through the parking lot.

"Did you enjoy dinner?"

She hugged his arm to her body. "It was fun. And they didn't hate playing golf with me, either."

He kissed the top of her head. "You parred two holes for us and at the most, we were two over. Considering who we were playing against, we did fantastic."

"Marie is amazing. The way the ball sails like it's being chased by the wind. Unbelievable."

"Ginny can hold her own too."

"Will she do the pro-am with Marie?"

Colin opened the passenger door for her. "She'll be Marie's caddy."

"They're really close, aren't they?"

"Ginny has been half in love with Marie forever and my sister is too blind to see it."

She got into the car and Colin closed her door and walked around to his side.

She clicked her seat belt. "I like Ginny."

He turned the engine over. "Ginny's good for Marie."

"Everyone needs to have someone who loves them unconditionally." She squeezed his hand. "Are you going to stay tonight?"

"I have to be at the hospital early tomorrow and you should sleep in, so can I have a rain check?"

"Stay tonight. We'll swing by your place and get your work clothes and then tomorrow night, we'll have dinner and you can stay again."

She could see his eyes twinkle.

"Now that sounds like an invitation I can't pass up." He gave her a quick kiss. "What's on your agenda for tomorrow? Kayaking?"

"Liza and I are going to one of the smaller lakes. We probably haven't been since before the boys were born, and spending time together the last few months, we've grown even closer."

"You two do seem to be very close."

"I think it's because Tessa and I were always competing to be the best at the winery. Liza never cared about the business."

He pulled out of the parking lot. "And now?"

"Tessa and I have matured and we stopped competing when it was crystal clear neither of us would ever occupy the CEO office; Don would. Then she bought Sand Creek."

"Which turned out to be the best decision for her. She met Max and married him because of that change, right?"

"Yeah." It dawned on her that sometimes taking a huge chance was just what was needed to live your best life. She knew they had a lot to talk about when it came to France, but she wanted to just be in this moment with Colin a little longer. The year abroad was going to change so many things; she just wasn't sure how.

"Earth to Anna." Colin drew her back to this moment. "What are you thinking about?"

With a shake of her head, she said, "Wondering what I should make for dinner since I don't want to poison you."

"Frozen pizza is fine as long as we're together." He slowed and pulled into his street.

"That was a quick drive."

"I'll run in and be right back unless you want to come in?"

"You've got ten minutes, buddy, and then I'm taking the car and heading home."

"I only need five." He chuckled.

Anna watched him disappear inside and closed her eyes, wondering how she got so lucky to have this wonderful guy in her life. Would things change while she was away? No, she would do everything she needed to do to keep things going strong with him.

The driver's door opened and he tossed a small duffel bag into the back seat. "I was just thinking, you live less than five miles from the club. Heck, if it was legal, we could buy a golf cart and drive back and forth."

She laughed out loud. "Could you picture that? Us puttering along the side of the road in a little electric cart."

"I'd let you drive." He bumped her shoulder with his and winked.

"Hmm, then maybe we should see if it's legal."

Each was lost in their own thoughts as he made the short drive to her place. When they arrived, she unbuckled her seat belt. "Are you coming?"

He pushed open the car door and hurried around to open hers. He took her hand before she could get out and pulled her into his arms. She slid her arms around his neck and interlaced her fingers. He gazed into her eyes and kissed her as promised until her knees grew weak.

The next morning, the air held a slight chill as the sun crested over the horizon. Liza waved at Anna and pointed to where their yellow and orange kayaks were ready for launch. The sisters agreed the early morning was the best time to be on the water. The surface was calm, and most people hadn't made their way to the lake for a day of boating. Yet.

Liza was wearing shorts, a zip-up sweatshirt, and a ball cap, with huge sunglasses covering her eyes and most of her cheekbones.

"Hey, sis. Thanks for getting the kayaks out."

"No problem. I was up early."

"Couldn't sleep?" She gave Anna a wink. "A handsome hunk hogging the bed?"

Anna squinted into the sun, which was behind Liza. "He had an early shift at the hospital, which worked out since we had plans. But I'll see him tonight too."

Anna buckled her life vest on and pushed her bright-orange kayak to the shallow water. Liza did the same with the yellow one.

They stepped in with one foot and pushed away from the bank with the other. As soon as the kayak was free, they each settled on the hard seat with legs extended.

"Comfy?" Anna asked Liza.

"You bet. Where are we headed?"

Anna pointed to the vast expanse of the lake. "Out there somewhere."

Liza cast a worried look toward Anna. "Let's skim the banks and stay out of the center. I'm out of shape."

"Whenever you're ready to go in, just give the word."

Dipping one side of the paddle and then the other, the girls set off at an easy pace, the kayaks skimming over the glass-like surface. They were side by side and conversation was easy.

After about thirty minutes of chatting about the boys and an upcoming event Liza had the following Saturday, she asked, "So when are you going to tell me what's on your mind?"

Anna paddled a little farther and then laid the paddle across her lap and glided. Liza worked her kayak so she was looking at Anna.

"What makes you think I'm stewing on something?"

"We've been sisters for thirty-two years. Don't you think I know you?"

Anna blurted, "Have you ever been presented with an amazing opportunity but the timing sucks?"

"What are you talking about, specifically? Something to do with Colin?"

"Yes and no." She looked into the distance, at the clear blue sky with zero clouds.

"Now I'm confused. Start at the beginning."

"You know when Colin and I went to London for the wine

conference, I met the Marchand Winery owner and his daughter."

"Yes, that's old news." She pushed her sunglasses up her nose.

"Henri asked me if I would spend a year in France working at his winery, and with Sophia, as her mentor. He likes how I approach every aspect of the cycle. I'm intrigued with the idea and after talking to him and Dad, I think I'll learn just as much as I could teach. Which, long-term, would benefit CLW."

"This is an incredible opportunity. Something you've always dreamed of without ever knowing it."

"I'm going to take it, and Dad, who is very supportive, said we could find a way so that I can stay involved with things here and he'd be my eyes on the ground, so to speak, for day-to-day stuff.

"Spending a year on a well-established French vineyard. That's an experience you'd never get from spending a week or two visiting, and it does have endless possibilities that could benefit CLW."

"From the business side, it makes sense."

"So what's the issue? Colin?"

Slowly shaking her head, Anna said, "Colin is a complication."

"What did he say when you talked to him?"

She dipped an oar in the water and held the kayak against the gentle current starting to move her. "He told me to go."

"Anna, look at me. He obviously loves you, so don't worry about him. You guys will be fine."

She looked at Liza. "I'm pretty lucky."

"He recognizes this is a once-in-a-lifetime opportunity and he's supportive. That's awesome."

"What if it strains our relationship? He was engaged to someone and they tried a long-distance thing. It crumbled and broke his heart."

"You're not that other girl and he's not the same guy he was. From out of something like that, people change." She gave her a reassuring smile. "Trust me. You don't want a guy who won't support your dreams one hundred and fifty percent. He's telling you to seize the opportunity, so do it."

"I know you're right but…"

Liza leaned over and paddle-flicked water in her direction. Her laughter was infectious, and Anna couldn't help smiling.

"You have heard of the technology called Skype, airplanes, and credit cards?"

She gave her sister a scowl. "What are you talking about?"

"You and Colin can Skype all the time. You can use your credit card to purchase airplane tickets to come home." She smiled. "Or he can go there."

"Henri did say they would give me a villa to use."

"I think the problem is solved."

Anna's heart felt lighter. "Thanks, sis, for the pep talk and reminding me I'm not going to Mars. Just France."

Liza beamed. "So, when do you leave?"

"I need to make arrangements, but in a couple of weeks, right after July fourth. I'll explain to Henri that I have a few things to wrap up here."

Liza wagged a finger at her. "For the record, you and Colin will be fine. I've seen that man look at you. It was the way Steve looked at me. Colin is in this relationship for the long haul."

"I hope you're right." She began to paddle and laughed over her shoulder. "Come on, Liza. You're going to the market with me. I have a romantic dinner date to plan with my smoking hot boyfriend."

32

After an early morning spent on the water with Liza and a relaxing afternoon, Anna had finished prepping dinner and lit the candles in the dining room. Wine was chilling and the table was set for two. She smoothed down the front of her sundress and wondered if she should put sandals on. She heard a car in the drive, which ended her debate. Padding in bare feet across the cool wood floors, she pushed open the screen door.

"Hello, handsome." She lightly kissed Colin's lips when he got to the top of the steps.

He handed her a bouquet of mixed flowers. "Something smells good."

"I made pasta for dinner."

"I wasn't talking about food." He nuzzled her neck.

She felt her face grow warm and she was sure it was a bright shade of pink.

He whispered, "I love it when you blush."

"Thank you for the flowers." She noticed he had a small duffel bag in his other hand. "Do you want to put your bag upstairs?"

"I'll take it up later."

They walked into the kitchen, where Anna put the flowers in a vase, which she then set them in the middle of the island.

"The flowers really are lovely. Thank you."

"I love the way you brighten when I give them to you."

"Flowers make a room." She was nervous. They had to talk about France tonight. "Shall we have a glass of wine before dinner?"

"Red wine tonight with pasta?"

"No, white. I love to challenge the status quo with pairings."

"And here I thought I was getting the hang of the wine thing." He glanced at her toes.

"Do you paint them in the winter too?"

She winked. "You'll have to wait and see for yourself."

Now, why did she say that? She'd be in France, but he would be joining her, maybe for Christmas.

He took the bottle of wine from her hand and poured. They moved to the love seat in the sunroom, then he tried the wine. "Nice. Which one is it?"

"It's our pinot grigio from last year. It goes well with shrimp fra diavolo." She sipped. "What do you think?"

"I like it; it's crisp and light." He took another sip. "Did you choose this one to complement the spices with the shrimp?" He put his arm around her.

She gave him a broad smile. "You are getting the hang of this." She pecked his lips.

He pulled her close. "I've been looking forward to this since last night."

"How was work?"

"Uneventful for a change." He set his glass down. "Did you and Liza have fun?"

"We did." She took a sip of her wine and then set it down and took his hand. "There's something I'd like to talk about. I called Henri today and I have a plan."

"I'm all ears."

If he was concerned, he didn't seem to show it.

Colin felt like his stomach was filled with lead. Anna was going to live in France for an entire year. Everything he had said, he meant. He would support her going and they'd plan trips so they would be together as much as possible, but he was also serious when he told her he had been waiting for her his entire life. The last thing he wanted was to not be able to see her on a regular basis, although that thought left him annoyed with himself. That was selfish. But the last time the woman he loved took a sabbatical for a year, it didn't work and he ended up broken-hearted.

If the shoe was on the other foot, he'd want Anna to be supportive of him. This was going to take the long-range ideas he had for their future and slow things down. He was already thinking of proposing, but he was a traditional kind of a guy. Maybe Christmas or Valentine's would be good days, but who knew if they'd be together on either of those days? Why couldn't they be together? Nothing was going to stop him from seeing her as often as their schedules allowed.

He held her close. He wanted it to work, but the past lingered.

"Let's relax and enjoy our wine."

"And you can fill me in on the details of what you'll be doing and when you're going?"

"I'll leave right after the Fourth of July and I'll still be doing some work for CLW. Dad and I have to work out those details, but he'll send me data to analyze, and I'll come back here in the early part of the year to check on timing for bottling and such." She picked up her wine. "I'm hoping that we could see each other every few months and we'll Skype all the time too. I know it's not ideal, but we can make this work." She touched his cheek. "Right? We can make this work, and a year isn't that long. Only twelve months."

"That soon?" The weight inside his chest just got heavier. He forced a smile to his face and raised his glass. He missed her already. "We should toast to the new phase of life."

They clinked. "To our future," Anna said.

"And wonderful adventures."

She glowed with excitement. "I've confirmed with Henri that I'll have my own villa, so when you come, we'll have privacy and be comfortable. Apparently, Sophia is struggling with judging how to tell when the grapes are ready for harvest. I'll need to be hands-on for those months."

"I'm already looking forward to seeing you in France and I know you'll teach Sofia a lot. You're brilliant."

"I know you haven't been exposed to much about winemaking, yet—" She leaned over and pecked his lips. "But in time, you'll be a pro. And you've got down what to pair the pinot grigio with."

He gave a short laugh. "I don't know about that, but I'm certainly going to try—if nothing else, just to keep up during a family dinner. From what I've observed, business is entwined in everything with your family."

She grew thoughtful. "I never really thought about it, but we're kind of like roots of the vines. We're a part of the greenery that is Crescent Lake Winery." Her eyes met his. "And you get that?"

"The first time I met Sam and he talked about his family and the vineyard, it seemed that one didn't exist without the other. It's easy to see it gave him life goals, to build on what his grandfather started before him, the legacy he would leave for future generations."

"I always knew it, but never put it quite like that."

He scooched closer to her. "Is this what you want for your future, or do you want more?"

"I want to leave a legacy for future generations of Prices."

"You already have with the winery, but what else do you want?" He wanted to see if she was thinking of a long-term future with him.

Her smile was tender, and her deep brown eyes were pools of liquid chocolate. "I don't know but I'm working on it, with you."

"How about we stop talking and focus on this beautiful night just for us?" He brushed her hair back from her face. "Dinner first, or later?"

The slow, sexy smile started at one side of her mouth and slid to the other and then filled her eyes with desire.

"How hungry are you?"

"For?" He knew the answer but needed for Anna to make the next move.

"To feed your belly or your heart?"

"I'm a heart guy through and through."

Her laugh was low and husky. "Good answer." She picked up their glasses. "Grab the bottle and follow me."

"My darling girl, I'll follow you anywhere."

Anna lay in Colin's arms, happy and content in knowing they were fine. It would take a little planning, but lots of working couples had to travel to keep their relationship going. Their long distance would only be for a year. Not so long really in the overall scheme of a lifetime together. She peeked at him under her eyelashes.

His arms tightened around her. "What are you thinking about?"

"Just how happy I am." She snuggled closer. "What about you?"

"Me too." He kissed her cheek. "But there is one other thing on my mind."

"What's that?" She eased up on an elbow and studied him.

"I seem to recall you promised me dinner, and I was hoping for dessert too."

She tapped her chin with her finger. "I gave you a choice of what you wanted. You chose to feed your heart first."

"If you want to have a replay, we'll need to fill my stomach next. I'm starving."

At that moment, her stomach let out a low grumble. She burst out laughing and he joined her.

"I certainly wouldn't want you to lose your strength."

He began to tickle her until she laughed so hard, tears flowed down her cheeks.

"You win. Dinner first." She got out of bed and slipped into her robe. "Are you coming?"

"We can't have dinner in bed?"

She placed her hand on her hip. "If you play your cards right, maybe we can have dessert up here."

In a flash, he threw back the blankets and pulled on his pants. "Am I dressed okay for dinner?"

She fluttered her eyelashes and gave him a half grin. "You're overdressed for dessert."

He pulled her to his chest and kissed her long and deep. "I hope you keep saying comments like that for years to come."

Her finger trailed down his cheek. "You can count on it."

33

Anna's plans for France were set. The last two weeks had flown by in a rush to get her visa in order and thank heavens for Henri pulling some strings to get it done. She also had to figure out what to pack for an extended trip. It was hard to believe she was leaving tomorrow. Her family's annual picnic was going to be a huge event with all the Price kids, spouses, extended family, and of course all the workers from the winery. This would be the first time Colin's family was attending a family event. Marie asked if Ginny could come, and she was bringing Drew too. Everyone was welcome; after all, the more, the merrier.

The back door banged, and Anna looked up from the sink of dirty dishes she was tackling. With soap-bubble-covered hands, she flung her arms around Colin and gave him a deep kiss.

Inwardly, she groaned. She was going to miss him walking through a door. But that wasn't something to dwell on today. This was a party.

"That was quite a hello."

"It's been what, two hours since I've been able to kiss that mouth of yours?"

He chuckled. "Ninety-seven minutes, but who's counting?" He looked around her mother's kitchen. "Do you have a few minutes to take a walk with me before things get crazy?"

"Let me just dry my hands." She pulled back and then laughed. "Oops." She turned him around. "You've got some big wet spots back here."

"I'll dry." He took her hand. "Come with me."

She walked into flip-flops on the way out the back door. "Are you looking for privacy? We can walk down the road toward the winery." With familiarity, he pulled her close as he slipped an arm around her shoulders. Her arm encircled his waist. If anyone was watching them, they'd see the couple's steps were in sync.

"Are you still taking me to the airport?"

"Of course."

The crickets and frogs were quiet as the day heated up, but in the early evening hours, they would serenade the stars.

They strolled down the gravel road with its canopy of large maple trees and leaves shading them. As they walked, the sun was streaking toward the high point in the sky.

"Things are going to get wild very soon."

He looked down at her. "I wanted to have a few minutes alone to give you something."

"You didn't need to get me anything." Her heart pounded. Was Colin about to propose? It was too soon, especially with her leaving.

There was a small wooden bench under an old maple tree. He steered her to it and they sat down. "You're on the cusp of an amazing time in your life and I want you to know I'm very proud of you."

"Colin, I couldn't do this without your support. It means a great deal to me." She was sure if she kept talking, she might start to cry. Leaving him was excruciating.

He smiled and looked deep into her eyes. "You will never be out of my heart."

He pulled a long, slim box from the deep pocket of his shorts. He handed it to her. "This is for you."

She took it and was thrilled at the gesture. "You shouldn't have."

"Open it." He let go of her other hand.

She eased the bow from the box and unlatched the clasp. The top folded open from the center. Lying on deep blue satin was a bracelet. She pulled it out.

"This is so pretty." The words caught in her throat. This was not just a bracelet. It held different charms.

He took it from her and secured it on her left arm. "Every charm has a special meaning and when you look at it, you can think of me."

She studied them one by one. He said, "Look. This is a golf club and then a tee"—she chuckled—"a raindrop, a sneaker, a flower, and a heart."

She looked at him through happy tears. "This is so sweet." She took his face in her hands and kissed him softly at first and then demanding more. "I could stay like this forever."

His face grew serious and he put his hands in her lap. "I wanted to talk to you about something else." He looked over her shoulder. "A few years ago, the woman I was engaged to, she lived on the West Coast. I told you about her. Well, it didn't just work out. She found someone else, and I discovered the truth when I went out there unexpectedly." He caressed her hand. "And as much as I love you and know I want a future with you, I think while you're in France, we need to cool things."

Confusion clouded her thoughts. "You're telling me this now?" She pulled her hands away and moved to the edge of the bench.

"I'm going to miss you like crazy, but I can't stand the thought of us being apart for much of the year, and the occasional long weekend just won't be enough for me. But I want you to go and make the most of this opportunity and know that when the year is over, I'll be here if you still want me."

"Do you want to be able to see other people?"

"No, that never crossed my mind. I'm devoted to you."

Before he could say anything more, she shook her head. "I can't believe you did this today, at my family's picnic. I'm going to pretend this conversation didn't happen. I can't deal with this or you now."

"Anna, please try and understand where I'm coming from." He reached out and brushed back her hair. "I've been trying to find a way to talk to you, to tell you how I feel."

She pulled away. "I'm not your ex-fiancée. I'm not a cheater." She wiped her damp cheeks with the back of her hand. "And you shouldn't have sprung this on me today." She plastered a smile on her face. No one was going to know her heart was breaking.

When they got back to the house, the music was blaring. Kate was sitting in a chair, rubbing her growing belly. It had been a surprise to learn she was pregnant. Unlike when she got pregnant with Ben, she said she had zero signs. The baby wasn't due for another five months, but with the heat and humidity, she needed to rest from time to time.

Anna sat down next to her. "How's everything going here?"

"I'm tired." She gazed lovingly at Ben running around the backyard, chasing his older cousins. Anna's own gaze followed them. "He's pretty excited." Kate's eyes grew wide. "A baby kicked. Do you want to feel?"

Kate took Anna's hand and held it against her tummy.

When she felt something thump against her hand, she was awestruck. "Does he or she do that often?"

"More and more until they run out of room."

Anna felt her mouth gape open. "Did you say *they*?"

Kate's eyes brimmed with tears. "We're going to make the

announcement today, but I wanted you to be the first to know."

She gave Kate a gentle hug. "Another set of twins. You and Shane, Leo and Liza, and now baby A and baby B."

"Our families seem to love to have babies in bunches."

"Like grapes." Anna laughed. "Do you know what they are yet?"

"Yes, but that news, you'll have to wait on. There have to be some surprises left."

"Things are certainly changing."

Kate said, "Change is necessary."

Out of the corner of her eye she saw Marie enter the yard with Ginny and Drew.

"Will you excuse me for a minute? That's Colin's sister and I want to introduce her to everyone."

"Bring her over. I'd love to meet her and her friends." She leaned over. "Remember, don't say anything about the twins."

"My lips are sealed." She made a zipper motion with her finger over her lips. "I'll be right back."

She met Liza crossing the yard. "Hey, come meet Marie, Colin's sister." She turned and checked on the boys before Liza did. "They're fine."

With one final look, Liza visibly relaxed. "Let's go mingle."

Marie was looking around and smiled when she saw Anna. "Hi. Good to see you." She gave Anna a hug. "Where's Colin?"

"Around here someplace." She gave Ginny a hug. "I'm glad you came. Make yourself at home. There's plenty of food on the tables and drinks in the coolers; they're labeled what's in each one." Her smile included Drew and Ginny. "Welcome."

Drew handed Anna a square box while his eyes were locked on Liza. "I brought some cookies."

"Thank you." She pulled Liza from behind her. "This is my sister Liza."

"Hi." She gave everyone a guarded smile. "I'm glad you came." She was still looking at Drew. "Cookies are good."

He said simply, "They're flags."

"Fitting."

Anna looked between Liza and Drew. The air was sizzling.

Stuttering, Liza said, "I need to go check on my kids."

"How many children do you have?"

"Two boys." She gestured to a bunch of kids who were playing a lawn game. "Johnny and George. They're six and seven going on thirty."

He laughed. "I'll bet they're good kids."

"They have their moments." She tore her gaze away. "I should go flip burgers."

"Do you want help?"

"No, you're our guest. Enjoy yourself." Color flamed Liza's cheeks.

Anna watched the exchange with interest. "Come on. I'll introduce you to the rest of the family and anyone else we come across and, Marie, if you have a minute, can I talk to you about something?"

The Grants arrived. Anna did the introductions without waiting for Colin. Things were awkward but despite that, the party was running smoothly and everyone seemed to be having fun.

Anna and Marie stepped to one side, and Marie asked, "What's going on? You look upset."

She kept her eyes on Colin, who was talking with Leo at the grill. "He said we need to take a break when I go to France."

"That idiot. Why would he do something like that?" She nodded and her eyes grew wide. "Daphne."

"I guess she cheated on him, but I can't believe he'd lump me into that category." She maintained her forced smile so no one would guess she was upset. "She really did crush him, didn't she?"

"In his defense, he was totally blindsided by what happened, and it took him a long time to get over it, not so much get over her but that he was naïve in thinking everything would be okay. He never saw her true colors. I wouldn't be surprised if she had cheated on him before she moved." She touched Anna's arm. "Give him some time. He's reacting to old emotions that don't have anything to do with you. It's easy to see how much he loves you."

As Anna was about to respond, Don said, "If we could have everyone's attention, please." He and Kate stood on the steps of the deck.

Anna and Marie, along with everyone else, turned their attention to Don. Ben ran over and dashed up the steps. Don picked him up and put his arm around Kate.

"On behalf of our family, we'd like to thank everyone for coming today. For those of you who don't know, our sister Anna is leaving tomorrow to spend a year working at Marchand Vineyards in France. We wish her safe travels. While Anna is off doing her thing with all things grape, Kate, Ben, and I will be welcoming..." He paused. "We will be welcoming a baby girl *and* a baby boy into the family in a few months."

"Twins!" Sherry rushed over to hug Kate, Don, and Ben. "I wonder what's in the water?"

Colin came up beside Anna. "Quite an announcement, don't you think? I never really thought about twins running in your family."

"Well, Kate has a twin brother in Loudon."

"But Liza and Leo are twins, so you might have that gene."

Anna had to wonder where this was going, but she didn't look at him. "Why?"

"I was wondering if we could get that lucky. Someday."

"You just broke it off with me and you're talking about having kids?"

His smile was strained. "I love you, Anna."

She shifted from side to side. This wasn't a conversation she was going to have now. She crossed her arms across her chest and arched a brow. "You have a funny way of showing it." She turned on her heel and walked away.

34

"Thanks for bringing me to the airport." Anna hugged Colin tight and blinked back the tears. She wasn't going to be a blubbering female getting on a plane, even if that was exactly what she wanted to do. She could feel him taking deep breaths as if he too were trying to keep his emotions under control. Maybe this hadn't been a good idea, him bringing her to the airport.

They stepped apart and stood on the sidewalk in front of the terminal. She wasn't sure what to say.

He took her hand. "Anna, I love you and I'm sorry for everything. We should have been celebrating this next step in your career."

She wanted to point out it was his choice, not hers, to give them space and she wasn't sure she could forgive him. She looked inside. "I need to go. Customs and all." The porter had already checked her bags and all she had left was a small carry-on and her laptop bag. "I'll touch base later if you want."

She kissed his cheek, but he cupped the back of her neck and kissed her like a man who did love her with all his heart. It was confusing. He was confusing.

"I do." When he gave her one last tender kiss, he searched her eyes. "Be safe."

She nodded. "Goodbye, Colin."

The plane taxied for takeoff and Anna watched out the window. Leaving things unsettled with Colin was hard, but it was all she could do. All she could see was his hazel eyes. It was only a few short months ago that Dad was in the hospital and she had run into him again. The man she had never forgotten and now had left behind.

How was it possible so much had changed in her life? What would the next twelve months bring? She shivered with anticipation. First stop Paris, then a train to Burgundy. Sophia would pick her up from the station and then thirty minutes after that, she'd be at the vineyard.

Her thoughts drifted back to her family. She might miss the birth of Kate and Don's babies. She sighed. There would never be a good time to take a year and leave. There would be more babies and weddings and family events that she would miss if she chose a different time. She hoped the drone of the plane's engines would lull her to sleep, but it eluded her. All she could think about was how each passing mile high above the Atlantic Ocean was taking her farther away from everyone she loved, to be with people she had met once.

Over the loudspeaker, the flight attendant said, "Welcome to Paris."

Excitement began to build. She was really in France. She continued to look out the window. The train didn't depart until early evening, so she had plenty of time to get through customs, have a bite to eat, and people watch before her next stop. She gathered her two carry-on bags and headed for the exit.

"*Merci beaucoup*," she said to the male flight attendant who stood near the exit door.

"*Au revoir, Mademoiselle*."

She hurried up the jet bridge and stepped out of the flow of traffic to get her bearings. She was really on this adventure.

Moving around the airport and catching the train proved to be very easy. Signs were in both French and English and after a light meal, she was anxious to see Sophia. Settled into her seat on the train, she sent a group text to her family. It was late back home and she just wanted everyone to know she was on her way. Minutes later, her cell rang.

"Hello, beautiful."

"Colin." The sound of his deep voice caused her heart to constrict. "This is a surprise. I didn't expect to talk to you."

"I was waiting until you were on the train before calling. I didn't want to distract you as you were navigating the airport."

"Thanks. I appreciate that."

"So tell me. Is the countryside as beautiful as all the guidebooks show?"

"From what I've seen so far, yes." She rearranged her bags at her feet. "Thanks for calling. I need to go."

"Oh." She could hear the hurt in his voice, but this had been his decision, not hers. "Can I call you again?"

"I might be busy." She looked out the window as the train picked up speed out of the station.

"I love you, Anna."

"You can't have it both ways. We'll talk about where things stand some other time. Goodbye, Colin."

She didn't wait for him to say anything else as she held the phone in her hand. Soon she began to see a familiar sight:

grapevines. Odd that something growing from the ground could give her comfort. The train pulled into the station and she grabbed her luggage. Talking to herself, she said, "A new phase of my life starts the minute I step off this train. I hope I'm up to the task."

Her first month had gone smoothly and Anna crossed the parking lot at Marchand's tasting room and got into the Peugeot Henri had deemed hers during her stay in France. He had certainly known her preference for automobiles, with the deep blue two-seater convertible. She gave a jaunty wave to some of the vineyard workers. It was the first weekend she was going to sneak away and explore.

The engine purred as she eased down the long drive and her tires kicked up dust as she turned onto the road. The wind teased her hair and she paused to wrap a scarf around it. She felt so European, almost like Sophia Loren, but wait—that was Italy. Now she had to add going to Italy to her bucket list. But for this weekend, it was all about wandering around Bordeaux, the cathedral, and tomorrow night the opera at the Grand Théâtre, where she was looking forward to seeing the twelve statues of muses and goddesses after dark. Sophia had said she needed to make that one of her first stops. Of course, there would be restaurants to dine at and shopping on Rue Sainte-Catherine, where she wanted to do some serious damage to her credit card.

The glimmer of the weekend dimmed a little when she thought of taking in the sights and sounds of Bordeaux alone. She had wanted to share this with Colin, but they had no concrete plans at the moment for him to come to France. In fact, they were barely talking. She tossed back her head and plastered a smile on her face. She was in France, and nothing was going to rain on her convertible.

35

Two more months had slipped by almost unnoticed as Anna settled into her new routine. Her villa was charming, and Sophia had done everything she could to see that Anna was comfortable. The two women had become fast friends and Anna's French was beginning to show signs of improvement. She could understand some conversations as long as no one spoke too fast, and she could make herself understood. But most conversations were like water rushing through fingers. She missed Colin like crazy and except for a few emails and texts, they hadn't talked. Each communication hurt as if the wound were fresh. Work kept her busy and for that, she was grateful.

Sophia and Anna walked through the vines, stooping to check the grapes by feel.

"It still amazes me how you do so much of this by touch." Sophia enunciated each English word slowly but without contractions. Her French accent was charming.

Anna was checking the plumpness of the cluster, feeling the weight in her hand. "It should feel like it has lots of juice in there and if the skin shrivels, we've waited too long." She took a step back. "Your turn."

Sophia bent low and mimicked Anna's movements. "I see what you mean. I have always gone more by the color and taste. But that can be disappointing when it comes to juice content."

Anna plucked two grapes from the vine behind them. "Close your eyes and tell me what you taste."

"Sweet, juicy, and warm." Sophia laughed and opened her eyes.

"Do you think they'll become sweeter with another week or two?"

"I am not sure. I would like to come out tomorrow and taste again."

"Excellent idea."

The women turned to make the long walk back to the compound, where activity was sure to be buzzing, getting ready for the harvest.

"So have you talked to Colin recently?"

She had shared what had happened with Sophia and it helped her to deal with the sadness. She looked off into the distance. "A few days ago, I got an email from him, but we haven't talked live. Just a few texts to touch base. I miss him."

"I can see in your face how much you care for him. I hope that is how I look when I talk about Gabriel."

"You get all dreamy when you talk about him, and when he walks into a room, you light up."

"He is a wonderful man. I am hopeful you and Colin will be able to work things out. Love is important in life."

"I understand that he was hurt, but I'm not that other woman."

"Insecurity is a difficult thing to overcome. I am sure he is sorry that he hurt you."

"He's said as much, but it still stings that he wouldn't even try." Anna paused. "Let's stop talking about something I can't change."

Sophia glanced at her wristwatch.

"Do you have another appointment?"

"No. Just checking the time. Before we go back, would you mind if we checked the grapes on the west side of the vineyard? I would like to plan our harvesting schedule." They moved down a new row of young vines. "How did you meet Colin?" She glanced at Anna. "Was it love at first sight?"

She laughed. "You are a true romantic, aren't you?"

"If you do not want to talk about him, I understand, but sometimes, I have found that talking brings clarity and I am French from the tips of my toes to my head, so I am a romantic."

Anna tipped her head back and looked toward the cloudless azure-blue sky. She closed her eyes and recalled the first time she had seen Colin when she was stretched out across her father's hospital bed.

"We met several years ago. He was a nurse when my father was in the hospital. I remember thinking how handsome he was and that he had the kindest eyes. I was tongue-tied. I will never forget that feeling when our eyes met. It was a feeling unlike any other before."

"Did he ask you on a date at that time?"

"No. I only saw him the once, and our paths never crossed again. Until last spring. Dad was admitted to the hospital with severe heart problems, and Colin and I ran into each other again."

"Did it feel the same as before?"

The corners of Anna's mouth curved into a smile. It came from deep inside her heart. "Exactly the same. It was as if I had known him for a very long time. We met for coffee, which slid into dinner and dessert. I knew after that night that he was the man for me."

She slowed her steps and drank in the sight of expansive fields of vines nearing readiness for the harvest. Even though she missed sharing a meal or a touch with Colin, she was glad to be a part of this harvest and she was looking forward to working on a new blend for Marchand and CLW.

"Did he feel the same, that you are the only woman for him?"

"I thought he did." She walked at a relaxed pace. Talking about Colin helped to make her feel he was nearby and that things would be okay. She held up her wrist. "He gave this to me before I left."

Sophia looked closely at each charm. "This is a very special and personal gift. He must love you very much."

Anna stopped to inspect a vine. Colin was never far from her thoughts and she loved him with all her heart, but it didn't change the truth. She was here and there were many months before she'd be returning to Crescent Lake. Who knew where they'd be by then.

Selecting a cluster of grapes, she closely examined the color and the skin, and then popped a dark-purple one in her mouth. She gestured for Sophia to do the same. "Tell me what you think."

"The color and skin look good. They are heavy with juice." She selected one and tasted it. "These are so much sweeter than the north side."

Anna grinned. "This is where the harvest begins. Let's go back and tell Henri and the others the good news." She glanced one last time at the cloudless sky. "All we need is for the weather to hold."

They set off at a brisk pace. After walking for a few minutes, Anna said, "Tell me how you met Gabriel."

"We were children in school. He used to tease me in the play yard until one day, a bigger boy pushed me down and took my swing. Gabriel rushed over to help me out of the sand and, much to my surprise, confronted the boy and made him give me back the swing. After that, we became inseparable."

"You've loved him for a long time." She sighed. "Now, that is very romantic."

Sophia slipped her arm through Anna's. "The heart knows."

"I guess you're right."

They reached the parking lot and Sophia said, "Let us share a glass of wine in the garden. It has been a good day."

"I should go into the lab and make some notes before I go home."

"No, we must enjoy the quiet moments of our day too. You work much too hard."

Anna allowed herself to be guided into the winery.

"A quick stop for a bottle, glasses, and an opener and we will savor the excellent news about the grapes. What would you like to try?"

"How about the Angeline rosé?" Anna walked to a rack and selected a bottle. She held it up. "Is this something you'll enjoy too?"

Sophia clasped her hands together. "It is *parfait*. Perfect." She took the bottle. "I have one in the cooler. It should be served chilled." She went into the back room. Anna was holding the glasses and corkscrew when she returned.

"Come. Let us go outside, shall we?" Sophia took the glasses from Anna as she opened the door.

They walked into the garden and Anna stopped in her tracks. Her heart pounded in her chest and tears pricked her eyes. "Colin!" Her voice was barely a whisper.

He opened his arms, and she ran into them.

"When did you?" She placed her hands on the sides of his face and studied every angle and curve. His eyes twinkled with happiness and love. "How did you?"

Using his thumb, he wiped her cheeks dry, and then he tenderly kissed her mouth.

"I couldn't stay away a minute longer. I've felt like a part of my heart was missing and I would find it in France, and you know how I feel when a heart is ailing."

With a half laugh, half sob, she threw her arms around his neck and clung to him as if they had been apart for years, not months.

"You may think I'm crazy, but I had to see you."

She covered his face with kisses. "I've missed you so much too."

A gentle clearing of the throat caught her attention. She slipped from his arms and held his hand.

"Come. Say hello to Sophia."

"Hello, Sophia. It's nice to see you again and thank you for everything."

He held out his hand and took the glasses. She gave him a hug and kissed both of his cheeks.

"I am so glad you arrived in time. I was not sure how much longer I could keep Anna away from the buildings today."

Anna looked from Colin to Sophia. "You knew he was coming."

Her musical laugh filled the air. "He needed help with his transportation from the train station. I was happy to oblige, as was Gabriel. Now if you will excuse me, I will leave you to enjoy the wine and spend some time together so that you can talk." She set the bottle and chilled bucket on the table and precisely at the same moment, Gabriel came through another door with a small platter filled with food.

Sophia took his hand and smiled at Anna. "Enjoy your evening and tomorrow, we will dine together."

Colin shook Gabriel's hand and hugged Sophia. "Again, thank you for your help. I couldn't have surprised my love without it."

Without further ado, they slipped away, leaving Colin and Anna alone. They sat at a small bistro table under a pergola and white twinkle lights came on overhead.

With a small laugh, Anna said, "Sophia does think of all the romantic touches."

They sat close together, holding hands and sipping wine.

"Are you happy that I surprised you?"

Anna looked at him. "This is the sweetest, but what are you doing here? I thought you didn't want to do the long-distance relationship."

He leaned over and kissed her lips. His hand cupped her cheek. "The last three months were very lonely, and I knew the moment we talked when you were on the train that I had to find a way to fix things."

Her heart constricted. Seeing him didn't change the fact that he would go home and they were right back to where they started.

"I know that sad face."

Colin's voice was almost her undoing. She drew in a shaky breath. "We're going to enjoy every moment you're here and not talk about when you have to leave."

"Well, I'm glad to hear you don't want to talk about my leaving, but I feel we must."

She dropped her chin to her chest. Might as well get the bad news over with.

Colin's silence compelled her to look at him. She searched his eyes. They were bright and full of mischief. "What are you up to?"

"Don't be mad, but I've had dinner with your parents a couple of times and asked for their help."

She set her glass down and gave him her full attention. "And…"

"I figured out pretty quickly I wasn't going to make a mistake and let an ocean come between us." He got up and walked a short distance away. He stuck his hands in the pockets of his jeans. "I told them I needed to be with you."

She nodded. "Go on."

"I talked to human resources at the hospital and asked for

a sabbatical so I could be with the woman I love in France as she finished out her year-long contract." He held up his hand. "Before you say anything, I talked with Henri and asked if he would mind if I came over and stayed with you. I've offered to help with the harvest or whatever might be needed, but he suggested that I could be the medical person on site. You know, help if there is an emergency."

"That sounds like a position he created for you." She got up and crossed the short distance between them. "Not that I'm complaining, but if you really want to stay here with me, I'm sure we can keep you from getting bored."

"I currently have a three-month tourist visa, but Henri will sponsor me."

"You've thought of everything, haven't you?"

He pulled her down to the stone step. "Anna, I love you and yes, I am okay with putting things on a slower track while you experience all that working at this winery has to offer you. But I've waited for you for a long time. The first time I saw you, I didn't ask you on a date."

She pulled back. "You really did want to ask me out the first time you met me?"

"In the worst way. I kept hoping our paths would cross, and then fate stepped in and I had the immense pleasure of seeing you again. I wasn't going to let you get away."

"Fate was my dad's heart attack?"

He squirmed. "I didn't mean I was happy your dad needed surgery. But it was fate I was assigned to his case. I don't want to waste another day without you in my life every single day, in person where I can see you, touch you, and share a life with you."

She took his hand and slipped her fingers through his. "I love that you did all of this for me. Are you sure you want to put your career on hold for a year?"

"When I'm an old man and look back at my life, I want to be able to say that I followed my heart and lived my best life." He held up their joined hands and kissed the soft underside of her wrist. "With you."

With that declaration, she sighed. "I want us to be together."

He lifted his face to her. "There is one more thing."

What else was left to be said? She searched his smiling face. "Okay."

He held out a small white box and popped the top open. Sitting inside was an amethyst and diamond ring. "We can have as long of an engagement as you want, but say you'll marry me."

"Yes." She melted into his arms. "Most definitely, yes."

The End

Thank you for reading Anna and Colin's story. I hope you enjoyed the story. If you did, please help other readers find this book: **Please leave a review now!**

Join Lucinda's Newsletter today to be notified about upcoming releases and specials just for you, my newsletter subscribers.

Read on for a Sneak Peek of
Blush, Book 3
Available August 2021
The Crescent Lake Winery series
Featuring feisty Peyton Brien and the handsome Jack Price

Order Here

Chapter One

"Peyton, are you in here?" Kate Price walked through the door that connected the Crescent Lake Winery tasting room and Kay-Dee's Bistro.

Peyton Brien looked up at her best friend. "Over here." She paused unpacking the box of glasses at the bar. "Look at you in your chef coat. Hard at work this morning?" There were a few stains on Kate's usually pristine coat that she wore over her slender prepregnancy figure.

"I'm trying some new recipes and knocked a bowl over." Kate's gaze took in the stack of boxes on the long wooden bar and on the floor. "What's all this?"

"The Finger Lakes wine trail spring season kicks off April fifteenth, which is less than two weeks away, and I ordered new logo wineglasses." Peyton held one up. "What do you think? I went with a new style for a new season—shake things up a bit." Spring was her favorite time of year, when she believed anything was possible, and she was excited to discover what was next in her life.

Kate took one out of the open box. "Nice, and I like that they're stemless. Classy. But you ordered a ton."

Peyton flashed her a grin. "You forget people come in droves to eat in a certain restaurant here at CLW and ever since you got back in the kitchen from having the twins, the tasting room is busier than ever."

Kate perched on a barstool. "Which brings me to the reason I stopped in. Any chance you want to try some of the new menu items?"

Peyton thought of the peanut butter sandwich in her bag. There was no contest. Lunch with Kate definitely had much more appeal.

Before she could answer, the back door to the tasting room opened and Jack Price strode in. "Did I hear someone say lunch?"

His tall, muscular body, blond hair, and golden-hazel eyes used to make Peyton's heart pound, but that was ten years ago when they were a couple. Now they were just coworkers and he was Kate's brother-in-law.

"Hey, Jack." Peyton returned to unpacking glasses.

"I didn't expect to see you today, Jack," Kate said. "Don mentioned you'd be in the fields all day, pruning vines."

He looked around the spacious room filled with small tables and wine displays. "Where is my brother?"

"He had a meeting at the bank about the new fermenting tanks you want to install this year."

Jack rubbed his hands together, and his smile crinkled the corners of his eyes. "Good. That means more food for me." He quirked an eyebrow. "That's if you don't mind me joining you ladies."

Peyton said, "No problem here." Thankfully, they had finally gotten past that awkward stage when they were in the same room. At one time, they had been friends, then lovers, and finally friends again years after he'd broken her heart. He'd asked her out a couple of times, but she'd turned him down. She doubted the feelings of renewal that came every spring would affect her and Jack.

Working for the Price family was more than a job to Peyton; it was her passion. And given how busy they'd been the past tourist seasons, that was a good thing. She was hoping for another successful season and maybe at the end of it, she'd talk to Don and ask for a raise.

Kate got up. "Give me five minutes and I'll meet you in the dining room."

"I'll give you a hand." Peyton stepped from behind the bar.

Jack held up his dirt-covered hands and gave Peyton a wink and smile. "I'll need to wash up."

Unaffected by his charms, Peyton walked with Kate through the inviting dining room. Small tables with two and four chairs filled the space. The large windows overlooking the vineyard allowed the warm sun to flood the room. Adding to the allure of the space, the French doors were propped open to the gazebo area, letting in the crisp spring air.

"This is one of my favorite views of the property. I'm glad you decided to build the bistro here."

Kate held open the swinging kitchen door for them. "I almost didn't. Sam was way too pushy and dangled my dream as a bribe just to get Don to take over the winery business. But it turned out to be a win for us. I have a wonderful husband, three healthy kids, and my own business."

"You're a lucky woman. I have one of the three."

"How is Owen?" Kate began to plate their lunch as Peyton watched.

"A typical almost eight-year-old. He's always on the move. His new love is fishing; it's all he talks about—well, except his birthday at the end of August."

"And how are things with Jerry?"

Peyton slashed her hand across her throat. "Dead. Turns out he was just another loser. I can't seem to pick a good guy who wants to take things at a slower pace."

"What about going out with Jack? He's a good guy and hasn't dated much since he moved back from Napa a couple of years ago." Kate set an overfilled plate on the shelf between the prep area and Peyton.

Slowly shaking her head, Peyton said, "That ship sailed a long time ago. When he took that job in Napa, it broke my heart. He left without even a conversation."

Kate paused. "I'm sorry. I had no idea he left that way."

Peyton gave her a smile. "Ancient history." She felt a pang of regret for what might have been. Back then, she had thought they had a forever kind of love. Life would have been very different if he hadn't left. But then, she wouldn't have Owen, who was the light of her life.

Kate filled two more plates. "Hungry?"

"Starved." Peyton balanced two plates and walked

through the swinging door backside first. Jack was on the other side of the room, looking at his cell phone.

Peyton said, "Lunch is ready."

Jack scanned his email. There was a forwarded email from the winery customer service team to his attention. The subject line: Urgent. Please call me. He dismissed it as a mistake and slipped the phone into his back pocket; he'd let them know later.

He flashed a wide smile at Peyton and made sure it included Kate. He didn't want to come off as being single-minded, but a very pretty petite brunette with soulful deep brown eyes was always on his mind. The biggest regret in his life was letting Peyton break up with him all those years ago, even if going to Napa was the best course of action for him and his father.

He took the chair next to her. "So, Katie, should I just eat and tell you what I like the best, or is this where I need to give a grade to each individual dish?" His fork was poised as he waited to dive in.

"Tell me as you go, please."

Peyton looked up from her plate. "I don't know if I can eat all of this food. But I'll do my best."

The trio enjoyed lunch and lighthearted conversation.

Jack said, "Peyton, I swung by the Little League practice the other night and saw you were helping out some kids."

"They lost one of the coaches; he broke a leg, I think. The league director asked if I'd lend a hand for a couple of practices until they get a new coach."

"Yeah, Liza filled me in. I was thinking of volunteering. I could spend time with Johnny and George."

"I'm sure they'd love it." She took a drink of her water. "I'm not sure if Liza told you, but there's another practice tonight if you're serious about pitching in. The kids have been improving over the last couple of weeks."

"I'll swing by. Is it at the middle school again?"

"Yes, and there's only six weeks left, except for the final playoff game."

He thought, That will give me six weeks to see her outside of work. "Would you happen to have the director's phone number? I could give him a call this afternoon."

"If you're serious, swing by the tasting room before you head back out into the fields and I'll write the number down. But to be an official coach, you'd have to get a background check." Peyton gave him a side-look. "That takes a week, usually more to get back."

"I should be in good shape; I coached the boys' basketball team last winter." He patted his stomach. "Kate, best lunch I've had in quite some time. Thanks for letting me crash the party." He jabbed a piece of frittata before he got up and popped it in his mouth. "This is a keeper. What wine would you pair it with?"

It didn't take Kate but a moment to turn the question around. "Peyton, what would you suggest?"

She took a bite and seemed to let the flavors mingle on her tongue. "The Pinot Gris. Unless you decide to add some heavier ingredients like sausage."

"There you go, Jack. Our tasting room guru has made her selection."

Peyton's cheeks flushed a sweet shade of pink. Jack was pleased to see that some things hadn't changed. He picked up the now empty plates. "I'll leave these in the kitchen and I'm going to see if Don's back yet." He looked at Peyton. "I'll stop back for that number."

"Sure. I'll be here until four."

Damn. She's completely unfazed by my presence. Is there any hope she might still have lingering feelings for me? He walked out of the dining room with the plates, leaving Peyton and Kate to enjoy the rest of their lunch.

Kate leaned back and crossed her arms. "That didn't stir up old feelings at all, did it?"

Peyton lifted her eyes. "What, having lunch with Jack? No. Why? Should it?"

"You loved him once and…" Her voice trailed off. "Huh."

"I've had years to get Jackson Price out of my system. As far as I'm concerned, we're coworkers and now, possibly, he might be Owen's baseball coach but really, it's no big deal. No sparks or embers here."

"I don't think I could be as chill around my ex as you are being around yours." Kate wiped her mouth on the napkin. "Especially a Price. When they get under your skin, they tend to stay there. I know from personal experience."

Peyton drank the last of her water before responding. How could anyone really understand that when she and Jack had dated, they were both different people than they were now? But she had loved him with all her heart. Did it even matter? "Who knows, Kate. Maybe it was because we were young, and life has taken us down very different roads. Besides, we agreed when he moved back that the past was just that, the past, and no sense dwelling on it."

Jack jogged into the dining room. "Excuse me, ladies. Kate, I didn't find Don. Will you tell him I'll catch up with him later? I need to get back outside."

"Sure."

He looked at Peyton. "Any chance you could get me that phone number now? I'd like to call the director this afternoon."

"I'll be right back." Peyton followed him into the tasting room. "Jack, it's really nice that you're going to help out. I wish more adults had the time to volunteer. It means so much to the kids."

She wrote down the phone number and handed it to him. "Here you go."

He stuffed the slip of paper into his shirt pocket. "I'm glad we can work together like this, for the kids."

She could feel her forehead crinkle. "Me too."

"Well," he hemmed, "I thought, given our history—"

"We should live in the present, Jack. The past doesn't matter." Peyton walked behind the bar. "I need to get back to work."

A flash of confusion hovered in his eyes. "Alright. See you around."

She went back to unpacking glasses, but her eyes followed him as he walked out the door.

Blush Book 3 Available August 2021

T

LOVE TO READ?

CHECK OUT MY OTHER BOOKS

The Crescent Lake Winery Series 2021

Blends

Breathe

Crush

Blush

Vintage

Bouquet

The MacLellan Sisters Trilogy

Old and New

Borrowed

Blue

It's Just Coffee Series 2020

The Matchmaker and The Marine

The Loudon Series

The Loudon Series Box Set

Between Here and Heaven

Lost and Found

The Journey Home

The Last First Kiss
Ready to Soar
Love in the Looking Glass
Magic in the Rain

A Dickens Romance Series
Holiday Heart Wishes July 2021
Holly Berries and Hockey Pucks November 2021

SOCIAL MEDIA

FOLLOW ME ON SOCIAL MEDIA

Follow Me on Social Media

Like my Facebook page
Join Lucinda's Heart Racer's Reader Group on Facebook
Twitter @lucindarace
Instagram @lucindraceauthor
BookBub
Goodreads
Pinterest

ABOUT LUCINDA

Award-winning and best-selling author Lucinda Race is a lifelong fan of romantic fiction. As a young girl, she spent hours reading romance novels and getting lost in the hope they represent. While her friends dreamed of becoming doctors and engineers, her dreams were to become a writer—a romance novelist.

As life twisted and turned, she found herself writing nonfiction but longed to turn to her true passion. After developing the storyline for The Loudon Series, it was time to start living her dream. Her fingers practically fly over computer keys as she weaves stories about strong women and the men who love them.

Lucinda lives with her husband and their two little dogs, a miniature long hair dachshund and a shih tzu mix rescue, in the rolling hills of western Massachusetts. When she's not at her day job, she's immersed in her fictional worlds. And if she's not writing romance novels, she's reading everything she can get her hands on. It's too bad her husband doesn't cook, but a very good thing he loves takeout.